D1475606

IN SEALED-OFF
INNER SANCTUMS

the best scientific minds join forces with giant computers to frantically search for a way to stop an irresistible force of destruction—a blazing planetoid on a relentless 100,000 miles per hour collision course with earth.

IN THE CAPITALS
OF THE WORLD

political leaders are torn between ingrained rivalries and suspicion, and a new need to work together or perish.

IN THE STREETS
OF NEW YORK

a panicked population plunges into fear and prepares to live out its last days loving in haste, despairing of salvation, and praying for a miracle.

ALL OVER THE
PLANET EARTH

the individual fates of men and women, their hopes and dreams, lusts and guilts, courage and cowardness, are all bathed in the hellfire illumination of—

FIREBALL

there are only eight days left for earth!

More Thrillers from SIGNET

☐ **THE BLOOD OF OCTOBER by David Lippincott.**
(#J7785—$1.95)

☐ **TREMOR VIOLET by David Lippincott.**
(#E6947—$1.75)

☐ **THE VOICE OF ARMAGEDDON by David Lippincott.**
(#E6949—$1.75)

☐ **THE SWARM by Arthur Herzog.** (#E8079—$2.25)

☐ **EARTHSOUND by Arthur Herzog.** (#E7255—$1.75)

☐ **FLUKE by James Herbert.** (#J8394—$1.95)*

☐ **THE FOG by James Herbert.** (#E8174—$1.75)

☐ **THE RATS by James Herbert.** (#E8770—$1.75)

☐ **THE SURVIVOR by James Herbert.** (#J8369—$1.95)

☐ **THE CATS by Nick Sharman.** (#J8654—$1.95)†

☐ **RATTLERS by Joseph Gilmore.** (#J8464—$1.95)*

☐ **EARTHQUAKE by George Fox.** (#Y6264—$1.25)

☐ **LAUNCH! by Ned Stewart.** (#J7743—$1.95)

☐ **THE DESPERATE HOURS by Joseph Hayes.**
(#J7689—$1.95)

* Price slightly higher in Canada.
† Not available in Canada.

To order these titles, please use coupon
on the last page of this book.

Fireball

by
Vic Mayhew
and
Doug Long

A SIGNET BOOK
NEW AMERICAN LIBRARY
TIMES MIRROR

NAL BOOKS ARE ALSO AVAILABLE AT DISCOUNTS IN BULK
QUANTITY FOR INDUSTRIAL OR SALES-PROMOTIONAL USE.
FOR DETAILS, WRITE TO PREMIUM MARKETING DIVISION,
NEW AMERICAN LIBRARY, INC., 1301 AVENUE OF THE
AMERICAS, NEW YORK, NEW YORK 10019.

COPYRIGHT © 1977 BY VIC MAYHEW AND DOUG LONG

All rights reserved. No part of this publication may be reproduced,
stored in a retrieval system or transmitted in any form or by any
means, electronic, mechanical, photocopying, recording or otherwise, without the prior written permission of Methuen Publications,
2330 Midland Avenue, Agincourt, Ontario, Canada.

SIGNET TRADEMARK REG. U.S. PAT. OFF. AND FOREIGN COUNTRIES
REGISTERED TRADEMARK—MARCA REGISTRADA
HECHO EN CHICAGO, U.S.A.

SIGNET, SIGNET CLASSICS, MENTOR, PLUME AND MERIDIAN BOOKS
are published by The New American Library, Inc.,
1301 Avenue of the Americas, New York, New York 10019

FIRST SIGNET PRINTING, JUNE, 1979

1 2 3 4 5 6 7 8 9

PRINTED IN THE UNITED STATES OF AMERICA

I have seen a comet strike our earth around the middle of the 1980's. Earthquakes and tidal waves will befall us as a result of the tremendous impact of this heavenly body . . . It may well be known as one of the worst disasters of the twentieth century . . .

Astrologer Jeane Dixon from
My Life and Prophecies

If you watch the sky for just fifteen minutes on any cloudless night you will see several shooting stars, probably three or more. These are a mere fraction of the 15,000 or so meteors which scorch through the atmosphere every day. Though they may blaze a trail of many miles, most are no bigger than a pinhead and burn up harmlessly above the earth. Larger meteors, occasionally bigger than an office block, can explode night into day over thousands of square miles. Such meteors are known, appropriately, as fireballs.

Fireballs hurtle debris over a vast area of the earth's surface; some crash intact to the earth, gouging out great craters. These impact craters are evidence that fireballs of awesome size have fallen.

The Chubb Crater in northern Quebec is two miles wide. The Canyon Diablo Crater in Arizona is a mile across. Australia's Wolf Creek Crater is a mile and a half in diameter. The Vredefort Ring near Johannesburg, South Africa, has a diameter of twenty-six miles.

In 1908, a fireball destroyed several square miles of forest in Siberia, charring mature pine trees and flattening them as if they were matchsticks. Wildlife was obliterated.

In 1947, another fireball burst over Siberia, pitting an area more than a mile wide with meteoric fragments.

A fireball can hit the earth at any place—virgin wasteland or populated city. It can zoom into the atmosphere at any time. Tomorrow or today. The next time you look at the sky.

Even now . . .

Fireball

Chapter One

Four hundred million years ago.

In the explosion of a collapsed star, fiery fragments hurtled helter-skelter through outer space. Among the debris, an oblong-shaped planetoid, 427 miles from end to end, was launched toward a distant galaxy. Within that galaxy was a sun circled by nine planets, one of which was to become known as Earth.

THURSDAY, 1 A.M.

Matt Young had almost managed to forget his anxieties about the Mars shot coming up on Saturday. He hadn't had an evening off in two weeks. Or was it three? For too long life had been all work and no sex, and he intended to redress the balance at the earliest opportunity. He checked his watch. Soon he and Jenny could leave the party and continue their celebrations in private.

Young, the youthful administrator of NASA, and Jenny Corbett, a reporter with the New York *Daily News,* were the guests of honor. After they had announced their engagement only hours before, their NASA friends had quickly reserved a dozen tables in the elegant banquet room of Houston's Rice Hotel.

Bob Bigelow, Young's second-in-command at NASA, had appointed himself joker-in-chief. Proposing the umpteenth toast, he hauled himself to his feet. "Here's to lots of thrust, Matt. May you always have lots of thrust." He slumped back to his seat as the laughter subsided.

Young winced, then smiled indulgently. He sometimes found his deputy's humor needlessly crude. He decided to propose a private toast of his own to Jenny. As he refilled their glasses with champagne she reached across the table and stroked the back of his hand. He raised his glass and grinned at her. "Here's to my child bride."

Her lips parted in a wide-mouthed, impish smile. Her eyes, a disconcertingly deep brown, glinted in the candlelight.

"You're flattering me again, lover, but keep right on. I love it."

At forty-six, Young was fifteen years older than Jenny. She invariably laughed off any hint of concern about the difference in their ages.

Looking over the top of her glass she winked, closing her right eye without moving any other facial muscle—a trick she had tried to teach Young without success.

A waiter suddenly appeared at his elbow and placed a phone on the table. "It's Mission Control, sir."

Jenny playfully waved a finger back and forth and slowly shook her head in mock warning. Young sat back in his seat, folded his arms and frowned at the phone. Surely, for once, HQ could spare him from a crisis. He wondered whether to pass the call to one of the other NASA executives at the party.

"Was I asked for by name?"

"Yes sir."

Young sighed and lifted the receiver. "What now?" he asked impatiently. As he listened he wedged the phone between his left ear and shoulder and toyed with the pewter ring he wore on the third finger of his left hand.

Less than three days remained before the launch of Apollo-Soyuz 1. The spacecraft, named in tribute to earlier space triumphs, was to land two Americans and two Russians on Mars. The planning and cost had been shared equally by both nations, and the NASA teams at Mission Control, Houston, and Cape Canaveral, Florida, had been bolstered by Russian technicians. It was the most ambitious space project ever, and had been plagued by countless problems—technical, political and, inevitably, personal.

"I'm on my way," Young announced abruptly, hanging up.

He looked apologetically at Jenny and shrugged. "I'm sorry, honey, but don't worry. It's only another damned crisis. I'll rush right back."

She smiled sympathetically but realized that his thoughts had already leapt ahead to Mission Control.

To Bigelow, Young said, "Look after Jenny for me. I won't be long."

"With pleasure." Bigelow shook his head, suddenly aware that he had drunk too much. "Are you sure you don't want me to come along for the ride?"

Young knew that his deputy's tipsiness would vanish instantly if there was work to be done—his lightheartedness was often contrived to conceal an introspective, complex character.

"No thanks, Bob. I'll yell if you're needed."

Smiling intimately at Jenny, he slid back his chair, rose and left, his long, easy strides disguising his brisk pace to the exit doors.

Jenny's newshound instincts were aroused by his hasty departure. She reminded herself that she was still on assignment to cover the Mars mission for the *Daily News*. He would surely have handed the matter over to someone else unless there was a real emergency. She checked the time—1.20 a.m. There was still time to catch the final edition if she could piece together a story in the next hour or two.

"There really couldn't be anything wrong, could there?" she asked Bigelow.

He chuckled, dismissing the idea. "Not unless someone's ripped off the rocket for a joyride . . . No, I'm sure Matt will soon have things sorted out."

He wondered fleetingly about the phone call he had received earlier from his son. Michael had been excited about something he had seen through his telescope.

"I wonder . . ." he said to Jenny, not bothering to finish the sentence. "No, that's crazy. It couldn't be."

Jenny seized on the half promise of information. "You wonder what, Bob?"

"Oh, it's nothing really. Michael called me earlier about something he'd seen through his telescope. He's a bright boy, but a bit imaginative. I told him to get some sleep and we'd solve his little mystery in the morning. He mentioned something about a star he couldn't track down on the sky map."

Jenny sensed intuitively that she had found a fragment of a major story. She took a deep breath in an attempt to slow down her quickening heartbeat. "What did he think it was?"

Bigelow laughed. "Well, like I said, he's an imaginative boy. He said it was a planetoid."

"A planetoid . . . a small runaway planet. Right?"

"Yeah. The boy's way off beam. He must be."

She lowered her eyes, hoping he would not detect her excitement. He just might clam up if he realized she was thinking of filing a story.

Thoughtfully he twirled his empty glass. "No, it's crazy," he added.

She was not so sure. If the boy was right . . .

The band began a waltz. "Come on." He took her arm. "That's one dance I can do without falling over."

The two made unlikely partners. Bigelow's tuxedo had suffered countless celebrations and had worn only slightly better than he had. Its crumpled fabric scarcely concealed his flabbiness. He held Jenny at arm's length as though trying to maneuver a glass door onto its hinges. Occasionally he released his tense grip on her waist to ruffle his unkempt, graying hair. Jenny, lithe, long-legged and slightly taller than Bigelow, glided with careless gracefulness across the floor.

As they danced she tactfully pursued the matter of the planetoid.

"Michael's a fine boy, Bob."

"Yeah. A great kid, but a bit quiet. I wish I had more time to spend with him."

"How long has he had this astronomy thing?"

"Oh, for years. I've bought him all the stuff—the best there is. Well, almost."

"And you don't think he just might have sighted a planetoid?"

"No way." He chuckled again. "He probably saw the moon and checked the wrong chart."

She refused to be discouraged. "But what if . . . I mean, what if he really did see a planetoid? What could it mean?"

Bigelow momentarily released his arm from her waist to ruffle his hair once more. "Almost anything, I suppose. The boy would get his name in the science magazines. That would give him a big kick. Ooops, sorry."

He stumbled, then struggled to pick up the beat. She gently eased him back into the rhythm.

"Still, what if he had discovered a planetoid?" she asked doggedly. "What could it do to, say, the Mars shot?"

"You must be kidding. Chances are it would be nowhere near the flight path, but if it was it could cause communication problems. Honestly, that reporter's mind of your is running away with itself."

She wasn't so sure he was right. As the waltz ended she excused herself, ostensibly to go to the powder room. She had decided it was time to make a few phone calls.

Bigelow had left for the party at 9 p.m., leaving his son to face another lonely evening at home. It seemed to Michael that every night his father either worked late or went to some social event. Proud as he was that his father had such an important job with NASA and an impressive circle of influential friends, he was ashamed of a side of Bigelow's character that those friends never saw. Though good-natured in company, he was frequently irritable and intolerant with those closest to him. His daughter had left home eight years earlier after one of many bitter arguments that Michael, then a boy of seven, had understood only vaguely. Now he hardly remembered what his sister looked like. His mother had walked out soon afterwards. At first, she visited Michael every weekend. Eventually, she brought another man with her. Gradually, the visits became less frequent. Now they were rare. Michael hadn't seen his mother for months.

He crossed the backyard of his home to the observatory his father had set up. Somewhat larger than a two-car garage and nearly as tall as the Bigelows' one-and-a-half-storey home, the structure housed Michael's most treasured possession, a massive telescope. The dome-shaped ceiling rotated on a track so that the scope could be fixed on any portion of the sky. His mother had once accused her husband of trying to buy their son's affection by building the observatory. Her remark was one of the few hints Michael ever received that his affection was even wanted. His father had retaliated by adding a darkroom for the development of photographs taken through the scope.

Michael pressed the button that turned the dome. After it had spun through about five degrees he removed his finger. He repeated the maneuver, pressing the button several times, allowing the telescope to move and stop at random.

He had become engrossed in astronomy in the hope of getting closer to his father. At first, father and son had spent hours together studying the sky. But the more Michael's interest grew, the more his father's declined. He apparently became as bored with his new toy as with his daughter, his wife and, now, his son.

Michael peered into the scope's tiny eyepiece, then referred to a map of the night sky on a table in the observatory.

Puzzled, he tried unsuccessfully to locate the strange, glimmering object that was now in focus. He peered again, more intently. He rechecked the sky map. His heart leapt. Incredulous, he looked once more through the scope. It was still there. Unmistakably. It had to be a new planetoid . . . He adjusted the lens to pinpoint the object as accurately as he could and marked down its coordinates, then made a final check of the map. Sure enough, that area of the sky should have been blank.

He whooped exuberantly and ran across the backyard into the house. Grabbing the telephone directory, he flipped to the number of the Rice Hotel, dialed quickly and was switched through a series of extensions. Finally his father's voice came over the line.

"Dad," Michael blurted out excitedly, "I think I've found a planetoid. It's . . ."

His father interrupted testily. "Whoa, slow down, son. I can hardly hear you because of the band. Say that again."

Michael paused, suddenly conscious that his checking had hardly been thorough. Perhaps he had made a mistake. "I've found something on the scope, dad, and I can't find it on the map. I wonder if I might have something."

"There are a lot of important people here, Michael, and I haven't got time to talk about stargazing. You've probably checked the wrong map, or you've got the wrong coordinates or any one of a thousand things."

"I suppose so." Michael was deflated by his father's belittling tone and eager now to change the subject. "How's the party going?"

"It's going fine." Bigelow felt just a pang of guilt at his impatience to rejoin the others. "Look, why don't you get some sleep and we'll talk this out in the morning?"

"Sure. Goodnight."

"Goodnight."

Michael hung up and took a pack of his father's cigarettes from a kitchen drawer—as he did several times each week. Once he had been afraid of being caught, but the cigarettes were never missed. He had even taken money, though only small amounts. It seemed that no matter what he did, good or bad, no one ever noticed. He was convinced that his father knew very little about Michael Bigelow, and cared even less.

He lit a cigarette and walked back toward the observatory, confident that his father would not be home for hours.

Young arrived at NASA headquarters shortly after 1:30 a.m. He studied the battery of television screens. Some showed Apollo-Soyuz on its launch pad at Cape Canaveral. Others displayed the circuits and instruments throughout the ship. One indicated the countdown to liftoff, scheduled for Saturday at 10:03 p.m. That screen now flashed sixty-eight hours, twenty-six minutes, twenty-three seconds. Another screen showed a faint flicker of light no bigger than a match head.

Pointing to the tiny dot, a technician informed him, "There she is. It's a planetoid all right, about five hundred miles in diameter. It just shot in from nowhere."

The picture was being beamed from INSITE—International Research Satellite—the largest and most complex observatory ever placed in space. On board was an impressive array of equipment, including radar and ultraviolet telescopes. INSITE could spot a golf ball at four hundred miles or a star the size of the moon thousands of light years away. Computerized data, photographs, oscilloscopic readings and a televised image pulsed continuously to Mission Control, Cape Canaveral and tracking stations around the globe.

Young gazed at the flicker of light and fumbled absentmindedly for a cigarette. Finding his pockets empty, he remembered that Jenny had persuaded him to give up smoking two days before. For a moment he wished she had not been so persuasive. His attention returned to the dot on the screen.

"Where the hell is it?" he asked.

"A bit less than twenty-five million miles away and moving fast. The sunlight it's reflecting indicates that it's pretty solid."

"What about the orbit?"

"That's the big question. We can't be sure yet, but it's certainly coming in our general direction."

Young frowned in annoyance at the unscientific answer. He chose his own words carefully, especially when he was on duty, and he expected others to be just as precise.

"What do you mean, 'in our general direction'? Exactly what information do you have, Winacott?"

Don Winacott flushed at the rebuke. Young achieved maximum effort from his staff by the judicious use of criticisms and compliments. But he imposed his own high standards as severely on others as on himself, and the compliments were hard won. "We've only had it under watch for an hour, sir. Our first estimates suggested that the planetoid's orbit could cut near or across the path of the Mars shot." He added defensively, "That's why we called you."

Young began to wish a more experienced team were on duty. Winacott was one of the two Americans manning that evening's skeleton shift. Neither had been with NASA for more than a year; neither showed any signs of being among the brightest sparks of the universe. Sharing the watch were two Russians, who had stood by, obviously bewildered, during the conversation.

"Have you conferred with the Russians?" Young asked.

"I'm afraid we let the interpreter go," Winacott admitted. "We thought . . ."

Young's glare cut short the explanation. "That wasn't smart. Let's see if we can make amends. Get the interpreter back, and a full team on duty here. Now or sooner. Alert all observatories. I want the most extensive worldwide watch possible. And have all sightings correlated every half hour."

"Yes sir," Winacott mumbled.

Young walked to his office and slammed the door. He picked up his direct line to the office of Bud Kennedy, the launch director at Cape Canaveral, and felt his irritation subside when he heard Kennedy's voice. At least someone was on the ball.

Kennedy had received news of the planetoid sighting at home and had immediately headed for the Cape. As the man primarily responsible for ensuring that the launch went successfully, his problems would end at liftoff. But his enthusiasm for the entire mission was such that few details escaped his scrutiny.

"I see the universe has thrown another curve, Bud," Young said. "What do you make of it?" He had presumed, rightly, that Kennedy would have been busily computing the mass and orbit of the planetoid. His judgment could be relied on.

"It's a hell of a headache, Matt. I make it that this thing will come too near the flight path of Apollo-Soyuz for comfort. At best there'll be a lot of static—possibly a total breakdown of communications between the spacecraft and the earth."

"How near is too near?" Young asked.

"I'd hate to commit myself at this stage. We just haven't made enough sightings, but we'll know better soon."

"Fine. Sit tight. I'll be in touch. Oh, and nothing to the press. We'll handle that from here."

Young's next call was to the Rice Hotel. He asked for Dmitri Akhmerov, administrator of Russian collaboration on the Mars program. The two men shared a mutual respect developed during two years of joint work in preparation for the shot. Young's respect would have been more grudging if he had known the Russian's true background.

In appearance, Akhmerov was unimpressive. With a bulging stomach, bald head, drooping mustache and florid complexion, he looked like a sad, overripe peach. In reality he was one of the most powerful officials of the KGB. He earned his first commendation as a junior KGB official after being assigned to discourage a dissident writer who was active on an underground newspaper hostile to the government. His brief was unspecific—a hint that he could use initiative to the utmost. The writer was felled in the street by what he imagined at the time to be a gunshot wound in the buttocks. Doctors discovered that he had been shot with a pellet of nitrogen mustard gas, which rapidly began eating away his flesh. Though the writer's life was saved, his recovery was slow and painful.

Akhmerov later helped plan KGB assassinations and earned further prestige by proposing the murder of President Kennedy. Though the plan was rejected, he was established as an agent who would unhesitatingly go to extreme lengths for his country. He now held realistic hopes of an appointment to the Soviet Union's highest authority, the Politburo.

All NASA personnel had been warned that liaison with the Russians on the Mars program would almost certainly allow KGB officials to infiltrate Mission Control and the Cape. Young frequently wondered if Akhmerov might be less benign than he appeared to be.

"Yes," the Russian eventually answered. "Why aren't you here at the party?"

Young detected a note of concern in Akhmerov's voice.

"I'll be back soon. Meanwhile, we've got a problem." After he had sketched out the situation, Akhmerov asked, "Is this serious enough to report any higher?"

Each man was directly responsible to his nation's chief executive. Young had already considered informing the President.

"I think not. We're not sure what we've got. I'm going to hold off until we know something more definite."

"Yes. Very good."

Both men had agreed to keep each other fully informed of developments concerning Apollo-Soyuz and to act only after consulting each other. Privately, each was ready to abandon the agreement if any situation threatened political embarrassment to either country.

"I take it you'll get your people in Moscow to zero in on the planetoid," Young added.

"Certainly."

"The sooner we get this thing tracked down the better."

"Yes, of course. Perhaps we should have a meeting first thing tomorrow morning."

"You bet. All hands on deck at nine."

"On deck?" Akhmerov struggled with the metaphor.

"Excuse me, I mean yes. We'll have a meeting of all senior personnel at nine in the morning."

He hung up and stepped into the outer office of Mission Control. He noted that the interpreter had arrived. The four men on duty were busily calling an extra staff.

Young interrupted Winacott. "Call me as soon as you get anything definite. I'll be at the party, at home or . . ." He hesitated then wrote down the number of Jenny's hotel. "You might get hold of me there."

With a final glance at the screen on which the planetoid still glimmered, he nodded a curt farewell. Winacott sighed with relief as the door closed.

The intense activity that typified Mission Control during busy periods was a direct response to Young's demanding, efficient manner. Tall, dark and athletic, he was the kind of man who automatically dominated any crowd. He was respected as a scientist who had risen through the ranks and earned his post on merit, not political connections. Young knew what he wanted and usually got it. Men found him brusque, but fair. Women, without encouragement from Young, were fascinated by his aura of power and authority.

Young had dedicated himself to work with a fierce determination since the death of his wife twelve years earlier. Patricia was petite, gentle and a talented artist. She had made the pewter ring he still wore and the figurine he kept on his desk. Her paintings decorated his home. Their child, a daughter, was born a year after their marriage. A mongoloid, she lived for just a day. Only a few months later, they had learned that Patricia had cancer. A succession of operations followed. She lost one breast, then the other. Eventually, she could only get around with the help of a walking frame. She died a week after their fifth wedding anniversary. Immediately Young had begun to work harder than ever, giving himself little opportunity to brood. He learned to live from day to day, cramming as much activity as he could into each twenty-four hours. There had been affairs—intense, sexual relationships—but Young had not felt the warmth of love again . . . until he had met Jenny.

Almost a year ago, the *Daily News* had sent her to interview Young on his appointment as NASA administrator. He had been startled by her close resemblance to Patricia. Though Jenny was taller, the two women could have passed as sisters and Young was at ease with her immediately. Soon he felt as though he had known her for years.

On their first date he took her to dinner at his favorite Italian restaurant. The place was pretentious, but the food was excellent. After the meal the restaurant's trio played "The Shadow of Your Smile," a song Young often requested when he ate there. A little sheepishly, he confided to Jenny that it was his favorite romantic ballad. At her insistence, he asked the musicians to play it again, and he and Jenny danced for the first time. The next morning twelve yellow roses were delivered to her hotel room. Attached was a simple note, "Thanks for a perfect evening." Other dates followed and, after Jenny returned to New York, Young flew to join her most weekends. Jenny taught him to laugh and to care again.

On the drive back from Mission Control to the hotel, Young tried to imagine what married life would be like the second time around. As sweet as the sweetest moments with Patricia, he hoped. And much less painful.

Jenny found a phone booth near the powder room and dialed the Bigelows' home. Despite the late hour, she hoped that Michael would hear the ringing. She had met him on several occasions when she and Young had visited Bigelow. Though about fifteen, the boy was unusually shy, with a too-ready, but beguiling, smile. His straight fair hair flowed over his collar. Jenny suspected that he grew his hair long in the hope of being accepted by other teenagers, rather than out of personal preference. Taller than his father, he walked with the gangling awkwardness of adolescence.

"Hello."

The one word betrayed Michael's surprise at the late call.

"Michael? This is Jenny Corbett."

"Sure. Hi."

"I hope I didn't get you out of bed."

"No, that's all right. I'm in dad's observatory."

"I'd hoped you might still be there. Your father's been telling me about your planetoid. It's really exciting, isn't it?"

Michael was grateful that Jenny couldn't see him blush
with pride. Perhaps his father hadn't intended to be as abrupt
as he had sounded. Maybe he had even been boasting at the
party at about how his son had . . .

"Yes, it is," Michael agreed.

"Well, you know I'm a reporter. I was hoping you'd tell
me all about it."

"Sure. Definitely it's not on the map and I've done a lot of
checking. I've still got a lot more checking to do but I'm sure
it's a planetoid."

Jenny slipped a notebook from her purse and began to
scribble. She had a story all right. A big one. She noted the
time—only 1:40 a.m. All the time in the world for the deskmen to give the story a big display. Ten minutes later she had
exhausted Michael's information.

"Thanks, Michael. You wouldn't mind if your name was
used in the paper, would you?"

"Er, no. Do you think they might print it?"

"Yes. I really think they will. I'll see you get a copy of the
paper. Goodnight."

"Goodnight, Miss Corbett. Oh, and a happy engagement."

"You're sweet. Thank you."

She hung up, convinced now that Michael's planetoid was
the reason for Young's call from Mission Control. But how to
check it out . . . ? She couldn't call Young. She knew he
would not want information released to the press until a carefully considered statement had been prepared for simultaneous release to all the media. She would have to chase the
story some other way. Her first duty was to try to get corrob-
oration of the story. She could decide later what she should
tell Young. Checking her notebook she called Bigelow's extension at Mission Control, hoping that Young wouldn't answer.

An unfamiliar voice came over the line. "Mission Control,
Don Winacott."

"Hello," Jenny said in her most seductive voice. "This is
the *Daily News*. What's the latest on the planetoid?"

"Christ. How did you find out?"

Jenny's heart raced. She now had all the confirmation she needed.

"Look miss. I can't say anything. We only spotted it an hour ago and . . ."

"I understand the Mars shot is in danger," Jenny lied shamelessly.

"Well, maybe, but we're not sure. Look, I really can't give you anything . . ." Realizing that he had already said too much, he added hastily, "You must know all information has to come through our press office. You'll have to talk to them in the morning. I don't know what planetoid you're talking about."

"But . . ."

Jenny couldn't continue. Winacott had hung up. She fumbled for more change and placed a collect call to the *Daily News.*

"Jenny, my love. I was beginning to think you didn't care about me now that you're promised to another."

The greeting was typical of Ken Reynolds, the ebullient news editor. His only interests were his five-year-old daughter, the *Daily News* and his considerable daily intake of alcohol. His marriage had been a disastrous failure. Because of his wife's frequent affairs, he won custody of his daughter and since the divorce she had been cared for by a nanny while he was at work.

"What's the front page lead, Ken?"

"Another gangland slaying, honey. Why do you ask?"

"Because I've got a better one. How about a planetoid threatening the Mars shot?"

"Shit."

"There's no time for that," Jenny joked. "Let me fill you in."

Reynolds quickly grasped the thread of the story.

"OK sweetheart. Let's have it. Go in hard on the boy-sights-planetoid bit, and play gently the speculation that NASA is concerned about a possible threat to the Mars shot. That seems a bit thin, but I'll get a few calls in to Mission Control and Cape Canaveral to see if we can catch someone off guard."

"Please don't, Ken," Jenny pleaded. "I haven't spoken about this to Matt, and I'd really like to explain it to him in my own way. Anyway, all you're likely to get from NASA is double-talk."

Reynolds considered the alternatives. What he had now was a top story. With more digging he might unearth a mass of official denials—or he might encourage NASA to issue a statement to all the press and thus rob the *Daily News* of a big-selling exclusive.

"OK, we'll go with your story. Have you got permission from the boy's father for the interview? We don't want any invasion-of-privacy problem if we can help it."

"I haven't got permission yet, but I'll have it before the paper comes out. And I'll see what I can do about pictures. Trust me."

"I do, honeybunch. Now get on to copy."

A typist came on the line and Jenny scanned her notes.

"Start it, 'From Jennifer Corbett, Houston, 2 a.m. Thursday.' And you can slug it 'exclusive'. I haven't had time to write this out yet so it'll have to be off the cuff . . ."

Twenty minutes later Jenny hung up and returned to join Bigelow, who was now chatting with Steve Dandridge, a career diplomat assigned to the Mars program to ensure smooth relationships with the Russians. Driven by a restless nervous energy, he was a tough-minded realist with a ready smile. The wearing of modest pinstriped suits was his only concession to textbook diplomacy. Few people suspected that he had a more significant role—with the Central Intelligence Agency.

"You look sensational," he told Jenny.

"How diplomatic," she answered, relieved to see that Young hadn't yet returned. She hoped Bigelow wouldn't make any remark about her own absence. With luck he might have assumed that she had been mingling with other guests.

"Where's the lucky man?" Dandridge asked.

"He had a better offer," she said lightly. "Mission Control asked him to drop in."

"Such are the penalties of power. And in the meantime I see you've been left without a drink. More champagne?"

"I'd love some."

"Count me in too," Bigelow said.

Dandridge clicked his heels, bowed with mock servility and turned toward the bar. As he ordered, he was aware that Sergei Krotkov, Akhmerov's personal assistant, had sidled alongside. A cowed individual, he had the disconcerting habit of looking directly at the chins of people he met. Dandridge was often tempted to duck down to the level of his own tie-knot, forcing Krotkov to look him straight in the eye.

"You have a very fine country," the Russian muttered hurriedly, his eyes now fixed on the bar and his lips scarcely moving.

Dandridge was taken aback. Krotkov opening a conversation was indeed remarkable. In the mirror behind the bar Dandridge saw that no other Russians were nearby.

"Yes, a fine country," he agreed. "I have also enjoyed my travels in Russia."

The Russian almost hissed, "We must meet."

Dandridge concealed his amazement with difficulty. In the next few moments he was to become even more puzzled. As he lifted the tray of drinks from the bar, Krotkov apparently quite deliberately knocked his elbow. The drinks crashed to the floor. For an instant everyone turned to look.

Dandridge bent to pick up the broken glass and Krotkov crouched beside him. Amid the confusion, the Russian whispered again, his head only two feet or so from the floor.

"You have a fine country. We must meet." In a louder voice, he added, "I'm so sorry, so sorry. How clumsy."

Good God, thought Dandridge. We've got a potential defector. The Russian continued his apologies as Dandridge ordered a fresh supply of champagne. Already he was pondering various ways to arrange a meeting with Krotkov without alerting other Russians.

"That's perfectly all right," he assured Krotkov with affected politeness. "Everything will be all right."

Dandridge, still bewildered, rejoined Jenny and Bigelow as Young approached from the banquet hall doorway. The administrator was obviously pleased to find all three together.

"Welcome back, Matt," Bigelow said. "I trust you put the fire out."

"Not exactly. It's still burning. We've sighted a planetoid and I'm afraid it could cause problems during the Mars shot."

So the story is right on the mark, Jenny thought. Her relief was overtaken by anxiety. How could she explain her deviousness to Young? And yet, she was a journalist, damn it. The story was one that any self-respecting reporter would have to reveal, by fair means or foul. She would tell Young she had filed the story as soon as they were alone together, but she would certainly make no apology for doing so.

"We'll be meeting at nine in the morning," Young added.

For an instant no one spoke. All knew that he would have been reluctant to discuss NASA business openly at a party. The fact that he had done so left no doubt about the seriousness of the situation.

"Oh, Christ," groaned Bigelow. "Michael phoned me hours ago to tell me he had sighted a planetoid on the scope at home. I told him he was out of his mind. I didn't even ask HQ to check."

"What time was that?" Young snapped.

"I don't know. Ten, maybe. I thought . . ."

"Had he fixed the coordinates?"

"I didn't ask him. He . . ."

"Too bad you didn't, Bob." The reprimand was one of the few Young had ever administered to his deputy. It had the effect of a bawling-out on a barrack square.

"I guess I could have checked it out."

"Exactly. It might not have helped, but it might have saved us many hours. As it is, observatories around the world are zooming in only now."

Dandridge relieved the tension. "I've had an interesting evening, too," he said. "I'd like to have a chat with you some time tomorrow, Matt."

"Sure." Young smiled at Jenny. "It seems like we'll soon have a story or two for you."

She swallowed, guilty at having pursued the lead without consulting him. She would have to tell him, but not now. To hell with permission from Bigelow for the interview with Michael. She could smooth that over later.

Young turned to Jenny as the band began to play "The Shadow of Your Smile." She was so preoccupied that she hadn't recognized the opening bars.

"That's our cue," he said. "Let's dance." On the dance floor he held her tightly and kissed her hair, breathing deeply the scent of her distinctive perfume.

Following his lead automatically, Jenny continued to worry quietly. Never before had her feelings for Young, or any man, conflicted with her passion for journalism.

Jenny had become a reporter at seventeen. While at college she pestered her local paper, the *Miami Herald*, for a newsroom job. After rejecting eleven of her applications, the paper capitulated. The news editor told her that it would be cheaper to employ her on staff than to keep answering her letters. Her parents protested only mildly when she announced that she was quitting college. They were divorced and each had remarried, and Jenny felt sure they were relieved to be unburdened of any financial responsibility for her.

Fiercely competitive, she quickly developed a total sense of duty toward her job. She first questioned the right of the press to report news vividly when she covered the story of a school building that had plunged into a disused mine. Forty-three children died, and Jenny was in tears when she interviewed the grief-stricken parents. Her graphic reporting brought her a fifty-dollar raise, and she was ashamed. How could she allow such a disaster to be her own good fortune? But sympathizers throughout the United States raised more than two million dollars for a disaster fund. The village got a new, better school. And abandoned mine shafts for miles around were reinforced with extra supports. Perhaps in some small way, Jenny thought, her efforts might have helped to minimize the possibility of a similar disaster.

She questioned, too, the right of her paper to publish in gory detail the horrific account of a three-month rampage by a hooded rapist. But she was proud to be a journalist when public indignation led to the setting-up of a vigilante group which trapped him.

She now believed passionately that it was the duty of the press to publish the truth, not to censor its own material. It was the privilege of the public to react to the news as it saw fit.

At nineteen Jenny fell deeply in love with one of the paper's senior reporters. They married after a courtship of only a month. In less than another month, she already regretted having exchanged the glamor of her newsroom job for a life of tedium in an apartment. The marriage was a disaster. One year, one miscarriage and one trip to Nevada later, she was free. She quickly buried her anxiety over her ability to have children and began to blitz the New York *Daily News* with a batch of job applications. If she was going to build a career banging a drum, she might as well perform before the widest possible audience. This time only six letters were needed before she got the job.

She soon found that, with guile and charm, she could open

doors that were closed to male colleagues and ruthlessly exploited the fact. Only once did she use her beauty more questionably. She had a brief affair with Reynolds after joining the *Daily News*. At the time, she persuaded herself that she was genuinely attracted to him. On reflection, she recognized that she had probably acted from ulterior motives. In any event, major assignments followed. And they continued after the affair ended.

On all the stories she covered, Jenny saw her responsibility as simply to report the truth as quickly as she could. Now, she felt strongly that it had been her duty to report the planetoid story.

Young broke in on her thoughts as the song ended. "Honey, you're not angry because I had to leave the party, are you?"

"No, Matt. It's not that. I have to talk to you, but not here. Please let's go."

"OK. I suppose they can run things without us at this hour of the morning."

He drew her toward the stage and gestured for the microphone. The chattering stopped as he announced, "Jenny and I are going home, folks. It's been a great party. Thanks, everybody, for a terrific time."

A loud cheer went up. Bigelow has earlier hidden a box of confetti and threw it on Young and Jenny as they left the banquet room. The cheering died down as the massive oak doors closed behind them.

In the foyer Young brushed the confetti from Jenny's hair and kissed her while his car was being brought to the door. She was unresponsive.

"I'm sorry, darling," she apologized. "I don't mean to be moody. I love you."

The car, a red rebuilt Thunderbird two-seater, now arrived in front of the hotel. Young pulled down the convertible top and played his usual joke of touching Jenny's knee, apparently by accident, as he reached for the gear shift. Jenny moved her knees out of reach.

"My place or the hotel?" he asked. Since arriving in Houston a week earlier Jenny had spent every night in his townhouse. He had playfully suggested that they should spend at least one night together in the hotel suite the *Daily News* had reserved for her. But that would not be tonight, Jenny decided. In view of the unwelcome news she had in store for him it seemed only fair to confront him on his home ground.

"Your place," she said. "If you'll have me."

"You bet I will."

Young shifted rapidly through the four gears, using every bit of the engine's 193-horsepower until he reached 80 miles an hour on the deserted road. Then he slipped the T-bird into overdrive. Ten minutes later he pulled up outside the townhouse, leaned across the passenger seat and opened the car door for Jenny. She thanked him uneasily.

In the living room, Jenny took Young's hand and pulled him to her. For a moment they simply held each other.

"Excuse me for being a bore, darling," she said, "but I'm very tense. I've got something to tell you and you might be angry with me."

"Impossible," Young assured her. "Anyway, it can wait."

"No, it can't, Matt. I called the office while you were at Mission Control."

"So?"

"I phoned in a story about the planetoid."

Young took a step back from Jenny, alarmed. He unconsciously played with his pewter ring.

"You what?" he asked incredulously.

"Darling, I am a reporter. Bigelow told me about what Michael thought he had seen and I called him up. I phoned in the story as a matter of course."

"My God. And just what the hell does it say?"

"Well, it says that there's a planetoid that might cause problems with the Mars shot."

Young whistled. "How did you find that out?"

"What Michael told me sort of added up with you rushing away like that. Then I phoned Mission Control and, well, one of the technicians . . ."

She stopped, hoping that Winacott wouldn't end up on the firing line.

"Matt, I'm sorry. No damn it, I'm not sorry. Everybody knows I'm a reporter and I have a job to do. The story's true, isn't it? What harm can the truth do?"

"A lot, honey. A hell of a lot. NASA information is given out to all the press at the same time. So you got a scoop—but who on earth is going to believe that you didn't take advantage of the fact that you're engaged to the NASA administrator?"

"I know, Matt. I know. But there were other reporters at the party, too. Any of them could have gotten it. And I'd sent my story over before you ever came back to the party."

"Any of them couldn't have gotten the story. Only one reporter was next to me when I got the call. And that was you."

"Matt, I had to do it. I . . ."

"You won't have to do it again. I'm going to have a hell of a lot of explaining to do—to the press, and possibly to the President—and I haven't got the time, damn it. I've got to be sure you'll never exploit your relationship with me again."

"But . . ."

"I mean it. I don't want your damned journalistic scruples getting in my way ever again."

Jenny was fighting a losing battle to win his approval, even his understanding.

"Hear this, Matt." She spoke softly but faced him squarely. "Marriage to you isn't going to stop me being a journalist. And I'm going to do the job as well as I can. That's the way it's got to be. Now what say we forget it and kiss and make up?"

He seemed about to speak, but kissed her dispassionately, then more warmly. She put her hand to his lips, resisting gently as he moved to kiss her again.

"Later, Matt," she said. "Let me get myself together again. I think I'll go and shower."

Young mixed two highballs, kicked off his shoes and sprawled on the sofa. As he heard the shower being turned on, he found himself trying to justify Jenny's actions. It was difficult for him to understand what she had done. Anxious to divert his thoughts to other matters, he decided to phone HQ to make sure everything was running smoothly.

He didn't expect the familiar voice that answered.

"Mission Control, Bob Bigelow."

Young laughed, delighted that his deputy had obviously dashed to HQ to keep an eye on developments.

"You sonofabitch," Young said, his earlier annoyance with Bigelow forgotten. "Having missed out with the boss's girl, I suppose you're after his job."

"I'd like the girl, Matt, but not the job. It looks as though you're in for a headache. The latest data indicate that this baby will certainly be near enough to the Mars path to cause serious radio interference."

"When will we know for sure?"

"In the morning. Hopefully, first thing."

Young hesitated, his concern growing as details of previous near-misses flashed into his mind.

"Bob, what are the chances that we have another Hermes on the way?"

Both men knew that Hermes, a minor planet, had narrowly missed colliding with earth in October 1937. Weighing about 500,000 tons and traveling at the speed of light, Hermes passed within half a million miles of the earth. A slight change in course, which could so easily have been caused by earth's gravitational pull, and Hermes would have smashed into the earth with incalculable force.

"I wouldn't lay any odds," Bigelow answered. "Let's just hope that it misses as neatly."

"I wouldn't complain about a wider margin."

Young paused, suddenly aware that Jenny was behind him. She gently massaged his shoulders.

"Uh, Bob? I've got to go. Keep in touch."

Young grinned expectantly as he turned and saw Jenny. She had let her hair down and was wearing a pale blue negligee, tied loosely at the middle. His eyes fell to her nipples, then followed the soft outline of her slender body to the dark area showing faintly.

"You look gorgeous."

"I feel it, Matt. What say we call a truce? And forget the drinks. Let's . . ." Her smile completed the unspoken invitation.

Jenny slid to the floor in front of Young and placed an arm over his knees. After a few silent moments she moved her hand forward along the inside of his thigh.

At Mission Control, Bigelow asked one of the technicians for more coffee. "And some for our comrade here," he said, indicating a Russian technician sitting nearby.

Bigelow found it difficult to be gracious with the Russians. Deeply patriotic, he resented that the Soviet Union would gain much more than his own country from the Apollo-Soyuz program.

He was grateful that, at least, details of the newest U.S. interplanetary vessels were being kept under wraps. Similar to conventional aircraft, they could take off and land at any big airfield, and dock with any spacecraft so far designed. The

Russians had offered to share in the development of the new vehicles, and had suggested that a cosmonaut should fly with an American test pilot proving flights. Congress had turned down the idea and proposed the Apollo-Soyuz Mars shot instead. The Soviet Union had leapt at the deal. The program appealed particularly because it suggested parity between the two nations, when in fact American space technology, since the 1969 moon landing and the Apollo-Soyuz docking of 1975, had spurted more than a generation ahead.

Each nation hoped the mutual contact would also pry loose information about the other's military strength. It seemed to Bigelow that most of the prying had been done by the Russians.

Bigelow raised his coffee cup to the Russian—one of the few who understood no English—and toasted, "Naz-der-over," giving a fair imitation of the Russian for "Good health."

"Na zdarova," the Russian replied, grinning sociably.

Noting that the nearest interpreter was some way away, Bigelow decided to amuse himself. "Say, you know this planetoid could hit Apollo-Soyuz?" he said, looking straight at the Russian. "Why don't we send your two cosmonauts up on their own? Good idea?"

"Na zdarova," replied the Russian, still grinning.

A secretary handed a telex to Bigelow. It was from the Central Telegram Bureau of the International Astronomical Union, located at the Smithsonian Institution's Astrophysical Observatory in Cambridge, Massachusetts. It confirmed that all major ground-based observatories in North America had the planetoid in view. Other nations throughout the world would maintain the watch as the earth spun around. The Union would coordinate all information from the observatories and dispatch it to Mission Control.

Despite the sophistication of satellite observatories, every available large telescope was used to help to determine the mass and orbit of any new body in the solar system.

Satisfied that nothing more could be accomplished for several hours, Bigelow picked up his coat and left for home to catch a few hours' sleep.

Tomorrow promised to be a busy day.

Shortly before daybreak over the east coast of America, darkness approached Japan. The Tokyo Observatory was already crowded. It seemed that every scientist with an official pass to the building had given up a night's sleep for a view of the new visitor to the solar system. While waiting to look through the eyepiece of the huge 74-inch reflecting telescope, they formed small groups and talked excitedly.

Soon an observer looking through the telescope turned to the assembled groups and gave a thumbs-up sign. The planetoid was in view.

Other scientists lined up to take turns at the telescope. Each time someone descended from the observation platform he was surrounded and bombarded with rapid-fire questions. Many scientists scribbled notes and punched computations on pocket calculators.

Two science writers, who had routine access to the observatory, flitted from one center of activity to another. The conversations the writers overheard made questioning unnecessary. Each scrawled pages of notes. There would be time enough to sort through the numerous contradictions and qualifications later.

At frequent intervals, a telex machine stuttered out a message to the Central Telegram Bureau. A copy of each message, posted on a bulletin board, drew eager crowds.

As dawn crept around the earth, similar scenes would take place in Russia, Egypt, Czechoslovakia, Britain and other countries in the northern hemisphere.

Soon the destination of the planetoid would be known.

Chapter Two

The tumbling planetoid sped on relentlessly at forty miles a second. First one end glinted in the sunlight, then the other. It was now 23,320,800 miles from the earth.

Michael stood in the middle of an ankle-deep pile of crumpled paper. He had spent the night jotting down one calculation after another, repeatedly checking for errors. On a map of the night sky he had plotted the planetoid's course. A dot marked each of the fifteen separate sightings he had made. The dots, closely grouped, were joined by a short, curved line, indicating a segment of the estimated orbit. Michael had extended the line, projecting the planetoid's eventual journey. He studied the map once more. If his calculations of speed and distance were correct, there could be little doubt about the result.

The planetoid was on a collision course with the earth.

Suddenly he heard his father's car skid to a halt on the gravel driveway. Snatching up the undeveloped photographic plates of sightings, he ran from the observatory and reached the car just as the driver's door opened.

"Dad, I've got it all here." Breathless, he slapped the plates. "It really is a planetoid, dad, and it's . . ."

"Hey, hold it, son," Bigelow said, forcing a smile. "We know all about it. We haven't exactly been asleep at Mission Control, you know. Let's have some coffee and we'll compare notes."

Michael's shoulders sagged as he followed his father into the house.

Not until the percolator had begun to bubble noisily did Bigelow give the boy his opening. "Now, let's hear it again, but slowly."

"I've made about fifteen sightings, dad. I've got the plates here. I make it that . . ."

"Fifteen sightings . . ." Bigelow interrupted. "What time did you make your first fix?"

"Just before ten. Nine-forty-seven, to be exact."

"That would give you about a three-hour start on NASA," Bigelow added thoughtfully. He squeezed his temples as though to strangle the hangover that had begun to thump away inside his head. He unplugged the percolator and raised his bloodshot eyes to peer quizzically at his son. Michael's confidence grew as he sensed his father's growing interest.

"I've been up all night checking, dad. I've checked and checked. It's . . . it's going to hit the earth, dad."

Bigelow turned sharply, too sharply, to look at his son. The contents of his head, dulled by alcohol, moved at a much slower pace. Wincing, he poured two cups of coffee and handed one to Michael.

"OK, son. Let's hear it all from the beginning."

Michael drew the back of his hand across his forehead, moving his hair out of his eyes. "Well, after I phoned you at the party I went back to the observatory and I checked and checked, and did all the calculations, and I made sure it was a planetoid. I figured out its orbit, dad, and it's scary. It's headed straight for us. It's going to collide with the earth, dad. I'm sure it is. You've got to help me check it out."

"Sounds as likely as a good woman, son. Are you sure I'm the only one who's been hitting the bottle?"

He smiled and ruffled Michael's hair, remembering too late that the gesture annoyed the boy. Michael drew away.

"Check it with me, dad. Let's develop the plates. We can be much surer then."

"True enough." He downed the rest of his coffee at a gulp and placed his cup in the sink. He shook his head slowly in another attempt to clear away the headache. "OK, son. Let's go."

As they crossed to the observatory Bigelow reproached himself again for not alerting NASA after his son's phone call. He was well aware that the amateur astronomer was just as likely as the professional to spot a strange object in space. The search was something like looking for a needle in ten thousand haystacks. Luck was a big factor. A slight adjustment in focus, or the angle of a telescope, and a whole new area of the cosmos would leap into view. Once an object had been sighted, sophisticated satellite telescopes were more likely to predict accurately its orbit. But at this stage Michael was hours ahead of any of the experts.

In the darkroom the two worked in silence until the outlines of the fifteen photographs gradually began to take shape.

"Are you sure all of these photos were taken with exactly the same exposure, Mike?"

"Yes, dad. And the same fix."

Both knew it was crucial that each picture be taken under identical conditions. Each negative and print had to be exposed and develoved in precisely the same way to ensure that any change in brightness or position on the prints indicated movement of the planetoid, not photographic error.

When the prints were dry, Michael marked on the back of each one the time it had been taken and arranged them in sequence. Each print showed a faint point of light in the upper left corner.

"This area of the sky should be clear, dad—at least, according to the sky map and considering the power of our scope."

"I know, Mike. This is the same baby we've spotted at NASA all right." He smiled wryly. "We were a bit slow off the mark, weren't we? Now where's that map?"

Michael fished a folded piece of paper out of a pocket and handed it to his father, who studied it for a moment, then wandered to the telescope and checked the setting.

"So far so good."

The next stage was to run the prints through the "blinker," a machine which enabled the viewer to look first at one print, then another, then back to the first again and so on, in rapid succession. A fixed object would show on the blinker as a steady light. A moving one would blink. Its speed could be estimated by measuring the distance the object had moved between the taking of each photograph. By projecting the angle of movement from several sightings, an approximate orbit could be worked out.

The machine blinked hurriedly as Bigelow fed in the first two prints. The blinking continued with the same frequency when he compared the second and third prints.

"Christ, she's moving."

"I made it more than 100,000 miles an hour, dad."

"You're way ahead of me, Mike. And NASA, too. They were still computing the speed of this thing when I left."

After putting all fifteen prints through the blinker, Bigelow made a few measurements and several calculations. "It looks like your figures are good—I get between 100,000 and 150,-000 miles an hour for sure. And your orbit checks out, too. Je-sus. Let's find out how big this thing is."

"I did that, too."

Michael fumbled through his notes and produced another set of calculations. By applying a formula to the estimated speed and brightness of the planetoid he had reckoned that it could be two thousand miles across.

Bigelow checked the figures and made some corrections.

"You've got something here, but I make it less than a thousand miles wide. Still, it's a big bastard."

He remeasured the distance the planetoid had traveled between the first and last sighting.

"Everything else seems to check out. It's definitely between twenty million and twenty-five million miles away. It'll cover that distance in a week or so. Now where will the earth be then?"

Michael snatched up an astronomical handbook which lay open on the front table. "That's the page you want, dad."

Bigelow paled as he read the text. "My God. We'd better redo these measurements as precisely as we can."

The two spend the next forty minutes repeating the calculations, this time with even more painstaking care. The results were just as frightening.

"It looks like you could be right, Mike. We just might be in for one hell of a big bang."

Michael struggled with the conflicting emotions of pride and alarm. Thrilled though he was that his father agreed with his calculations, he was anxious about their significance. So he was right . . . the planetoid was on collision course with the earth. . . .

"Son, I'm going to have to get back to the office. I'd like to take your pictures with me."

"Sure."

"Meanwhile, you'd better get some rest. I guess neither of us is going to want to leave the scope tonight."

Michael wondered whether to mention the call from Jenny. It could wait, he decided. Anyway, his father seemed to be in a hurry. "Can I stay up?"

"Why not? I'll make a Galileo of you yet."

"Thanks, dad. Goodnight—I mean, good morning."

Just in time, Bigelow remembered not to ruffle Michael's hair.

Young managed to slap off the radio alarm as soon as it blurted out its raucous greeting. Jenny slept on while he showered. He slipped into a bathrobe and decided to prepare a special breakfast to give her a relaxing start to the day.

Awakened by the smell of fresh coffee, she tossed back the blankets and rolled over to Young's side of the bed. She blinked as sunlight fell on her face.

"Hi," she called sleepily.

"Morning, honey," Young answered from the kitchen. "Be with you in a minute."

He set breakfast on a quaint tea wagon she had bought for him the summer before at an auction sale and rolled it into the bedroom.

Jenny lay naked on her back, still half-asleep. Her negligee was on the floor at the bedside, where she had let it fall during their lovemaking.

Young gazed at her for a moment and stroked her hair. She moaned and stirred.

"Matt!" she protested, squirming away. "Give me time to wake up."

"Here, this will help." He handed her the glass of orange juice.

She drank it quickly, then climbed out of bed and stretched her arms above her head, loosening her sleepy body. She put an arm around his neck, leaned her forehead against his shoulder and held him tightly.

"Oh, Matt, I'm sorry about last night. Still want to marry me?"

"Of course I do," Young assured her. "No more apologies. Let's have breakfast."

She put on her negligee while he poured more orange juice. He found himself unable to crowd out memories of similar scenes he had shared with his first wife. He supposed that the memories would endure, but at least they were no longer painful. An image of their child flashed into his mind. That anguish, he had vowed, would not be repeated.

He and Jenny had talked about the question of children early in their relationship. He had told her about Patricia and the baby and his reluctance to risk loss of that kind again. She had held his hand sympathetically and then, suddenly, found herself confessing her own unhappy past. She made it clear that she did want to try pregnancy again, but with someone she loved, at the right time.

They had moved onto a more comfortable subject and the issue had remained at an impasse. When they began to discuss marriage seriously, she remembered the conversation uneasily. Yet she felt confident that she would be able to persuade him to try starting a family. So many of his emotional wounds had been healed already that she hoped the surgery would eventually be complete.

She stood to clear away the breakfast dishes and kissed Young on the forehead.

"Matt, about last night . . ."

"Honey, as far as I'm concerned that's over. You know where I stand. I'm not going to budge, honey. I can't."

"I'm sorry, but it's important to me—and to us—that you understand. I want to play fair and I have to say I'd probably do the same again. I want to be sure you don't let anything slip, or if you do you must emphasize that it's in confidence. It's just that . . . well, you know how seriously I take the responsibility of being a reporter. I don't believe that anyone has the right to hush things up."

"Honey, if . . ."

Young was relieved when the ringing of the phone prevented him from having to finish the threat for the moment. Bigelow, sounding a good deal huskier than usual, was on the line from Mission Control. Young noted the time—7 a.m.

"Good God, Bob. Have you been there all night?"

"More or less. And it promises to be a hell of a day, too. For certain the planetoid is going to be too damn near the path of the Mars shot. And worse, it looks like it might be heading for good old Mother Earth."

"Christ."

"That's a thought," said Bigelow flippantly. "Let's hope He's on our side. I'm not sure the Russians are."

"What do you mean?"

"They've been huddled in private meetings. They know the score as well as we do. I'm not sure what it all means, but they're plotting something."

"Have you heard from Akhmerov?"

"Yes. He's been here for hours."

The news seemed to support Bigelow's suspicions. Akhmerov seldom arrived at HQ before 8 a.m.

"Can we hold the meeting earlier?" Young asked.

"Well, I can call the others in. I guess we could start at eight."

"Make it seven-thirty," Young ordered, hanging up.

He dressed and kissed Jenny hastily.

"I have to dash," he said. "All hell could break loose today—and that's not for publication."

The door slammed behind him.

Jenny sighed, went into the bedroom and returned with her notebook. She checked Bigelow's home number and dialed, hoping that the ringing would awaken Michael. After a wait of several minutes her patience was rewarded.

"Michael?"

"Yes?"

"It's Jenny Corbett again. Well, you've certainly got things hopping at Mission Control." It was just a hunch, but perhaps the boy had learned more since she had last spoken to him.

"Oh, I think they were already onto it," Michael said, "but I think I was first to work out the orbit."

So he had been able to calculate the orbit. Jenny puzzled over how to question him further without giving away that she knew so little.

"And at what point were you able to be certain, Michael?"

"Well, when dad checked with me, I suppose. I mean, it seemed so unlikely."

"What seemed so unlikely, Michael?" Jenny asked desperately.

"Well, that it might collide with the earth. It just sounds unreal, doesn't it? I hardly believe it."

Jenny silently mouthed the words, "It's going to hit the earth . . ." No wonder Young had fled to Mission Control.

"And your father confirmed all your figures?"

"Yes. Well, most of them. Then he went back to the office. Hey, I didn't tell him you'd called. Do you think I should have?"

"No, I suppose not. It wasn't necessary. Look, my paper is delighted with your story and they'd like to have a picture of you. Do you think you could sort one out for me and I'll call around and pick it up?"

"Sure, Miss Corbett. No problem."

"Oh, and do you have pictures of your scope?"

"Sure, and of the observatory, inside and out. You can have them too if you like."

"Thanks, Michael. That would be great. I'll see you soon."

In her excitement Jenny misdialed her next call. At the second attempt she placed a collect person-to-person call to Reynolds at the *Daily News*. She guessed, correctly, that because of developments at NASA he would still be on duty, even though his shift normally ended at 4 a.m.

"Ken? I've got a fantastic follow-up. It's a blockbuster."

"Honey, I'm just going home. I need my beauty sleep. Let me put you on to the day news editor."

"If you like, Ken. Just tip him off that the planetoid is on collision course with the earth . . ."

"What?" Reynolds shouted.

"That's right. The planetoid is right on course for the earth. I was going to try for quotes from NASA but I'm sure we'll only get the runaround. I can give you what I know for sure, and you can probably get more information from a friendly observatory or two somewhere."

"You bet. OK, to hell with my beauty sleep. Shoot."

Sergei Krotkov was in the habit of taking a variety of detours each morning on his way to Mission Control. That morning at dawn he crossed to a city park and sat on the third bench from the park entrance where he had a clear view for several hundred yards in any direction. He took a transistor radio from his pocket, turned in to a music station and unfolded a morning paper.

Within minutes a stocky, bespectacled figure in a track suit jogged by, paused at the bench and slumped down to rest. Outwardly nothing distinguished him from any of millions of American keep-fit enthusiasts.

Krotkov turned up the volume on the transistor. This had become standard procedure for KGB agents making a rendezvous. The music would prevent any chance of a conversation being overheard, even if a highly efficient directional microphone were being operated from some distant vantage point.

"I think that at last we have something," the jogger announced.

Russian agents were continually shadowing key figures at

NASA. Few intimate details escaped their scrutiny. Until now, the KGB exercise had been fruitless.

Krotkov shiftily scanned the horizon. No one was in sight.

The jogger continued, "One of our contacts in New York has met with a hooker who confided that her father was 'something at NASA.' It was a simple matter to check further. Her father is the deputy administrator, Bob Bigelow."

Krotkov flinched involuntarily at the enormity of the news. Bigelow would certainly have access to classified information about the latest interplanetary vehicles and, possibly, sophisticated weapons. If he could be coerced into helping the Soviet Union, either now or in the future, the rewards for Russia could be immense.

"You have done well, comrade," Krotkov complimented his colleague. As suddenly as the jogger had arrived, he leapt to his feet and continued his morning run.

Krotkov weighed the information. Clearly, it could be of great importance. His role in succeeding developments could considerably enhance his prestige with the KGB . . . or ruin it. Krotkov wavered only for a moment in his resolve to defect. Even if he were able to exploit this new development fully, he would still be unable to reconcile what he had learned of the American way of life with the doctrine to which he had been subjected in Moscow. And since his wife had died there was no one with whom he could share his triumph—or who might suffer as a consequence for his defection. All his life he had been taught that the American political system was totally corrupt. But experience in the United States told him that capitalism was no more corrupt than communism. Here the truth was unveiled; in Russia it was not. And Americans enjoyed such unbelievable freedom. They could travel without permits. They could change jobs at will.

Krotkov knew that he had no choice—he would have to tell Akhmerov about Bigelow's daughter. To fail to do so might even put his life in jeopardy. But perhaps there might be a way in which he could place the Americans under obligation . . .

He continued to weigh his options throughout the journey back to Mission Control. He sought out Akhmerov and peered nervously at his chin.

"I have something to report," Krotkov announced.

Akhmerov pulled at the ends of his drooping mustache.

His bulbous eyes were heavy from lack of sleep and he looked sadder than ever. But Krotkov's greeting sent the adrenalin in a familiar rush through his system. So many of his great adventures had begun in such an innocuous way.

He directed his colleague to an exit door. When they had walked a safe distance from the Mission Control compound he said simply, "Well?"

When Krotkov finished his brief explanation Akhmerov's already florid complexion was bright with excitement. Thoughtfully he flicked away a few specks of dandruff from where his jacket bulged over his stomach.

"I think, comrade, that it is time for you to make a short journey."

Krotkov was ordered to travel to New York with another KGB official on the next available flight. On arrival, he would be met by the contact who had been in touch with Bigelow's daughter.

"Between the three of you, I suggest that you arrange to take some photographs of Miss Bigelow," Akhmerov instructed. "Then you will return at the earliest opportunity. We must not keep the deputy NASA administrator too long in ignorance of the well-being of his daughter." Akhmerov chuckled and his many rolls of fat quivered.

Krotkov understood perfectly what his superior had meant by "photographs."

Young strode into Mission Control at 7.29 a.m. The television screen showing the countdown for Saturday's Mars shot flicked to sixty-two hours, thirty-six minutes. On the screen which kept the planetoid constantly in view the speck of light had grown almost to the size of a fingernail.

Young nodded to his secretary as he entered his office.

A twelve-foot square map of the sky had been placed on the wall facing his desk. A red line showed the estimated orbit of the planetoid. A blue line indicated the orbit of the earth. The two lines crossed at a point in the bottom right hand corner of the map. A card pinned alongside the intersection read, "Probable impact: Wednesday p.m."

Dandridge was dressed immaculately in a pinstriped suit and white shirt. Bigelow had taken time only to exchange his tuxedo for a rumpled sports jacket. Despite the bow tie he still wore, he had the elegance of an unmade bed.

"Good morning Steve, Bob," Young said, motioning to two chairs on either side of his own.

"Well, Steve," he added. "It looks like your diplomacy might be needed today. How are our comrades reacting to the situation?"

"Mysteriously. They're less open than they've been since the Mars program started, though they seem to acknowledge the current dangers readily enough."

John Sykes, the director of flight operations at Houston, entered the room. He was not the type to make hasty decisions. There was always another side to any situation. Once he began brainstorming he would usually discover multiple facets to any problem faster than others could assimilate them. Although Young had great respect for him, the two men often argued bitterly. When Young faced the need for decisive action, Sykes might well have a score of theoretical reservations against any particular decision. Still, Young acknowledged that Sykes helped clarify the risks involved in a crisis and had helped to keep NASA one step ahead of disaster in many space emergencies.

As though at a signal, Akhmerov and three senior Russian technicians arrived and sat at the four remaining seats.

"Good morning, gentlemen," Young began. "If our comrades have no objection we'll hold the meeting in English."

Akhmerov nodded in agreement.

Young continued, "I'm afraid that Bigelow's little jokes, which I'm sure we won't be spared even on an occasion such as this, may be untranslatable."

Bigelow understood that his obscure metaphors would serve to convey any subtleties that Young would wish to conceal from the Russians.

"Bob, you start by explaining what that damn map on the wall really means," Young said.

Bigelow picked up a ruler and stepped toward the map. "The planetoid is some 400 to 500 miles across. Its point of origin is unknown, though it's definitely from outside the solar system. All computations of its orbit do not yet coincide—we still need more time—but indications are that the planetoid will follow this path."

He pointed to the red line on the map. Then with a chalk, he marked a third line.

"This is the intended flight path of Apollo-Soyuz," he explained. "You will note that at this point the two lines are very close. In fact, they're a mere whisker apart in terms of outer space. Radio contact would be seriously jeopardized by static caused by the planetoid."

Bigelow pointed to the blue line.

"Meanwhile, we may have an even bigger problem. This blue line marks the earth's orbit. As you see, the blue line and the planetoid's red line eventually meet. If our preliminary calculations are correct—and there is some disagreement—this planetoid would strike the earth some time next Wednesday evening."

Silence greeted the statement.

Returning to his seat, Bigelow added, "If our boys in Apollo-Soyuz are still up there when the planetoid hits, they might discover that there's no one left when they get back home."

Young took over and looked at Sykes. "John, how do you assess the situation?"

"If the estimated orbit of the planetoid is accurate, and if the Mars launch goes ahead, and if . . ."

"Please try to cut out as many 'ifs' as you can, John," Young interrupted impatiently. "This is a preliminary meeting. If . . ." He paused, emphasizing the word," . . . if we have to listen to all the 'ifs' the planetoid might hit the earth before you've finished speaking."

Sykes coughed in embarrassment. "To be perfectly blunt, I recommend we hold the Apollo-Soyuz countdown. We can easily reschedule the shot. In the meantime we can get the scientific facts we need and stop dealing with uncertainties."

"What about radio problems if we launch as scheduled?" Young asked.

"They'll be a damned menace," Sykes replied curtly. "Even a body half the size would cause communication problems. We'll have to talk through an extraordinary volume of static and we'll probably lose radio contact for a while."

"Dmitri, what's your view?" Young asked. "Do your people want to delay the countdown?"

The Russian shifted in his chair. "We do not. Our country and yours have invested millions in this project. Interrupting the countdown would mean unnecessary complications. I'm not convinced that a hold would gain us anything."

"Only time," said Sykes, "and a degree of certainty. That could count for quite a bit with four men in the capsule, and as you know the launch can be delayed up to eighteen hours without hurting the mission. For all we know at this stage the planetoid may even be on a course which could cause it to collide with the spacecraft—not that I'm too worried about that danger. Apollo-Soyuz is well able to take evasive action. We could even take a ride to the planetoid and land on it."

Bigelow remarked, "If there are any spare seats on the spacecraft you can book one for me. It sounds as though I'd be better off up there than down here."

Sykes ignored the joke. "Nevertheless," he persisted, "I'm extremely concerned about radio interference. That could jeopardize the safety of the entire mission."

"I agree with Dmitri," Young said. "The countdown continues. We'll have time to reconsider later. Now for the sixty-four-thousand-dollar question. What action do we take if it is confirmed that the planetoid is on collision course with the earth?"

Throughout the night, Bigelow had raised that same question with the acting chief of operations at the headquarters of NORAD—North American Air Defense—at Ent Air Force Base in Colorado Springs. "I have some information on that one," he volunteered. "We obviously have to deflect the planetoid from its orbit, or destroy it. At this point . . ." Bigelow paused, looking directly at Young, ". . . it's a problem of what eggs we have to put in the basket, and whether or not the other grocers will add a few for good measure."

So that was it, Young thought. He and Bigelow were among the few key men in America who knew that at Florida's Tyndall Air Force Base, NORAD stockpiled conventional nuclear bombs and its newest baby—a plutonium bomb no larger than a suitcase and a billion times more explosive than the atom bomb dropped on Hiroshima. Its sophisticated delivery system could carry the bomb to a target well beyond Mars. It was by any standards a superbomb— America's first interplanetary defense weapon. If the United States revealed such weaponry, détente would crumble. The cold war of the sixties would seem like a heat wave.

"I'm sure we have the technology to destroy the planetoid, but I doubt that we have the hardware," Young said cautiously. "Since ratification of the non-proliferation treaties, the U.S. government has naturally moved swiftly to reduce its stock of nuclear materials."

"The same applies to my government," Akhmerov said.

Young and Akhmerov looked steadily at each other, each suspecting the other's predicament.

Yes, this was it, Young realized. A macabre kind of Russian roulette. Each nation would want first to determine which area of the earth was threatened, hoping to compel the other to take action. If America was the target, the Russians would sit tight—and vice versa. And while this grim game of politics dragged on the planetoid would continue to speed toward the earth at more than 100,000 miles an hour.

Young turned to his deputy. "When will we know the precise orbit of the planetoid and its potential impact area?"

Bigelow answered unhesitatingly. "I checked that out with the Minor Planet Center at the University of Cincinnati. They should have that information by tonight after a fix has been made at Mount Palomar."

"Very well, gentlemen. I guess we'll take matters further this evening."

Dandridge, Sykes and the Russians rose to leave. Young signaled Bigelow to remain.

Akhmerov hurried to the room which had been set aside as his office and dialed Young's extension. From an inside pocket of his jacket he took a miniature harmonica and blew two sharp blasts into the mouthpiece before Young's phone could ring. The notes activated a bug which had been wired months ago to a phone company terminal outside Mission Control. Barely detectable except when in use, the bug prevented Young's phone from ringing and acted as a microphone, broadcasting to Akhmerov all that was said in Young's office. If Young made a call while the bug was in use, Akhmerov was able to listen in. A transistorized electronic booster prevented any loss of quality on the line.

The first part of the conversation Akhmerov overheard was innocent enough. Young and Bigelow were discussing preparation of a press release.

"You handle it," Young said, "but lay off the threat to the earth, for God's sake. For the moment just say we anticipate minor communication problems with Apollo-Soyuz but it's all systems go. That sort of jazz."

Akhmerov heard the door close as Bigelow left the office. Then Young's intercom buzzed as he called his secretary.

"Have a plane put on standby for Washington," he ordered. "I expect to be leaving soon."

"Yes sir."

"And get me the President."

"Yes sir."

Akhmerov smiled, then crossed the floor with surprising quickness for his bulk to lock his office door. This was one conversation he wanted to listen to without fear of having to hang up if an unexpected visitor should arrive. He returned to his seat, heaved his feet onto the desk top and cradled the phone to his ear.

A click on Young's private line signaled that the call had finally been connected to the President's office.

"Matt?"

"Yes sir."

"What is it?"

"We have a major problem concerning national security, sir. A planetoid spotted yesterday could endanger the success of Apollo-Soyuz and may even be of some threat to the earth."

The President did not reply for a moment, then asked, "How much time do we have?"

"Very little. We have a number of options but we'll have to move fast."

Again the President paused. "You'd better get over here with the details."

Young hung up and buzzed his secretary. "You can tell the pilot I'll be right there. Immediate departure."

Akhmerov again drew the miniature harmonica from his pocket and blew the same two notes to deactivate the bug. He frowned, irritated that Young had been so discreet. However, he still had sufficient information to justify a call to Moscow, he decided.

In the Oval Office the President greeted Young coolly. "I've something to show you, Matt. I received this after your call."

From his desk he took a copy of the New York *Daily News* and handed it to Young. In massive type on the front page, the main headline read, "Boy, 15, sights planetoid." In smaller type beneath, Young read, "NASA alert over threat to Mars shot."

"It seems, Matt, that the press of this country is better informed than its President. What the hell's going on?"

Young hastily turned to page three and scanned the details of the story, considering a reply.

"I had no knowledge of this, sir, until after the event. And I had no idea that the information was so detailed."

"A pity, Matt. The name above the story, of course, is not unknown to you."

Young had already noticed the byline—"By Jennifer Corbett."

"Yes sir," Young said listlessly. "I am afraid she overheard a conversation at our engagement party last night and acted without consulting me. She told me later that she had filed a story. It seemed that . . ." He abandoned further explanation. "I will do all I can to see that this does not happen again, sir."

"Do that, Matt. I need hardly tell you this is a most delicate situation. If you are unable to silence Miss Corbett, I shall help you. Now let's have a drink and get on to other matters."

The President opened a cabinet. "What will it be? I'm in need of a stiff bourbon on the rocks."

"Me too, sir."

The President laughed, his anger already evaporating.

Young accepted a cigarette from a silver box. To hell with giving up smoking, he decided.

"Now let's hear the rest of it," the President said.

Soon Young had explained the problems.

"And what do you suggest, Matt?"

"I favor holding our nerve for the time being," he recommended. "If we calculate that this planetoid will land on their side of the globe, we can let them deal with it."

"And if it appears that North America is the target?"

"We could pepper it with our latest space weaponry, of course. But I suggest we don't do that."

"Tell me more. What are the options?"

"We could call off the Mars shot, sir, then load the spacecraft with some of the old-fashioned stuff. Conventional hydrogen bombs. Then hit the planetoid with Apollo-Soyuz. It should be quite effective. The Russians would be angry if we scrapped the Mars shot, but they'd be angrier if they knew for sure that we'd been producing superbombs."

The President smiled, obviously pleased. "Ingenious. Yes, it's ingenious. I'll explore the possibilities further." He thoughtfully sipped his drink. "What are your immediate plans?"

"To get back to Mission Control, sir. We'll have more meaningful information on the orbit tonight."

"Very good. Keep me informed. And . . . congratulations on your engagement." The President grinned. "She seems to be quite some girl."

"Thank you, sir." Young decided it would be imprudent to be drawn into further conversation about Jenny. "Unless there's something else . . ."

"No, I guess that's it for now. Have a good flight back."

Before returning to his plane Young stepped into the visitors' office at the White House and phoned his deputy.

"Bob, your son is big news."

Bigelow groaned after Young had outlined the *Daily News* story. "Oh God. I knew something was in the air. Calls from the press have already started flooding in here. But I had no idea . . ."

"For Christ's sake keep the boy quiet, Bob," Young interrupted. "You'd better get home and handle any calls there. And make doubly certain that Jenny gets no further information. I want a memo to all senior personnel ensuring that she is given access only to official statements issued through the press office. Send her a memo, too—tell her that all statements for publication must come through regular channels or her press privileges at Houston will be withdrawn."

"Right away, Matt. I'm sorry about this."

"I understand. And I know it's not your fault. Let's just make sure things don't get any worse. I'm on my way back."

After dressing, Jenny took a cab to the Bigelows' home and collected the photographs Michael had sorted out for her. She took the cab on to the airport and arranged for them to be flown directly to New York. Jenny then called the *Daily News* picture desk and gave the details of the flight. A courier would be sent to meet the plane. Her next call was to Young's office. She had hoped that he would be able to meet her for lunch.

"Mister Young is in Washington," his secretary hold her. "He should be beck some time this afternoon. I'll tell him you called."

Washington, she thought. Again she called the *Daily News* and this time asked for the news desk. Reynolds was still on duty.

"Ken, I think the President has summoned Matt to the

White House. Certainly he's in Washington. 'Top level summit' and all that. I want to get over to Mission Control, but it might be an idea for you to get someone to place a call to Matt at the White House. Some dumb secretary just might let the cat out of the bag."

"Darling, you're a genius. I'll do that."

"How does the paper look, Ken?"

"As beautiful as you do, honey. And the next one looks better. We're rushing out a special edition to hit the streets at about six tonight. It's an update of this morning's story with 'Planetoid threatens the earth' in a three-decker headline of the biggest type you've ever seen. We've got backup from a number of observatories. There's no way anyone can put the gags on us now."

"Sounds great. I only hope I still have a fiancé when this is all over."

"If the worst comes to the worst you can have me. Bye, honey."

Jenny took another cab and paid the driver at the entrance to the Mission Control complex. She cheerily showed her press pass to one of the guards. His face was familiar, but his manner wasn't. Instead of waving her on as she had expected, the guard said, "Just a moment, Miss Corbett. I've been asked to escort you to the administrator's office."

"Oh, that's alright," Jenny said. "I know my way."

"Yes, I realize you do, but I have been asked to escort you there."

"I see. And are you being asked to escort other journalists to the administrator's office?"

"No, miss. Shall we go now?"

Jenny resisted the temptation to show her anger to the guard. Clearly the situation wasn't of his making.

At Young's office his secretary formally handed over an envelope bearing the NASA seal and smiled with obvious embarrassment. Jenny tore open the envelope and read, "I wish to take this opportunity of reminding you that only the Press Office of the National Aeronautics and Space Administration is authorized to give official information of NASA affairs. Interviews with members of the staff can be allowed only with specific approval of the administrator."

The note was signed by Bigelow on behalf of Young.

"See if you can get Mister Young on the line, will you?" Jenny asked the secretary.

"I'm afraid he's unavailable. He'll be in the office shortly."

"I see. Then where is Mister Bigelow?"

"I'm afraid I'm not authorized to release such information," the secretary said guardedly. "Perhaps the press office . . ."

"This is outrageous," Jenny snapped. Nevertheless, she realized there was little she could do. There would be no point in protesting further to the secretary.

"Please tell Mister Young that I do not wish to arrange any interviews at this stage—particularly with the NASA administrator," Jenny said, determined to retain what dignity she could. "And you can tell him that if he wishes any further information about my intentions it can be obtained through my hotel switchboard. Good day."

Jenny tore up the envelope and letter she had been given, tossed it onto the secretary's desk and walked quickly out of the office.

Bigelow arrived home to find his driveway blocked by several cars. He parked on the roadway and strode into the house. Michael was talking to a battery of newsmen in the living room. Several photographers were busily taking pictures of him from various angles.

"Get out," Bigelow snarled. "Every one of you, get the hell out of here—and you can quote me. You're all trespassing."

"But sir . . ." a reporter began to protest.

"But nothing. I call the cops in five seconds."

Michael blushed in shame at his father's outburst. More than once Bigelow had laid on such performances, but never to an audience of strangers.

The newsmen ambled to the door, several photographers pausing to put away their equipment.

"Get out . . . out," Bigelow hollered, "or I'll throw those damn cameras onto the driveway."

He slammed the door behind the last newsman, catching the man's heel. Turning on Michael, he grabbed the boy by the shirtfront, hauled him to his feet and threw him down into a chair. "You stupid, mindless, brainless, meddling, idiotic fool." He raged at Michael relentlessly for almost a minute.

The boy felt tears trickle uncontrollably down his cheeks. He was bewildered by his father's outburst. Only a moment before he had basked in the attention of the newsmen; now he felt hurt, humiliated and angry.

"I don't want you to go near that observatory ever again." Bigelow spoke in a low, threatening voice before hurrying to the observatory where, with much stamping and banging, he padlocked the door. On his way back he stopped, breathless, in the kitchen and poured a large measure of Scotch.

"The observatory is locked and out of bounds," he yelled. "Don't you understand what you've done? Your stupid blabbing makes NASA look like a bunch of idiots in a lunatic asylum, and it's all your fault."

"I think I'll go to bed," Michael said weakly. "I'm tired."

"You do that, and stay there. I don't want to see you again."

Michael resisted the temptation to shout back that the feeling was mutual. In his room he wiped his tears with a shirtsleeve and wandered around aimlessly. He opened a drawer of his night table and rummaged through. He had some money there. Perhaps he would sneak out of the house and take a taxi downtown. As he searched through the drawer he came across a forgotten birthday card. It had arrived with other cards on his last birthday. Michael had hidden it from his father, uncertain but suspicious of what his reaction would be. On the card was written, "I still love my baby brother, Eleanor." Then followed a phone number, beginning with the New York area code. Michael had been meaning to call her for months, but had never known quite what to say. Suddenly he felt that he and his sister might discover they had a lot in common, despite all the years since they had last seen each other. Clutching the card, he flopped face down on the bed and buried his face in the pillow. Sobs heaved his body until, totally exhausted, he fell asleep.

A scene of chaos greeted Young when he returned to his office from Washington. Workmen had stripped it bare. Panels had been hauled from the walls and ceiling and the carpets had been rolled back. One man was methodically sweeping a small electronic gadget inch by inch across the walls. The device emitted a low, monotonous tone. If it swept across an activated electronic bug the tone would increase dramatically in intensity and pitch.

Dandridge stood by as the sweeping continued. "I'm afraid we're in the middle of a big clean-up, courtesy of the CIA," he said as Young entered. "If we can take a walk I'll fill you in."

"This sure is a great time for a bug check," Young complained. "How long will this take?"

"We'll soon be finished here and I'll get one of the boys to help you check your desk and cabinets. Then we're going through the entire building."

"Forget the walk. Let's take a drive instead. We'll take my car . . . if you're sure that mightn't be bugged, too."

"It isn't. We've already checked it out."

Young picked up his secretary's cigarettes from her desk as he left the office and handed her a dollar bill. "I'd like to buy these from you, sweetheart. I've just made a resolution to try to start smoking again."

At the Mission Control garage he found two men sauntering conspicuously nearby.

"They're our boys," Dandridge assured him. "As of now we're going to have to step up security all around."

"Nice to be surrounded by friends," Young said cynically, pulling down the T-bird's top.

He headed the car for open country, maneuvering through the city traffic with a series of rapid bursts of speed. Dandridge glared nervously at the speedometer as Young gunned the car to a hundred-and-ten on the open road. Finally Young pulled up on a deserted hillock near Galveston, overlooking the Gulf of Mexico. For a moment both men watched the sun glinting on the cobalt blue waters.

"OK, Steve. What do you know?"

Dandridge handed him a folded sheet of white paper. On it had been written in capital letters with a felt-tipped pen, "NASA administrator's phones bugged. Hook-switch bypass fitted." The note went on to give the location of an IT&T terminal where the bug would be found.

"We tested the terminal, of course. The bug was exactly where the note says it would be. It was one of the most sophisticated types there is—impossible to detect unless we'd used a sweeper while someone was listening in. As you know, we haven't done that for quite a while. I'm afraid your phone has been about as private as a public address system."

Young hurriedly replayed scores of phone conversations in his mind, trying to evaluate what might have been overheard.

"The eavesdroppers could have listened in whenever they wanted to," Dandridge continued. "All they had to do was dial your number from anywhere, blow the appropriate sounds into the phone to activate the bug and stop your phone from ringing, and as of that moment your office was beautifully wired for sound."

"Who tipped us off?"

"I can't be sure. The note turned up in my secretary's in-tray. Someone must have dropped it there in passing. How-ever, I suspect our friend is Sergei Krotkov."

Dandridge described his encounter with Krotkov at the en-gagement party. "He suggested that I arrange a meeting, but I don't think I will just yet. I'd like to see just how deter-mined he is. Anyway, now isn't the time for a defection."

"It certainly isn't."

A defection at any time threatened acute political embar-rassment. In view of the uncertainty over how the planetoid threat was to be handled, a defection at this time would un-necessarily complicate an already intricate situation.

Dandridge added, "I know you have enough problems, but I thought you should know about this so you can be on guard in case Krotkov acts unpredictably."

"I appreciate it. I guess we'd better get back to HQ. Like you said, we do have other problems."

Young's office was back in order when he returned, and the debugging team, apart from one technician, had moved on to other offices in the complex. The remaining man asked Young to open his desk and cabinets, then made a meticulous check with his electronic sweeper.

"All seems clear, sir," was the verdict. "I'm sorry we had to trouble you."

As soon as the technician left, Sykes entered, carrying a bulky red folder. "Bob Bigelow had this report routed directly to me in your absence. It details probable impact damage should the planetoid collide with the earth."

Young noted that his flight director was subdued, presum-ably still smarting from the mild reprimand he had been given at the morning meeting. He decided it was time to restore his colleague's morale.

"Thanks, John. I know it's not strictly in your province, but have you had time to read it yet?"

Sykes relaxed visibly, responding to the friendly approach. "I have, and if you haven't eaten yet I warn you it's going to take away your appetite."

Young struggled to keep his frustrations under control.

"John, I don't really have time to plow through all this. Can you brief me?"

"Well, if this thing hits, we've had it. Boom . . . finished. The force would shift the earth's axis and even a minor shift would be disastrous. Polar and equatorial regions would be radically changed. Glaciers a mile thick would cover Canada within months. Unprecedented hurricanes and tornadoes would ravage the earth. Oceans would shift in response to the altered pull of the moon's gravity. The British Isles would be swamped."

"My God, if the press gets this there'll be mass panic."

"True enough. And I haven't given you the half of it. If the impact is on land, an area the size of New England would be wiped off the face of the earth. Devastating earthquakes and volcanic eruptions would occur throughout the world. If in the ocean, impact would cause earthquakes, tidal waves and massive floods. Water would surge hundreds of miles inland, deluging and reshaping large areas. The toll in human life and suffering would be staggering. Survivors would succumb sooner or later to climatic changes and disease epidemics. And so on . . ."

Sykes closed the red folder with a slap. "The plain truth is that the earth as we know it would cease to exist. I'm sorry to be the carrier of such bad news, but that's what the experts tell us."

"I don't need to ask you to keep this report under wraps, I'm sure. Let's buy some time with another news release saying everything's under control."

"Done. I'll get the press office on it now."

Sykes almost bumped into Akhmerov's ample stomach on leaving the office. The Russian stood back to let him by, then closed the door.

"Hello, Matt. We haven't seen much of each other today." Twenty-four hours ago Akhmerov's cheerful manner would have pleased Young. Today it merely put him on guard.

"Hello, Dmitri. I was just about to check the latest sightings. I guess we'll soon have to consider whether we take this problem any higher."

"Yes," Akhmerov agreed. "Perhaps, if we get definite news."

Cunning devil, Young thought. He was sure that by now the Russian premier knew as much as the President of the

United States. Guiltily, he acknowledged to himself that he had been equally cunning.

"Our country may well need the further cooperation of the United States if the planetoid poses a threat to our continent," Akhmerov said. "Our nuclear resources, as you know, are limited."

Young decided he needed another drink. "What will it be, Dmitri? Vodka?"

"Of course. Thank you. As you say, on the rocks."

Young helped himself to his second bourbon of the day.

"I'm afraid we're faced with exactly the same dilemma, Dmitri. With the development of friendship between our countries, war with the third world has been our only fear of major conflict. And we've been confident that, with the Soviet Union as our ally, we could hold such a threat in check with conventional weapons."

Young found himself wondering just how long the Russians would dare carry on this war of nerves.

"My position is . . ." Akhmerov seemed about to play his hand when Sykes returned.

"The sightings are all building up a fairly consistent picture," he announced.

"OK. We'll meet now," Young said, looking inquiringly at Akhmerov. The Russian nodded. Young added, "Round up everyone else, John. The same team as this morning except for Bob Bigelow." To the Russian he explained that his deputy had gone home to attend to a personal matter. Akhmerov grunted suspiciously.

When the group had assembled, Young asked Sykes to detail the latest information. The flight director went to the map on the wall.

"You'll notice that the red line marking the planetoid's course has been adjusted," he said. "But only slightly. The concensus—and I'm afraid it's still opinion to some extent—is that the planetoid will, unless deflected or destroyed, collide with the earth at about 2300 hours next Wednesday."

"That would give us a fairly definite impact area," Young commented.

"It does. The planetoid would strike the earth somewhere between the Atlantic Ocean and the west coast of North America."

"On the continent or in the ocean?"

"Either. We can't be sure yet. But whether it hits ocean or

land, the results would be catastrophic." Sykes referred to a clipboard he had brought to the meeting. "All observatories agree that the planetoid is solid, elliptical and spinning on its long axis. Its speed and mass will prevent it from bouncing off the atmosphere into an orbit around the earth or the sun. If this thing is on target for the earth, we're going to have to do something drastic."

Young turned to the Russians. "How do your people see the problem, Dmitri? I'm sure we all realize that wherever the impact area, prospects for survival would be bleak worldwide."

Akhmerov fumbled through some papers on his lap. Young wondered if the Kremlin had told him exactly what to say. Probably, he decided.

"Our sightings and deductions are similar to your own," the Russian said. "As I've already indicated, even if the probable impact zone were in Russia we would be dependent on the technology of our American colleagues to deal with the problem. Our nuclear resources are insufficient to deflect the planetoid."

So the war of nerves is on with a vengeance, Young thought.

His secretary knocked on the door and handed him a telex message from the Central Telegram Bureau. He skimmed it quickly, then read the message aloud. "Data confirmation: planetoid. Mass nickel/iron. Maximum diameter 400–500 miles. Estimated speed 144,000 mph. Expected impact 2257 hours Wednesday, July 28. Impact area North America."

The others received the news in silence.

Young added, "The situation is obviously clear. I suggest we adjourn."

As the last of the group closed the door behind him, Young called the President. After hearing the telex message the President said, "I think it's time for a television address to the nation. I'll have a statement prepared for broadcast at 11 tonight. My staff will clear the text with you."

"Very good, sir."

"Matt," the President added, "it's now crucial that you make no decisions without consulting me. In turn, I will have to take into account other considerations. But for the time being, the Mars launch goes ahead."

"Yes sir."

Young learned of Jenny's latest story from the President later that evening.

"My broadcast has been scooped, Matt," the President said gruffly. "Miss Corbett has struck again. I'm afraid I shall have to take steps to render her inoperative."

Young drummed the desk with his fingertips. His annoyance with Jenny mingled with despair—and concern for how she would face whatever action the President had in mind.

"I understand, sir."

"Fortunately, the paper contains nothing that I hadn't meant to spell out on TV, except that it fails to make clear that we have the technology to blow up the damn thing. I'm bringing the broadcast forward to 7:30. We can't risk mass panic setting in. Meanwhile, I suggest you and Miss Corbett spend what time you can together this evening. I expect she'll be back in New York soon covering fashion shows."

"Yes sir."

Young went to the Mission Control press office and warned the director that no further information was to be released without his personal approval. Within twenty minutes of speaking to the President he was at Jenny's hotel. He decided against announcing his arrival and strode to the elevator. Jenny kept on the door's safety chain when she answered Young's knock.

"I'm afraid Miss Corbett isn't available for interviews," she said sarcastically as she released the chain.

The jeans and heavy white sweater she wore warned Young that she was in a practical, no-nonsense mood. Her blonde hair shook loosely as she dropped into a chair.

"So how goes the battle against the freedom of the press?" she asked.

"Not well enough, Jenny. Why didn't you tell me you'd sent another story?"

"I didn't get a chance," she protested. "All I get from Mission Control is, 'You'll have to speak to the press office, you'll have to speak to the press office.'"

He realized the President's broadcast was about to begin and switched on the television set. "Before you get too bitter, honey, I want you to sit down and watch something with me. Have you been watching TV?"

"No, I've been catching up with some notes. I'm going to nail down this story, with or without your help."

"Well, make yourself comfortable, sweetheart. This is one show I particularly want you to see."

The sound of the set blared through at the end of a news announcement: ". . . but the government is confident that disaster can be averted," the broadcaster said. A commercial followed, then the face of the President filled the screen. Stern but visibly relaxed, he clasped his hands on his desk.

"My fellow Americans and people everywhere. By now you are all probably aware that a planetoid one-fifth the size of the moon is on collision course with the earth.

"This morning, as preparations continued for the launch of Apollo-Soyuz 1 to Mars, mankind was on the brink of discovery and international cooperation. Tonight the world is on the brink of disaster. But we will not stand helplessly by. I have conferred with our Russian friends and my message to you is this. The United States and the Soviet Union have joined forces. Together we have the resources to meet this challenge. The planetoid will be destroyed in outer space.

"This is a time of danger. Let us meet it with composure. Thank you."

Of the millions watching, Young was one of the few who noticed that the President had avoided giving an assurance that all was well with preparations for the Apollo-Soyuz launch. The President, he realized, had already decided how the planetoid would be destroyed.

He flicked off the set and sprawled in a chair facing Jenny's. "Like the man said, let's meet this with composure. Now I want to make a short speech, strictly off the record."

"OK," she agreed. "Off the record it is."

"We have a number of weapons we can use to deal with this problem, and mass panic in the streets isn't one of them."

He went on to recount his previous conversations with the President and explained the political maneuvers calculated to persuade the Russians, if at all possible, to deflect the planetoid. He did not tell her of the possibility that Apollo-Soyuz might be used as a bomb-carrying vehicle.

"There are various options, and the release of information has to be carefully controlled to ensure the minimum of embarrassment to the United States. This isn't a plot to gag the press, Jenny. It's a grave situation with dire implications for national and international security. Please, can I ask you from now on to keep your damned pencil in your purse? If there's anything for the press, we'll give it out. But some secrecy is vital."

Jenny avoided his penetrating gaze. "I don't know, Matt. Secrecy might be part of your business. Mine is truth. Honestly . . ."

"You're going to have to play ball," he interrupted. "You've got no choice."

Hesitantly, he wrestled to find a way to tell her that she was likely to be recalled to New York.

She studied his face searchingly, sensing the uneasiness.

"There's something else, Jenny. You mustn't give any hint that I've warned you, but I suspect that the *Daily News* is likely to recall you to New York."

"But . . ." Jenny leapt to her feet. "They wouldn't do that. They couldn't. My assignment is to cover the launch."

"I think they could do it, and I think they will."

"I see . . ."

She felt a strange sense of fear. She had heard of many instances when people in high places had manipulated the press. But this was the first time she had been directly involved in such a situation. The consequences for her career could be disastrous.

"Look, honey, if it helps, I'm sorry. Let's drop this until tomorrow."

"I'm not going back, Matt. Not just like that. I'm going to have to think things out."

"Jenny come here."

"Go to hell."

He laughed in an attempt to lighten her mood, hauled her to her feet and held her closely.

"I love you, Jenny."

"Sure . . . Sure . . ." Despite her anger she felt comforted by the strength of his arms. "I love you too, Matt, I think I'll let you marry me after all."

She took his hand and drew it to her breast. He realized that she was not wearing a bra. Gently, he eased her sweater upward and moved his hand beneath the thick wool, stroking her soft skin tenderly.

"This marriage bit," he said. "How about some more practice for the real thing?"

Michael, exhausted by his hours at the telescope through the night, awoke after several hours of fitful sleep and crept cau-

tiously downstairs. He heard the voice of a TV news broadcaster giving an update of events at Mission Control. Bigelow
lay slumped on the sofa, snoring loudly. At his side was an
empty Scotch bottle. Michael moved warily nearer the screen
as the President's broadcast began. The statement was followed by an on-the-scene report from outside the Mission
Control complex. The reporter repeatedly mentioned sightings
and calculations made by NASA, the Russians and other observatories around the world. No word was given of
Michael's involvement. He wondered if Jenny would remember her promise to let him have a copy of the *Daily News*.

Bigelow spluttered noisily and Michael froze, fearful of a
continuation of the morning's violence. His father turned vigorously on the sofa and sank once again into a heavy slum-
ber. Michael looked at him with disgust. He remembered
Eleanor's birthday card, and the sketchy plan that had begun
to take shape earlier in his mind. All he knew for sure was
that, for a while at least, he needed to get away.

On an impulse he went to the basement and collected his
backpack, sleeping bag and other camping equipment. He
carried his bundles to the kitchen and helped himself to two
packs of his father's cigarettes. Then from his bedroom he
collected the birthday card he had received from his sister,
the $45 he had been saving and an assortment of clothes
from his dresser. Back in the kitchen he opened the fridge
and took bacon, eggs, cheese and some apples. Then he went
to the food cupboard for bread, canned milk and coffee. As
he placed the last of the food in his pack he noticed that the
keys to his father's Chevrolet were on the kitchen counter.
What if . . . ? His father had given him several driving
lessons, and he was sure he could handle it on his own. Still
undecided, he picked up the keys, went into the garage, slid
into the driver's seat of the car and flicked on the ignition.
The fuel-gauge needle swept across to the "F" mark. His decision was made.

He walked stealthily to the kitchen, grabbed his backpack,
returned to the car and slung it on the back seat. His scalp
tingled with excitement as he started the engine, moved the
lever into the "R" position and backed slowly out of the garage.

In the house, Bigelow slept on undisturbed.

Billy Galiardo had been patrolling Manhattan's East 42nd

Street for more than an hour in search of a likely mugging victim. Neither he nor his three brothers had made a hit in weeks. He was flat broke and desperate.

A prosperous-looking middle-aged man walked through the swing doors of a nearby hotel and headed toward him. Galiardo eyed the prospect approvingly. Not the kind to put up a fight, he thought. He tensed his muscles. He was about to pounce when a police car turned into the street and crawled slowly along the curb.

"Shit," said Galiardo.

He allowed the middle-aged man to pass him by.

"Shit, shit, shit."

There was nothing else for it. He would have to wait for another victim.

Sergei Krotkov was amazed by New York's skyline as his cab approached Manhattan. It was his first visit to the city. Though movies and countless photographs had given him an idea of what he would see, he was startled by the sheer size of the towering, brightly lit buildings. In the cab with him were the KGB escort from Houston and the contact who had met them at the airport.

"She's a versatile performer," the contact man reported. He knocked ash from his fat cigar into one of the ashtrays. "She caters to all tastes, though not always enthusiastically. We should produce an intriguing movie."

Krotkov found himself wishing that he could cast himself in the starring role. His sexual appetite had been unappeased since his last night in Moscow. Unfortunately for him, his instructions were that the part should go to an American. The KGB did not wish to risk being accused of coercing Eleanor Bigelow into prostitution—as might happen if one of its agents were subsequently recognized in the photographs.

The cab halted outside a hotel on East 42nd Street. Krotkov paid the fare while his companions walked into the lobby. As he turned toward the cab he was suddenly grabbed roughly from behind.

"Your billfold," a voice growled.

Krotkov's two colleagues witnessed the incident and acted instantly. Billy Galiardo was struck by a karate blow to the back of the neck. Twenty minutes later his eyes flickered open. His arms and legs were tied to a bed in a modest hotel room. Sitting beside the bed were the man he had tried to mug and two companions.

"I take it you are in need of money, my friend," Krotkov said sneeringly.

The mugging attempt had been an answer to Krotkov's dreams. He had considered various ways in which a client for Eleanor might be persuaded to assist in securing suitable photographs. None was altogether satisfactory. But the muscular, swarthy brute who now cringed on the bed would suit his purpose admirably.

"What the hell gives?" Galiardo answered. "Let me out of this dump."

"We shall, friend. Eventually. But first I have a proposition to make."

Galiardo listened with frank amazement as Krotkov outlined his proposal.

"You've got to be kidding," Galiardo said. "You mean that you'll give me five bills to lay some broad and we call it quits? Brother, you got a deal. Lead me to her, guys. I'll give her one for you, too."

"Excellent," said Krotkov. "For the time being you will remain tied up here. We want to be sure you get plenty of rest before your exertions of tomorrow."

He nodded to the heavy-set contact man. "You stay here and see that our friend gets a good night's sleep. We shall be in the next room if you need assistance."

The contact man reached for a fresh cigar. "OK. If he tries anything I'll remove his teeth."

Krotkov gestured to the other agent to leave the room, then followed. Not for the first time, he hoped that his part in the plot could be kept from the American authorities. This was to be his last job for the KGB, he had decided. By now, the bug on the NASA administrator's phone would have been found. There were other services he could provide for the U.S., and making surreptitious obscene movies wouldn't be one of them.

Chapter Three

In outer space, the pitted surface of the planetoid, which had been at absolute zero since aeons before the birth of man, began to warm slightly in the increasing glare of the sun's rays.
It was now 19,864,800 miles from the earth.

The *Daily News* office was eerily silent when Ken Reynolds awoke. He had fallen asleep at his desk. Now he was alone in the newsroom. Throughout the night, cleaners had shifted masses of scrap paper, galley proofs and old newspapers from the floor to clear a passageway between the desks. Soon Reynolds would be joined by the first reporters and deskmen on duty and the newsroom would come to life again with telephones jangling and typewriters clattering out the daily chronicle of events—tragic and comic, significant and trivial.

Reynolds' deputy had phoned earlier complaining of flu, and asked for the day off. Reynolds approved readily. When there was big news in the air he delegated authority with reluctance.

On Reynolds' desk a messenger had place six copies of the morning edition. Picking one up, he smiled, pleased at the dramatic front page. It had been changed only slightly from the front page of the special edition to accommodate a cross-reference to the President's speech and other inside-page stories about the planetoid.

He had already read the paper from cover to cover at least a dozen times. Now he settled in his seat to enjoy the exercise one more time. He leafed through the paper page by page. "Brilliant," he announced to the empty newsroom. "Damn brilliant."

He was still admiring the paper and preparing a list of possible follow-up stories when he was startled by the ringing of a phone in the managing editor's office. He was even more surprised when, seconds later, the managing editor opened his door. Reynolds had assumed he was alone on the newsroom floor.

"Have you busted up with the wife or something?"

"Cut the small talk, Ken. The Old Man's up bright and early too and wants us in his office."

Reynolds pushed back his chair and got up hurriedly to follow the managing editor to the elevator. The Old Man. The publisher himself. Reynolds had spoken to him only once—at a Christmas party.

"What on earth is he doing in the office at this ungodly hour?"

"God knows. Perhaps he wants to tell you you're a genius—or give you the bullet."

On the way up to the executive floor Reynolds adjusted his tie and ran a comb through his hair. He noticed that his hands were moist.

The two men reached the top floor and found the publisher's door open. He greeted them with a gruff, "Come in, boys," and waved to two luxurious armchairs. Though in his sixties, the publisher looked ten years younger. Slim and still strikingly handsome, he had a mass of wavy silver hair. "Congratulations on a great paper. Unfortunately, that isn't the reason I called you both here."

Reynolds nervously rubbed his moist hands on his thighs. Soon his anxiety gave way to anger. Twenty minutes later he and the managing editor were dismissed from the publisher's office with a cursory, "That's the way it's got to be."

As the two men returned to the elevator, Reynolds was silent, not trusting himself to speak. He was furious, not only because of what he had been told but because it had been made clear that he had no choice. He had threatened to resign at one point during the meeting but he knew only too well that his resignation wouldn't change the publisher's decision. Without waiting for the elevator, he took the exit stairs two at a time down to the editorial floor, went straight to his desk and picked up the phone. He held the receiver for several minutes, trying to compose the speech he would have to make. Then, hesitantly, he dialed.

"Holiday Inn."

"Miss Jennifer Corbett, please."

"One moment, please."

After a few seconds he was switched to the hotel desk clerk, who told him that Miss Corbett had left a number where she could be reached. He hung up, then dialed Young's townhouse. When Young answered, Reynolds apologized for making the early call and asked for Jenny.

"Hello," Jenny said huskily.

"How's our gorgeous star reporter this morning? Sorry to wake you up so early."

"Cut the crap. How're things back in the lion pit?"

"The special edition went like hot cakes. It was our biggest ever run and the public's clamoring for more. Great stuff, Jenny. Great stuff. But that's not what I called about."

"Oh, what's up?"

"Well, I don't know how to put this, but something important has come up. I've been asked to call you back to the office."

"You're crazy. What could possibly be more important than a planetoid on collision course with the earth in the midst of an Apollo-Soyuz Mars shot? What's up?"

"Something important enough that we want you on the next flight back to New York."

"And who's going to cover the shot? And who's got the contacts I've developed here to handle the planetoid coverage? Come on. You've never pulled me off a big story like this before. What's up?"

"Tell you when you get here, Jen. OK?"

"It's damn well not OK, and you know it. I smell a rat, Mister Reynolds. What's going on?"

"Jesus, Jenny. I didn't call you for an argument. Just get on that plane. I'll talk to you when you get here."

"Terrific, Ken. The biggest story of my career and you say, 'Drop it.' No explanation that's worth anything. Do you really expect me to buy that?"

"No, actually I don't, Jen. But why don't you just get back here and make life a little easier?"

"Two reasons. First, it's not like you to be so secretive and you know it. Second, if I believed everything I was told I wouldn't be much of a reporter, would I? Now, what gives? Is my stuff not holding up? Is somebody after me for libel?"

"You don't give up easily, do you?"

"You know I don't. You're going to level with me, because if you're not I'm staying put on this story to the bitter end."

Reynolds sighed heavily, then paused for a long while.

"Well?" Jenny asked.

"OK, I'll give it to you straight, but remember you asked for it. The M.E. and I just met with the Old Man. The President's office has put on pressure because of your reporting."

"What do you mean, 'because of my reporting'?"

"Well, apparently the White House wants a low profile on this story until they've decided what action to take. I'm told that your yarn about that kid spotting the planetoid first was an embarrassment to NASA. Apart from that, the powers-that-be seem to feel you're too close to NASA bigwigs for the government's own good."

"I assume they mean Matt."

"Undoubtedly. Anyway, they've sold the publisher a line and he's bought it. If it's any consolation I was ready to resign, but you and I both know that wouldn't have stopped them from taking you off the story."

"I thought something like this might be in the wind."

"What do you mean?"

"Skip it. But I'm not letting go of this one, Ken—even though I've had a stern lecture about going through proper press channels and my free access to NASA installations has been curtailed. I'm not going to slow down one bit."

"I was afraid you'd say that. You don't have any choice, you know."

"I do, Ken. I can always play the card you didn't play, and I think I will. As of now you can consider my employment with the *Daily News* to be terminated."

"Just like that, eh?"

"Just like that. I quit. I'll continue covering the story as a freelancer. If the *News* wants my copy it can pay standard rates. I'll give you first crack at it. If you don't want it, there are lots of other papers in this country."

Reynolds recognized that his responsibilities as news editor required him to try to change her mind. Secretly, however, he admired her spirit. "I don't suppose I can talk you out of this," he said.

"You know you can't, Ken. I'm a big girl now."

"You're a smart one, too. I'll pass your decision upstairs. And keep the copy coming. They can't muzzle you if you don't work for them."

"Thanks, Ken. You'll be hearing from me."

"OK, Jen. Good luck."

"So long. Hold tomorrow's front page for me, will you?"

"You've got a deal sweetheart. 'Bye."

As he hung up he noticed that he had been joined by the picture editor.

"Morning, you ugly slob," Reynolds said exuberantly, for no good reason that he could think of. "You know," he added proudly, "that girl Jenny Corbett's got balls."

Sergei Krotkov placed "Do not disturb" signs on the doors of his room and the adjoining room shared by Galiardo and the Russian who was guarding him. The ropes which had held Galiardo to the bed had been untied and he was stalking about, rubbing his wrists in an attempt to stimulate his blood circulation. The contact man lounged disinterestedly, puffing on yet another fat cigar. On his knee rested a .38 automatic.

Krotkov returned to his own room and picked up a hammer and chisel which he had purchased that morning from a nearby store. He wrapped a face towel around the handle of the chisel, then gently marked an area about a foot square at eye level on the wall between the rooms. The towel effectively muffled the sound of the hammering and within half an hour he had neatly knocked out a hole.

"Good morning, gentlemen." He spoke through the opening to the two men in the next room. "I trust you are well."

His remarks were ignored.

Leaving the other agent to clear away the chipped plaster, Krotkov took an oval-shaped mirror from a slim suitcase which the contact man had given him the night before. Holding the mirror at arm's length, he studied his reflection. He looked fairly uninteresting, he had to admit. The bags under his eyes sagged and his lower lip drooped, exaggerating his sulky expression. He turned the mirror around and noted with satisfaction the crystal-clear view that he now had of the area of the room behind the mirror.

"Not an original device, but still an ingenious one," he commented. Through the hole in the wall he called out to the contact man. "Open up. I'm coming in."

He stepped into the adjoining room and tapped a nail above the hole in the wall, then hung up the two-way mirror to cover the opening.

"That should serve our requirements," he said. "Now, if our friend will be kind enough to rearrange the furniture . . ."

The contact man casually waved the pistol, making clear that Galiardo had little choice. He was ordered to haul the bed, which had been placed alongside the wall on which the mirror now hung, against the opposite wall so that the foot of the bed faced the mirror. Chairs and the two small tables in the room were repositioned to ensure that there was no obstruction between the bed and the mirror.

"Very good," said Krotkov, when the task was finished. "The love nest is all nice and cosy. Now let's be perfectly sure that you understand exactly what you have to do."

He detailed the sexual acrobatics that Galiardo was required to perform. As one particular feat was described, Galiardo involuntarily licked his lips. The bulge of his trousers betrayed his growing excitement. The contact man stood slowly, then suddenly punched him in the crotch. Galiardo fell to the ground with a scream, holding his hands between his legs.

"What was that for?" he moaned, his eyes moistening as he writhed in pain.

"To keep you cool for the big moment, lover boy," the contact man said. "We don't want you to overdo things before this evening."

Galiardo struggled painfully to his feet and hauled himself into a chair. He decided not to risk further protest.

The contact man stubbed his cigar in an ashtray and turned to his companions. "If you guys can handle this jerk, I'll get over to the Plaza."

Eleanor had been tailed to the Plaza Hotel the previous evening. The contact man had arranged to take over the shadowing at 9 a.m. He would wait in the hotel lobby until she came on the scene. Later, he would call for Galiardo to be brought to the hotel. A meeting of the two would then be arranged.

"I'll call you at six tonight," the contact man said. "Then you can bring this punk over to wherever she is and he can make his proposition. I'll keep her company to make sure no other joker complicates matters."

"Good," Krotkov said. The plan, he concluded, was perfect.

In the streets of New York, life bustled and bumbled along in its usual bumptious manner. Eight million priorities divided eight million people, each person unconcerned about the priorities of others. Soon, however, New Yorkers would share a common obsession . . . a mounting fear of catastrophe.

In Sally's bar and grill on East 27th Street, Sally bawled out one of her characteristic requests to her clientele as she turned up the radio to listen to the news.

"Shaddup!"

Her good plain food at reasonable prices, not her civility, kept her customers coming back for more.

"Meanwhile, at Cape Canaveral, the Apollo-Soyuz countdown continues," the newscaster reported. "Speculation is mounting that the Mars mission may be delayed because of possible communication problems. America and the Soviet Union are conferring today to determine how to destroy the planetoid, which threatens to collide with the earth next Wednesday. It is expected that nuclear weapons will be used."

The customers diplomatically remained silent during the remainder of the newscast. A hubbub of conversation built up again as the music resumed.

At a window table sat two of Billy Galiardo's three brothers. Rick, the bagman of the outfit, disconsolately thumbed the wad—three dollars. He wondered how Sally would react to the news that once again she would have to stake them for breakfast.

Sparks, the safe-cracker, nonchalantly surveyed his left hand, minus three fingers lost in one of the group's many fiascos.

The third brother, Willie the wheelman, marched into the restaurant and slapped a piece of paper onto the table. It was a speeding ticket.

"You dumb bastard," said Rick.

Sally's approach saved Willie from further insult.

"Why don't you guys do the world a favor—me in particular?"

Rick tactfully rose to the bait. "A favor like what, Sal?"

"Make like them other guys and go to Mars. And stay there."

A few nearby customers snickered dutifully.

"Sally, my darling," said Rick. "Make four big breakfasts for the journey and you've got a deal."

"I've already got a deal—with the bank. They don't sell grub and I don't lend money. And which one of you smart guys is planning to eat two breakfasts?"

"C'mon, Sal, you know it's for Billy," Rick said. "He'll be here any sec."

"Yeah, well, he can try to weasel grub outta me when he gets here."

But she wrote down the order just the same and placed the slip on the serving hatch between the dining area and the kitchen.

"I thought Billy was with you guys," said Willie.

"Naw, we ain't seen him since yesterday," Sparks replied.

"He'll show up," Rick said, "unless he's mugged a cop. In the meantime, things ain't getting any better."

The last whiskey heist had flopped because somebody, probably Billy, had blabbed. Craftily, they staged the raid a day early. Even craftier, Old Mac of Mancini's had planted a whole stack of whiskey crates handily near the rear entrance. The raid went without a hitch until the mob reached Willie's garage in the Bronx. There they discovered that each bottle was filled with water.

"One of us might have to take a job," grumbled Rick.

No one took up the idea.

"I say let's bang another safe," said Sparks. "Why don't we hit Mancini's? We owe that guy a favor."

"I say let's put Sally on the streets," said Willie, patting her bottom as she served the pancakes.

In response, Sally nudged a glass of water with her elbow as she reached across the table. The glass tumbled into Willie's lap. Rick and Sparks applauded while Willie snatched handfuls of napkins and sponged the water from his trousers.

Rick took up the idea of hitting Mancini's. "I reckon Old Mac's our best bet."

"Yeah, let's pay the sonofabitch back," Willie added. "Just shout when you screw it up so I can bugger off with the car."

"You just handle your end, wise guy, and we'll handle ours," Rick said. "OK, then. The Mancini job it is."

The gang who never did anything right got down to details.

In room 903 of the Plaza Hotel, Eleanor Bigelow awoke with the usual bad taste in her mouth. She had been up most of the night, smoking and watching television. She looked with revulsion at the snoring body beside her. It had been another trick, another dollar.

She moved stealthily from the bed and rifled through his billfold. Credit cards galore and a mere $22 in bills. Still, with the $100 he had given her in the elevator on their way up last night, not bad. He had drunk himself into a stupor and had been hopelessly unable to enjoy the service he had paid for. After a few minutes of futile fumbling he had turned onto his back and said, "Come on, you do the work."

"Catch your breath a minute while I have a cigarette," Eleanor had suggested.

Before she had finished smoking he had fallen asleep.

She glanced at the television. The color bars of a test pattern wavered on the screen, accompanied by a soft hiss. She decided not to turn off the set—she had read recently that the interruption of a soft, steady sound, such as the ticking of a clock, could awaken someone more surely than could a sudden loud noise.

She walked past the foot of the bed and noticed that the man's bloated face had an unhealthy pallor. She reached the window and pulled the drapes slightly apart. Sunlight reflected off the peaks of some distant skyscrapers but the long narrow streets below were cloaked in bleak, cold gray shadow.

Eleanor stretched, picked her clothes off a nearby chair and headed for the bathroom. The man in the bed rolled over heavily, resumed his snoring and spluttered saliva onto the pillow.

"Pig," Eleanor muttered. "Damn you. And cops and ginks and . . . the whole goddamn world."

Eleanor saw the gynecologist once a week and had an appointment to see him this morning at ten. The week before he had raised his fee to $100. She hated his malicious, sneering manner, but he was the brother of the precinct sergeant, who ignored her business in exchange for the odd favor. Regular visits to the gynecologist was one of those favors. "I run a clean precinct," the sergeant liked to boast. "Not honest, but clean." He charged the same as his brother.

She ran the hot water into the sink, then bent over and splashed some on her face. It stung but felt good. She took a deep breath and plunged her head into the water. She blew bubbles and splashed water over the floor, as she had often done as a child. Maybe she should breathe in deeply and simply float away. She wondered if her father ever remembered the day he caught her, face down in the sink, blowing bubbles and splashing the floor. He had grabbed her hair, yanked her head back and slapped her hard across the face. "Christ," he had yelled, "look at the mess. Are you trying to drown yourself in the goddamn sink?" The recollection of her father's roughness made her shiver. She shook her head, stood up and dried herself vigorously. Her face was flushed, hot and tingling. Her anger had gone. Sadness rushed to take its place.

She dressed quickly, tucked the $22 into her purse and stepped quietly out of the room. Soon, in some noisy, dark bar, she would again be selling a smile for a drink, more for $50 or so. But first she had to see that gynecologist.

As she walked quickly down the carpeted hall, she had the uneasy feeling that someone was watching her. She glanced over her shoulder. The hallway was empty. In midstride, she pushed the "down" button of the elevator, lit a cigarette and wandered restlessly back and forth, looking up and down the hall. The door to 903 remained closed. The arrow above one of the elevators clicked on. A thin line of light flashed under the door and the elevator whirred to a stop.

She looked down the dimly lit hall as she stepped into the car. The doors clicked shut. Eleanor slouched into the far corner, dragged deeply on her cigarette and flicked ash on the floor. She stared at the numbers as they blinked on, off, above the door. 9 . . . 8 . . . A dull, heavy, weariness pressed down on her as she pondered how cheap her services were for the large part of her soul she sold each day. 7 . . . 6 . . . 5 . . . Another hooker had once described one possible way out. A few downers, then a few more. A lot more. 4 . . . 3 . . . No pain. No guilt. 2 . . . Yes, that was the way it would be, Eleanor assured herself. Simple. Any day now. No more days of nothing; no more journeys to nowhere. 1 . . .

The hotel lobby smelled of disinfectant and stale smoke. A man in gray trousers and shirt was swishing a thick wet mop across the terrazzo floor. An elderly woman dozed in a corner on a sofa. A stocky, balding man, reading the *Daily News*, leaned against a wall. He held the paper at arm's length, as though he were unusually farsighted. Cigar smoke wafted up between his face and the paper. A bellhop and the desk clerk, hunched over another copy of the *Daily News*, talked in hushed voices.

Eleanor saw the huge, three-decker headline as she passed the cigar smoker. "Planetoid threatens the earth." Beneath the headline was a picture of an astronomical observatory and to the left of that was a small, single-column picture of a young boy. She was too far away to distinguish the features of the boy, but the larger picture looked hauntingly familiar. She crossed the lobby, picked up a copy of the paper from the newsstand and stared at the front page.

"Michael!" she exclaimed.

"Can I help you, miss?" the news vendor asked. The stocky thick-set man with the cigar looked over his newspaper.

Embarrassed at being overheard, Eleanor looked at the news vendor. "Oh, I'm sorry. I'll take the *News*."

She reached into her purse and paid for the paper. "Can you believe that's my kid brother on the front page? Christ, I haven't seen him for years."

"Uhuh," he grunted, handing Eleanor the change. She put it into her purse while hurriedly reading the newspaper.

"It says here that he discovered that planetoid before NASA did. Hell, I was up most of the night watching the newscasts and not once did anyone mention my kid brother."

"Terrific, sister. So what's that make him? A hero? If he can do something about it, now that would make him a hero, I'd say."

"The whole thing gives me the creeps," she replied. "You really think it's big trouble, do you?"

"Big, big trouble." He shuffled some newspapers on the counter. "You saw the TV, sister. Ain't nothing the government can do in my opinion. By the time they get off their asses, kaboom—forget it."

She winced. "Well, I guess if your number's up, your number's up. If you don't get it one way, you get it another."

"Tell you what I'm gonna do, sister. I'm not sticking around for the fireworks. No sir. I'm closing up this place tomorrow and me and the wife and the kid, we're flying to Canada to stay with my brother. Hell, I ain't had a vacation in years anyway and I sure ain't staying to watch this hotel crash down on top of my head. No sir, not me."

A bell rang at the nearby bank of elevators. A middle-aged

couple got out of the car and walked to the newsstand. Eleanor heard the couple talking excitedly as she headed for the front doors of the hotel.

"Look at this, Agnes. 'Planetoid threatens the earth.' What'd I tell you? The world could come to an end and you'd probably sleep right through it."

As Eleanor reached the hotel's front entrance, the stocky man who had been reading the *Daily News* ground out his smoldering cigar into a sand-filled ashtray. Eleanor hailed a cab. The man tossed his paper onto a table, hurried out of the hotel and climbed into a waiting rent-a-car.

"I know I don't have an appointment, but I'm sure Doctor Peters will see me."

The receptionist hid her distaste for the tubby woman cuddling a ridiculously pampered poodle. "Well, I know he's busy—and dogs are not allowed in this office, Mrs. Winstanley."

With each visit to the doctor's office she received the same reminder. It never had any effect. On her next visit, as ever, the poodle would be trotting obsequiously behind her. The receptionist directed Mrs. Winstanley to the empty waiting room, then called the doctor on the intercom. He had only five minutes before his next appointment, she reminded him.

Peters was well aware of his 10 o'clock appointment. It was to be Eleanor Bigelow. A fast $100 . . . or perhaps he could arrange for payment in some other form. Meanwhile, Mrs. Winstanley, one of his more persistent "respectable" clients, was also a regular source of income. He could get rid of her quickly and chalk up another fat fee.

"Show Mrs. Winstanley in," Peters said.

The receptionist announced, "The doctor will see you now."

"Do take care of Cecil for me," Mrs. Winstanley pleaded, handing the dog to the girl. As soon as Mrs. Winstanley turned her back the girl bared her teeth and growled angrily at the nervous animal.

"Ugly mutt," she snarled, and promptly tied its leash to a chair leg in the waiting room.

Mrs. Winstanley beamed as she greeted the doctor. "I know I look well, doctor, but I've had the most disturbing heart flutter."

"Perhaps you're in love," he joked, assuming his most flattering manner.

Her blush was scarcely noticeable under the heavy pink makeup.

"Oh, doctor, how could you?" she said coquettishly.

"Whatever the problem," Peters said, "I'm not sure I can help. As you know, I'm a gynecologist. Perhaps you should see a heart specialist."

That apparently wasn't what Mrs. Winstanley had in mind. She admired the doctor and made frequent excuses to see him and relieve the boredom of her lonely existence.

"I know, doctor, but I would be so grateful if you could just check my heart for me. I really don't want to see another doctor unless I have to."

What the hell, Peters thought. He summoned a nurse to accompany Mrs. Winstanley to the examining room. When he listened to her chest the heartbeat, as he expected, was normal.

"You know, you really must take things a little easier," he lied soothingly. "You're in the prime of life but you can't go galloping around like a teenager."

The most beneficial therapy having been administered, he wrote a prescription for a mild sedative as Mrs. Winstanley buttoned her blouse.

"Take one of these with a glass of water when you feel weary, but not more than three times a day. And do take more care of yourself."

Mrs. Winstanley flounced back to the waiting room and greeted her yapping poodle as though she had not seen it for months. "Did Cecil miss mommakins? Poor baby, all tied up like an animal." With much fussing and cooing she untied the dog and bustled out, pointedly ignoring the receptionist.

Peters strolled into the outer office. "If that painted, blue-haired old hag brings that stupid animal here again, shoot it," he said to the receptionist.

"Yes, doctor, with pleasure," she replied, handing him the mail—a stock of circulars and advertisements. He glanced at the top brochure, a booklet circulated by the Civil Defense Preparedness Agency entitled, "In Time of Emergency: Natural Disaster."

"A damn waste of the taxpayers' money," he grumbled, pitching the booklet into the wastebasket.

Eleanor arrived at Peters' office ten minutes late for her appointment. The receptionist immediately ushered her into the examination room.

"Good morning, my dear," Peters said with mock politeness. "I must ask you to try to be punctual in the future."

"Go to hell," Eleanor said tiredly.

"How unladylike." Peters tutted, took Eleanor's arm and directed her to the examining room. This time he did not invite the nurse to accompany him.

"Remove your clothes, and let's make sure that all is well, shall we? After all, yours is a hazardous profession."

Eleanor undressed, obviously repulsed by Peters. "I hate you, you bastard," she said.

"Now, now, then. None of that. The bra, too, please. Then let's have you up on the bed."

She tensed as he pawed at her, grabbing a breast with one hand while he made his "examination" with the other. He bent his head suddenly to kiss her. She compressed her lips tightly and turned her head away.

"OK, that's it," she said, lowering herself from the bed and beginning to dress. "One more stunt like that and I'll scream this place down."

"That really wouldn't be wise," he drooled. He decided to repay Eleanor for her rejection.

"I'm afraid I have bad news for you, sweetheart." He clapped his hands mockingly. "You've got the clap."

"You lying bastard." Eleanor zipped her skirt.

"I'm afraid so. You're going to have to tell your boyfriends you've got the applause."

"Oh, Christ, are you not funny? I've no more got VD than you've got an MD."

"Now, now, sweetheart, we can't be too careful, can we? It can be very painful and very expensive if we don't treat it in time. Now, that will be $100 and I'll have to charge another $100 for the medication you need."

"Pig," Eleanor said, reaching into her purse.

"Of course, a reduction could be arranged . . ."

"Go play with yourself," Eleanor told him, throwing two hundred-dollar bills on his desk as she stormed out of the office. Breathing deeply in an attempt to control her racing heartbeat she wandered listlessly across the street.

In the park Eleanor lingered behind a group of people listening to a soapbox evangelist. On his makeshift pulpit were scrawled the words "Fearsome Freddie."

An ex-boxer-turned-preacher, he was predicting gloom with uncanny irony. News of the planetoid's approach had inspired him to prepare a powerful sermon.

" 'And there fell a great star from heaven,' " Fearsome boomed, condensing a favorite passage from Exodus, " 'burning as it were a lamp, and many men died . . . and the sun was smitten, and the moon, and the stars were darkened.' " Fearsome had stuck since his boxing days. His followers felt that it was equally appropriate to his new career.

"I tell you, brothers, that's how it will be. Behold, that star, that planetoid, will be cast down upon the earth. They that sin shall be destroyed. They that believe shall be saved. Repent now, sinners. Be saved here and now. Otherwise you shall surely perish."

Fearsome paused, breathing heavily.

"Men," Eleanor sneered softly. They were either sex-crazy—or just plain crazy, period.

" 'And I beheld,' so the Bible goes on to tell us, 'and heard an angel flying through the midst of heaven, saying with a loud voice, Woe, woe, woe, to the inhabiters of earth.'

"And I say unto you," Fearsome continued, borrowing a few phrases popular with his peers, "that it will be woe unto you all lest you now turn your eyes to the Lord."

Eleanor shuddered. The preacher's message had begun to alarm her and she moved closer to the crowd. She failed to notice the heavyset man watching her intently from the edge of the group.

" 'And all the people saw the thunderings and the lightnings, and the noise of the trumpet, and the mountain smoking: and when the people saw it, they removed and stood afar off,' " Fearsome quoted from Exodus.

He repeated, " 'Stood afar off,' brothers. For they were sore afraid. You bet your sweet life in the hereafter they were sore afraid. This, brothers, is the vengeance the Lord took in the days of Moses. This, brothers, is the vengeance the Lord will take in the days to come. We are warned that this mighty star might endanger the rocket ship that man, in his vanity, hopes to send to Mars. I warn you that this is a visitation of the Lord to those who dare challenge the wonders of his creation. This mighty star shall indeed smite the earth. It shall smite the sinners on the earth. And they shall be sore afraid."

Eleanor was jostled as more people stopped to listen. A fervent follower shouted, "Hallelujah."

Fearsome thoughtfully chewed a fingernail, then quoted from the tenth chapter of Joshua.

" 'And it came to pass, as they fled before Israel . . . that the Lord cast down great stones from heaven upon them . . . and they died; they were more which died . . . than they whom the children of Israel slew with the sword.' "

Fearsome surveyed the crowd once more, then continued in an even louder voice. "This, brothers, was the Lord's punishment in the days of Joshua. The good book tells us, He slew with great stones from heaven those who stole, who fornicated, who coveted their neighbors' wives. I say, beware. Another day of judgment is at hand. I say that this time the Lord's vengeance will be every bit as mighty as in the days of Moses and Joshua."

Eleanor had heard enough. She moved away from the crowd and headed for a park exit. The heavyset man followed at a discreet distance.

At 4 p.m. the precinct sergeant who was on Eleanor's payroll decided to call it a day. He patted his billfold contentedly. Two hookers on his list had coughed up within the last two days, and a third was due to pay off this evening. Sergeant Winston Peters decided to tour several bars on his way home.

In his lapel, as ever, was a flower—this time a white carnation. "Flower Power," the guys at the precinct called him. None knew that each day he stole a flower from one of the window boxes near his home in Queens on his way to the subway.

Sergeant Peters crossed the road to Fridays and greeted the barman with, "The usual, Jim."

The "usual" was a Jack Daniels with a 7-Up chaser.

"Sure thing, lieutenant."

The "lieutenant" was their private joke. Both knew that Peters, after eighteen years with the New York Police Department, would never make lieutenant.

A jazz group, rehearsing for an evening jam session, pounded out a lively rhythm in a discotheque beneath the bar.

"What's new on the tube, Jim?" The sergeant nodded to the set behind the bar.

"Aw, it's a bore. They've been on about that planet thing all day. I turned it off. They say they can stop it, but there's screw-all you and I can do about it. So when the President says, 'Don't worry, America,' I don't worry."

"Let's hope the rest of New York feels the same way. A panic we can do without. Panic just wouldn't be good for business."

Peters preferred as much peace and quiet as possible. He never volunteered for overtime and resented the occasional crisis that made it compulsory. He no longer needed the money, and sought only time to spend what he had.

He ordered a second drink as the hooker who was due to pay him this evening slinked over to the bar and stood beside him. She took a cigarette from a pack which she turned toward Peters, who glimpsed the wad of bills inside. He struck a match for her. She lit the cigarette, then wandered away to join another group at the far end of the room. She left the pack on the bar and Peters slipped it quickly into his pocket. He spent a few more moments finishing his drink, then popped the carnation into the empty glass.

"Goodnight, Jim," he said, moving toward the door.

"Goodnight, lieutenant."

Ken Reynolds' hopes for a giant sellout looked as though they would be fulfilled. A wild cheer went up in the editorial room when the managing editor announced that the print had been a record run of more than five million copies, and that sales were running high. The jubilant air was heightened further by the anticipation of a party for one of the reporters who had married earlier in the day. John Hutton and his bride had agreed to stop by at Costello's before they left on their honeymoon. Reynolds decided to hurry home to share the evening meal with his daughter before joining the rest of the staff at the celebration.

When he reached home his housekeeper told him that Susan was playing in Central Park, near the entrance directly opposite his apartment. The girl still hadn't returned half an hour later and he decided to look for her.

He spotted Susan standing back from a group of friends who seemed to be taunting an old derelict sitting on a park bench. She was holding her hands self-consciously behind her back and swaying her shoulders slightly to left and right.

Intrigued to see what might develop, Reynolds decided to

watch for a moment as a boy aged about nine approached the old man and said boldly, "Excuse me, can I have a dollar?"

The old man shifted uncomfortably on the bench and drew his tattered overcoat tightly around him.

"Let's have a dollar," the boy persisted.

The other youngsters began to chant, "We want a dollar, we want a dollar."

"Go away," said the old man with a tired wave of his hand.

Another boy sneaked behind the bench, tied a piece of cord around the old man's feet, then ran backward from the bench, leading a new chant.

"Smelly chops. Lazybones. Smelly chops. Lazybones."

The old man, angry now, stood up, leaning heavily on a stout branch he used as a walking stick.

"Go away," he growled again. He wielded the stick above his head, took a step forward and tumbled helplessly to the ground.

The children shrieked with glee and fled—except for Susan. She stepped hesitantly toward the old man as he struggled to his feet. She stopped suddenly as he glowered at her. Reynolds shouted and ran forward as the old man seemed about to raise his stick again.

"What the hell do you think you're doing?" Reynolds said threateningly.

"I'm sorry," the old man said. "I didn't mean . . ." He sat wearily on the bench "I wouldn't have hurt her. I . . ."

He got no further with his explanation. Reynolds picked up Susan and carried her toward home.

The old man sighed sadly.

John and Alice Hutton were more than a little drunk by the time they reached John F. Kennedy International Airport. It had been a riotous party at Costello's. The newlyweds had left at eight, but no doubt the drinking and singing would continue well into the following day.

Alice reached for John's hand. "We'll have to be on our best behavior at mom's place," she cautioned. "I mean, the walls are so thin . . ."

"You mean we won't be able to . . ."

"No, John. What if they should hear us? I'd feel awful."

"Come on, Alice. It is our honeymoon." John drew his hand away.

They had married after a whirlwind six-week courtship. Alice's parents had missed the wedding because only two days before her mother had suffered a severe asthma attack. Alice, a waitress, had wanted a honeymoon at a top hotel— where she would be waited on for a change "in real style." But because of her mother's illness she had persuaded John that they should spend a few days with her parents, who lived in the dusty Arizona village of Winslow. John was more eager to see the nearby mile-wide canyon Diablo Crater than he was to meet his in-laws. His interest had been aroused by a photo of Canyon Diablo that accompanied one of the *Daily News* reports about the planetoid.

The couple planned to return to New York on Wednesday for a lavish meal at the top of the Pan-Am building. Then Alice would get her wish to stay at a first-class hotel.

John counted the days remaining until he and Alice would be able to make love. Saturday, Sunday, Monday . . . "Alice, do you realize you're asking me not to touch you for five whole days? That's unreal. Couldn't we sneak out and make it in the desert?"

"What about the rattlesnakes?" Alice joked.

"What about my trouser snake?" John said.

"John, please. We've got years and years."

"Yeah, and I've been cut off already."

Alice stroked his hand teasingly. "Think of those men going to Mars, John. What will they do?"

"I dunno, but God help any Martian in a skirt when they get there."

"John, I'll make it up to you when we get back. Honest."

"Promise?"

"Yes, promise."

"Wow! Roll on Wednesday."

An airport announcer directed passengers for Phoenix to board at Gate 12.

"Shit," said John. "Not even time for a quick one."

Eric Sinclair had toured all of Eleanor Bigelow's usual haunts. Finally he despaired of finding her and returned to his apartment to continue his drinking marathon with his roommate.

Vernon Cooke's relationship with Eric had reached a crisis.

For years the friendship had flourished, with Eric never suspecting the other's real motives. Sometimes Vernon had joined Eric on double dates, bravely trying to hide the truth and talking himself out of situations when his date seemed to expect more than a passionate necking session. Eric had offered to fix him up with Eleanor, but he had declined. Even necking revolted him. He would make light of jibes that where women were concerned, he would never have what it takes. At first, he hadn't minded Eric's women. After all, their inclinations were somewhat like his own. Lately though, his feelings for Eric had become disturbingly intense.

Vernon was drying dishes when Eric arrived home.

"I couldn't find that broad anywhere, damn it. Let's have more booze."

Vernon stacked the dishes, then prepared two gin and tonics. He handed one to Eric and joined him on the sofa, wondering if this might be the moment. "Listen, screw you and your women."

"Excellent idea—at least about the women."

"Christ, that's not what I mean and you know it. It's not my scene. I've tried it out. The whole bit. And it turns me off."

Eric took a long slow drink. "You're the quiet type, mate. You need a shy little virgin you can come on strong with. What about that little chick at the bank?"

"I don't want any type. Can't I make you understand? Surely you've noticed. I'm different, Eric . . . different."

"Yeah, but . . ." Anxious now, Eric gulped the remainder of his drink. "Look, you must be a bit zonked, Vern. Don't talk bullshit."

"I don't want women, Eric." Embarrassed but determined to finish what he had started, he gazed disconsolately into his glass. "I want you."

It had been said. At last.

"Come on," said Eric, leaping to his feet, startled. "You'll be telling me you want a goddamn kiss next."

Vernon didn't answer. He raised his head to look at Eric. "I'm sorry. That's the way I am. I know it's the way I'll always be. You're the only person who turns me on."

Not even attempting to hide his disgust, Eric noticed tears welling in Vernon's eyes.

"I knew when I was a kid," Vernon went on. "My old man used to knock the living daylights out of me and, you know, I really liked it. The pain was exquisite. It got so that I'd get into trouble just to get a thrashing. It hurt like hell but it was incredibly exciting.

"Later it was a whole new routine. With boys, not girls. 'I'll show you mine if you'll show me yours . . . I'll touch yours if you'll touch mine.' Then, at boarding school . . . oh, to hell with the details."

Eric was astonished. "But what about all the women I've fixed you up with? You've screwed your ass off!"

"You thought I did. I tried it once or twice. It's just no good."

Eric stomped into the kitchen and slopped a large measure of gin into his glass.

"So much for my big buddy," he accused. "I thought we were great friends and all the time you've been thinking . . . you dirty bastard. You can get the hell out of my life, damn you."

His immature sense of masculinity was outraged. He wondered if his own sexuality had been somehow challenged. He stormed into the bedroom, hurriedly stuffed a suitcase with Vernon's belongings and flung it at his feet.

"Get the hell out of here. I'm not staying with any stinking fag. Come back for your TV and the rest of your things when you're shacked up with another weirdo like yourself."

Vernon picked up the suitcase and headed for the door. "So long, pal. It was great while it lasted."

The door clicked behind him. Eric turned on the TV, flopped onto the sofa and muttered, "Christ, Jesus Q. fucking Christ."

On the TV a panel of experts was discussing ways in which the planetoid might be diverted.

"Not that rot again," he said angrily. He flicked the channel selector switch back and forth, but each program dealt with some aspect of the planetoid story.

"Planetoid, planetoid, planetoid," he complained, switching off the set. He poured another drink and flopped once more on the sofa.

Krotkov, his fellow agent and Billy Galiardo made their way down to the bar of their hotel and sat at a corner table. The thick-set contact man was nearby, talking to Eleanor. At a nod from Krotkov, Galiardo walked over to her.

"Hi, beautiful. Why don't you tell this creep to blow and I'll buy you a drink."

"Don't push your luck, sonny boy," the contact man answered, bristling. Galiardo's aggression was not part of the script.

Eleanor found neither man a particularly appealing prospect. The newcomer was neatly spruced and dressed, but had an apelike profile.

"Honey, I've got to blow anyway," the contact man said. "See you around."

To Galiardo he said ominously, "Next time I see you, punk, I'll give you some surgery, without anaesthetic."

Galiardo realized he had gone too far. "No offense, buddy," he said appeasingly.

As the contact man walked away Galiardo grinned at Eleanor. "You and me could do big things together, sweetheart. How about a little drink?"

"Then what?" she asked warily.

"Then whatever you're offering for top rates."

Why not, thought Eleanor. The brute was well muscled and, almost certainly, otherwise well equipped too. Tonight she might treat herself as well as the customer.

"I'm expensive," she cautioned. "It'll cost you $100."

"I was thinking of $300, lover—for every trick in the book."

Three hundred dollars. Jackpot.

"I don't go in for the rough stuff," she warned.

"Nor do I, honey."

Three hundred dollars. She hesitated for hardly a second.

"OK, lover boy. I'll have a gin and tonic."

About an hour later he escorted her to the room where he had spent the last twenty-four hours. Krotkov and his companion followed moments later. In the room next to Galiardo's, Krotkov looked through the two-way mirror. When he saw that Eleanor had removed the last of her clothing he signaled for the movie camera to roll.

Chapter Four

In outer space, light and shadows rushed across the rough, scarred surface of the planetoid as it whirled in the sunlight.

It was now 16,264,800 miles from the earth.

Young was awakened by the ringing of the phone at his bedside table. He sleepily untwined himself from Jenny and rested the receiver on his pillow. On recognizing the President's voice he flung back the covers and sat on the edge of the bed. Jenny wriggled toward him and put her arms around his waist.

"I want you at the Cape today," the President said.

The order startled Young. On every previous launch the NASA administrator had directed operations from Houston.

"Sealed orders are on their way to you there by military escort," the President continued. "Be prepared for any eventuality."

"Yes, sir. I understand."

The call had confirmed his suspicions that the Mars shot was to be called off. He was curious for specific information, but realized it would not be given over the phone.

"By the way, what's your view of Dandridge?" the President asked. "I'm familiar with details of his career as a CIA agent, of course, but I haven't met him since his appointment as a diplomat attached to the Mars shot."

"He's first class, sir. He's respected by the Russians and his judgment is sound. He thrives on problems. I'd trust him unreservedly in any situation."

"In that case, I'd like him up here as soon as possible." The President ended the conversation with a friendly, "Have a good day."

In view of the circumstances, Young thought, that seemed highly unlikely.

He told Jenny, now wide awake, of his schedule. He would have to take a military aircraft to the Cape and suggested that she follow on a commercial flight.

"Another thing," he said uneasily. He recalled that he had recently approved an order that residential quarters at the Cape were to be used only by NASA staff and their families, except in specific contingencies. That meant no mistresses sleeping on the compound . . . and no Jenny. "I'm going to have to sleep at the Cape. I have to be on the spot. You'll have to get a hotel."

She laughed at his obvious fear that she would be annoyed. "I think I'll survive. I have slept alone before, you know."

"To make amends, I'll get you a grandstand view of the launch at the VIP lounge."

She thanked him by hugging him tightly.

Dandridge was already awake when Young phoned him at his apartment. He received the news of his summons to the White House with typical calm. "I assume our Russian friends will not be told of my whereabouts."

"The less they know the better, particularly in view of the decisions likely to be made. I suggest you tell your secretary you'll be unavailable, without hinting at the details. The Russians will find out you've gone soon enough."

Within half an hour Young and Dandridge had boarded separate airplanes.

The flat Florida landscape fried like a giant pancake in the shimmering heat. Young's vertical takeoff jet banked steeply over the Atlantic into a tight turn toward Cape Canaveral. The pancake was tossed suddenly upward, then dropped away as the jet levelled out. The VTO now decelerated sharply, hovered over the Cape's Patrick Air Force Base and floated to the ground. Young stepped from the jet and was greeted by the launch director. Bud Kennedy, lean, athletic and deeply tanned, shook his hand vigorously.

"Welcome back to where the action is, Matt. It's good to see you again, especially now."

"Good to see you, too. You look as fit as ever. I see you still haven't learned how to grow hair."

Kennedy laughingly drew his hand through his crew cut.

"We don't have time to sit around and watch hair grow like you guys at Mission Control. Got too much to do. As you know, it's bedlam here on the day of a launch."

"The action has barely started, Bud. There'll be a hell of a lot more bedlam before the day's out."

Kennedy's craggy features furrowed in puzzlement as he and Young climbed into a waiting jeep.

In the distance Apollo-Soyuz towered above the vast, sand-swept scrubland bordering the Cape. The spacecraft, a third higher than the Statue of Liberty, was held securely in the grasp of its umbilical tower on Launch Pad 39-A, the same pad from which Apollo 11 had blasted off to land man for the first time on the moon.

The first stage of Apollo-Soyuz, the Saturn rocket, had been hauled out of mothballs and converted for the flight. The Saturn was the most reliable launch vehicle ever developed—the only one that had never failed. A new propellant provided greater thrust than previous fuels. A new method of pressurization enabled the Saturn to carry more fuel and travel further than on earlier voyages. The Saturn's valves were as big as oil barrels, its fuel pumps bigger than refrigerators, its pipes big enough for a man to crawl through and its five engines each the size of a bulldozer.

The second-stage rocket weighed more than a million pounds, ninety percent of which was fuel. After the spacecraft had been propelled into orbit fifty miles above the earth, the first stage would be discarded. The second stage would kick the spacecraft toward Mars at 70,000 miles an hour.

The third stage, the Soyuz command module, was designed to land on Mars, boost itself from the planet's surface, rejoin the orbiting second stage and finally make a hard landing on the earth—near the Russian cosmodrome at Tyuratam. In case of a launch malfunction, a release rocket would lift the Soyuz and its crew from the first two stages and dump the command module safely in the Atlantic Ocean.

On the outside of the spacecraft glinted the Stars and Stripes, the Hammer and Sickle and the words, "Apollo-Soyuz 1."

The Cape's administration buildings were dominated by the vehicle assembly building, known as the VAB. Young recalled its staggering statistics—at 524 feet high, 513 feet long and 418 feet wide, it was twice as large in volume as the Pentagon and the tallest building south of New York City.

Nearby was the launch control center, a white structure of reinforced concrete and metal set deep into the ground on a complete hydraulic system designed to absorb the shock waves that would result if a rocket exploded on the launch pad.

The jeep halted and Kennedy directed Young toward the medical block, housed within the launch control center. "Our spacemen are having their final health checks," Kennedy said. "I thought you might like to say hello."

Young nodded to the astronauts and cosmonauts and to the two doctors examining them.

One of the cosmonauts grumbled in Russian to his colleague.

"What was that?" Young asked Kennedy. "I couldn't quite hear."

Kennedy laughed. "He's complaining that the stethoscope's cold."

"He'll soon have more than that to complain about," Young confided. "Let's go to your office. I must speak to you privately."

In the office, Kennedy rummaged uneasily through a desk drawer as Young crossed the carpeted floor, sat in an armchair and lit a cigarette.

The men had developed a lasting friendship during their post-graduate years at Cornell University. They shared an absolute commitment to the success of Apollo-Soyuz and pride in having significant roles in an operation that had cost America and Russia a total of more than $2 billion. The two men believed that such joint ventures did more than all the diplomacy in the world for international understanding.

Kennedy found his pipe and tobacco in the desk drawer and sat in a chair next to Young. "OK, let's have the bad news, Matt."

"Well, I know this project means more to you than anything you've ever been involved with at NASA."

Kennedy nodded and lit his pipe. "True."

"I also know your loyalty to this country is as great as your dedication to this job, and that I can rely on you to act fast in a crisis."

"Also true. What are you getting at?"

"Just this. We're going to be facing a crisis today and I'll need you to act quickly—and probably against all your instincts."

"I suppose this has something to do with the planetoid."

"What else, Bud? In the strictest of confidence, our Mars shot is unlikely to take place."

Kennedy sat back, blew a cloud of smoke into the air and watched it spiral toward the ceiling. This day was to have been the fulfillment of a brilliant career. Since the go-ahead for the Mars shot he had personally checked every component of Apollo-Soyuz. Virtually every conscious thought had been about some aspect of the mission. When he slept, he dreamed of the moment when that massive, metal monster would become alive with a thunderous, throbbing roar at liftoff. To Kennedy, Apollo-Soyuz was no longer a machine; it was a being that he loved with a possessiveness he had never felt for any man, woman or child.

"I see," he said, tapping the bowl of his pipe in an ashtray. "But frankly, I don't see. What do you have in mind?"

Young explained the plan to use Apollo-Soyuz as a bomb-carrying vehicle.

Kennedy stood up and walked to the window. He peered at Apollo-Soyuz and imagined the moment of obliteration when the bombs would be exploded on the surface of the planetoid.

"She deserves a better fate, Matt. Surely there's got to be another way."

Young paused sympathetically. "No one way is ideal, Bud. But Apollo-Soyuz is our best shot."

Kennedy turned from the window and returned to his desk, resigned to the situation. "So be it. But when that baby is loaded with all that blasted weaponry, I'm not going to enjoy watching her lift off to self-destruction."

"Look on the bright side, Bud. I can see your epitaph now—'one of the men who helped to save the world.'"

Kennedy laughed and relit his pipe.

"Meanwhile, I want your complete discretion," Young continued. "Everything goes ahead as normal. But if I issue any orders there won't be time for discussion. I'll need you on the spot ready to act fast."

"I'm with you. You can bank on it."

A knock at the office door brought a sharp "Come in" from Kennedy. His secretary entered. "Sorry to disturb you, sir. There's a military detail here from the White House to see Mister Young."

"Show them in, please."

A dispatch rider marched in briskly, flanked by two heavily armed military policemen. All clicked to attention.

"Sealed orders for the NASA administrator from the President, sir," the rider announced.

Young stepped forward and handed over his security card. The dispatch rider checked it quickly, handed Young a receipt to sign, checked his signature on the security pass and finally gave Young an envelope bearing the Presidential seal.

The three men stood at attention while Young broke the seal and read the message.

"There will be no reply," he said, dismissing the messenger and guards.

"OK, Bud," he said, when the two men were alone again. "Stay close. I might need your help in a hurry. The chief hasn't made a final decision, but my guess is we'll have to abort."

Kennedy turned slowly once more to face the spaceship. The phone buzzed, interrupting his thoughts of what might have been.

"It's Bob Bigelow," he said, passing the phone to Young.

"Yes, Bob."

"We've just had word from the Central Telegram Bureau. They've pinpointed the target area. Quote. Impact: Wednesday, 2257 hours 12 seconds. Location: longitude 30 degrees north and 45 degrees north; latitude 60 degrees west and 90 degrees west. Unquote."

"So where the hell's that?" Young snapped.

"Somewhere between Chicago and the Atlantic Ocean, and Montreal and Jacksonville, Florida. They can't be more precise because they can't be certain how much the planetoid would be slowed down by the earth's atmosphere."

"OK. Get all that to the President immediately—with the translation. In case he's in conference mark it 'For the urgent attention of . . . top priority.' Follow up with a phone check."

"Got it. I'll keep in touch."

Kennedy looked quizzically at his boss.

"Looks like that planetoid has decided to blast hell out of northeast North America, Bud. Like I said, the action here has barely started."

In the main operations room of the launch control center the countdown to liftoff clicked to precisely 13 hours, zero minutes, zero seconds.

Bigelow lunched alone in the cafeteria at Mission Control, agonizing over Michael's disappearance. Daughter, wife and son. All gone. All gone with good reason, he admitted to himself painfully. He had loved all three, and yet he had been compelled to humiliate them as though trying to convince himself that their love was great enough to tolerate his worst excesses. At first, it had been. But slowly, stupidly, wretchedly, he had poisoned all traces of the affection his family had felt for him. But perhaps he could still make things up to Michael. Perhaps, Bigelow thought, he could regain his son's respect . . . if he could only get to the boy before he came to harm. At one o'clock, he decided, he would call home. If Michael had not returned he would call the chief security officer at Mission Control. He would know how to instigate a search for the Chevrolet without alerting the press.

Bigelow returned to his office and found Krotkov sitting on the edge of a chair—like a small boy afraid of being caught in class after hours, Bigelow thought cynically.

"What do you want?" He scowled at the Russian. Krotkov was to Bigelow by far the most insidious of the Russians contingent in Houston. Bigelow grunted sneeringly as Krotkov's eyes focused somewhere around his middle.

"I need some time with you," Krotkov said. "Perhaps you should ask your secretary to ensure that we are not disturbed."

"This sure is my lucky day," he said bitterly. "I'm being disturbed as it is. Say what you've got to say and get it over with."

Bigelow noted that it was one o'clock. Suddenly his heart raced at the thought that Krotkov's visit might be connected with Michael having left home.

"What the hell's this all about?"

"I had hoped that this would be no more unpleasant than it has to be," Krotkov said ominously, raising his eyes defiantly to about the tip of Bigelow's nose. "I thought you might wish to know that your daughter is alive and well."

A wave of nausea swept over Bigelow. A tingling sensation sped through his body to his scalp. He pulled open a drawer of his desk and poured a Scotch without offering a drink to the Russian. Krotkov rose and placed a small package on Bigelow's desk.

"I'm sorry about this," the Russian said almost convincingly, "but you might find these photographs of interest."

Bigelow downed the Scotch. His composure returned as the taste lingered in his throat. He poured another Scotch and tore open the package. On top of the pile of photographs was an eight-by-ten portrait of Eleanor's head and shoulders. She was smiling seductively.

"Eleanor," Bigelow whispered. "Eleanor . . ."

Her face had changed only slightly from the girlish one he remembered. He gazed at the photograph for more than a minute, painfully recognizing each contour of the smooth skin, the dimple on each cheek, the tilt of the nose. Then he turned to the next in the pile.

"You bastards," he said, tears welling in his eyes. He sprawled forward and dropped his forehead to the desktop. "You filthy, dirty bastards," he sobbed.

The first print was a close-up of a portion of the second, which showed Eleanor standing naked, her hands holding her breasts. On his knees in front of her was a swarthy, muscular man. He wore only his socks. His hands were around her buttocks. His face was buried in her pubic hair.

Krotkov stared at the floor as Bigelow continued to sob. He stopped suddenly and swallowed his drink. He stood at his desk and his eyes narrowed.

"I could kill you, you filthy . . ."

"There are more pictures," Krotkov interrupted without shifting his gaze from the carpet. "Some are more . . ." He began to say, "more interesting." Instead, he said, "Some are worse."

Bigelow picked up the package and flung it at the Russian. Photographs fluttered about the room. One fell directly in front of Bigelow's feet. It showed Eleanor and the man in profile. This time they had reversed positions. The man's fingers were interlocked behind Eleanor's head.

Bigelow bent down, picked up the picture, shredded it into tiny pieces and dropped it into the wastebasket.

"There are, of course, many more," Krotkov simpered. "And we have the negatives."

"Get out . . . get out . . . get out." Bigelow's voice rose to a shriek. He rushed at Krotkov, grabbed his lapels and shook him roughly. The Russian sat passively. Bigelow slapped him across the head, then stood back, alarmed at his own violence.

Krotkov looked Bigelow directly in the eyes for the first time. "This will achieve nothing." The Russian began collecting the pictures. When he had picked up the last one he placed them in a briefcase. "These pictures need not receive wide publicity," he said.

"Do what the hell you want with them," Bigelow growled. "So my daughter has a lover. What the hell?"

"Your daughter has several lovers, Mister Bigelow," Krotkov said. "In fact, many lovers. Any man can be your daughter's lover, for a modest fee. We have irrefutable evidence that she is actively engaged in prostitution. As you see, she serves her customers in a very uninhibited way."

The statement cruelly confirmed fears that Bigelow had only half acknowledged. "I wish she were dead," he muttered. "I wish you were dead . . . I wish I were dead."

Krotkov decided to hurry along the confrontation. "Perhaps there might be some occasion on which you may be of service to my country," he began. "Perhaps . . ."

"Get out of here." Bigelow tried in vain to control the quiver in his voice. "Do what you damn well please with your pictures. I shall report this meeting immediately to my superiors. Now get the hell out of here."

"Very good. I too have to report to my superiors." Krotkov paused at the door. Without turning he said, "I'm sorry. I'm really sorry. I had to do this."

Bigelow hardly heard. He had already picked up the phone.

As he told Young about Krotkov's visit his voice choked over the most repulsive detail.

"And there's something else, Matt," he continued before Young could reply. "Michael's gone. He took the car. I don't know where the hell he is . . ." His voice trailed away.

Young struggled to find words that could ease his deputy's grief. "I'm glad you told me this, Bob. Michael is the most important problem, so let's get the police on it right away. Leave the Krotkov thing with me and not a word to anyone else. I'll report that matter to Dandridge."

"Thanks. I'll call the police now. Christ, I hope they find him."

"They will, Bob. You know they will."

Young reached Dandridge at the White House shortly before he was to go into conference with the President and told him of Krotkov's approach to Bigelow.

"I'll get our boys to pick up Krotkov as soon as they can," Dandridge said. "The Russians would deny complicity in this set-up. At best, Krotkov is a potential embarrassment to them. At worst, he's in big trouble. I really think that he will now be regarded as superfluous to their requirements."

Young hung up and shook his head at Kennedy. "It's a funny old world, Bud," Young said. "I can't help wondering if it's really worth saving, but I guess we'd better try. Let's see how the launch checkout is going."

The countdown to liftoff now clicked to eight hours, thirty-three minutes, zero seconds.

Akhmerov received the news of Krotkov's failure with obvious displeasure. "You have not done well, comrade," he said. "First, the Americans removed our bugging devices. Now they have the opportunity to accuse us of a squalid attempt at subversion. Both failures reflect poorly on your performance. Your value to us is in question."

Akhmerov had suspected that the American debugging operation was the result of a leak. The Politburo would require an explanation. Krotkov was now the most suitable scapegoat.

"I suggest you wait in your office for further instructions."

"Yes, comrade."

Krotkov sullenly left the room. He realized only too well the danger of his situation. Instead of returning to his office, he left the Mission Control complex and hailed a cab. He would hide in some downtown motel until he could reach Dandridge by phone. He still carried his briefcase containing the photographs and negatives of Eleanor Bigelow. If necessary, he would offer them to Dandridge in return for help in defecting. Alternatively, he would destroy them. No matter what his fate, he decided, he would have the satisfaction of ensuring that the KGB would be unable to make use of the pictures.

As his cab pulled away from the curb, a pale blue Pontiac drew out of the Mission Control garage and followed. Some ten minutes later Krotkov's cab pulled up near a cluster of motels. He chose one and booked a room on the ground floor.

The pale blue Pontiac drew into the motel moments afterward. The driver walked to the reception desk behind Krotkov and booked the adjoining room.

The Russian called Mission Control as soon as he entered his room. He asked for Dandridge.

"Mister Dandridge is unavailable," a secretary answered. "Is there a message?"

"Yes. Give him this number as soon as you can, please." Krotkov read off the figures from the dial. "Tell him it's Sergei Krotkov. It's urgent."

He decided to take a shower in the hope of fighting off his growing sense of anxiety. The noise effectively muzzled the sound of a high-speed drill with which the man in the next room made a small hole at the junction of the floor and the wall. Into the hole he placed a small microphone. Any further calls by Krotkov would now be overheard. The task had been completed when Krotkov returned from the bathroom and lay naked on the bed. He stared at the phone.

"Please ring, damn you," he said in Russian. "Please ring . . ."

In less than five minutes his wish was granted.

"Hello," Krotkov answered nervously.

It was the secretary he had spoken to earlier. "Mister Dandridge is still not here but he has ordered someone to pick you up. Where are you?"

Krotkov gave the address of the motel and his room number. "Tell them to get here fast," he pleaded. "Tell Mister Dandridge I've got something I think he'll want. And tell him I want to defect."

"We're on our way."

Krotkov began to dress hurriedly. He had just belted his pants when he was startled by the sound of breaking glass. The man who had driven the pale blue Pontiac pointed an innocent-looking fountain pen through the broken window. He pressed the top of the pen. A dart, a quarter of an inch long and no thicker than a human hair, struck Krotkov in the stomach. The dart was tipped with a smear of shellfish toxin—colorless, odorless and undetectable in the human body. Krotkov's fingers began to tingle, then his lips. He slumped to the floor, too stunned to feel shock at the realization that he couldn't move. The strange tingling spread throughout his body. Seven seconds later, Krotkov died painlessly.

The blue Pontiac halted momentarily at the motel entrance as an approaching car swept in at high speed. All four doors were flung open and four men hurried to Krotkov's room. As

one of the men knocked on the door the Pontiac pulled out
and merged into the stream of traffic.

The doctor who carried out the autopsy would in all probability have decided that death was due to heart failure. But
one of the CIA agents who had failed to reach Krotkov in
time suggested beforehand that the doctor should look carefully for a puncture wound. The dart was eventually found
with the aid of a microscope.

In Moscow, the seventeen members of the Politburo met for
an extraordinary session. Five of the men seated around a
plain circular table, including the Russian premier, had at
some stage served with the KGB. Any decision reached at the
meeting would inevitably reflect the best interests of the communist world, though not necessarily the best interests of the
world itself.

The premier called the meeting to order. "Our information
is that the planetoid is headed for the northeastern United
States," he announced.

A spontaneous round of applause broke out.

"My sentiments exactly," the premier continued. "But we
have to take into account that impact would threaten the existence of the entire planet."

He gestured to a small, studious man to his left. Doctor
Alexis Nureyev—known to the CIA as The Dancer—was the
senior man in charge of weapon research and an authority on
impact damage.

"What are your findings, Alexis?"

The Dancer rose, though he was so small that his head was
scarcely higher than when he had been sitting.

"Impact might well shift the earth's axis, comrades—possibly by as much as three degrees. This would produce catastrophic earthquakes and floods. The snow and ice of Siberia
would reach southward to Moscow. All life on the earth
would be seriously endangered."

As The Dancer sat down, the premier continued, "We have
to determine, comrades, whether the Americans have the capability to eliminate this threat, and whether we can be abso-
lutely assured that they will perform the task satisfactorily. I
need hardly add that it would be embarrassing if we were
forced to take matters into our own hands."

The premier looked at Nureyev. "What further light can
you throw on the matter for us, Alexis?"

"Our information is that the Americans have been working on an interplanetary missile. Though undoubtedly inferior to our own, it would have the capability of at least deflecting the planetoid. As their continent is threatened directly, my judgment is that they will be compelled to take action."

The scientist put on his glasses and read from a dossier in front of him. "The planetoid would hit the earth next Wednesday. We ourselves have the capacity to divert it at any time up to twelve hours before impact, though there would be no room for delay."

The premier took over. "I suggest, comrades, that we prepare to divert the planetoid with a missile to be launched precisely twelve hours before impact—but let's hope the Americans take effective action earlier.

"When the capability of American weaponry is exposed I shall protest, in the strongest terms, against their defiance of the non-proliferation treaties."

To a bespectacled figure on his right the premier added, "I take it that appropriate people throughout the world can be relied upon to organize suitable demonstrations."

"Yes indeed, premier."

In the Oval Office, the President introduced his closest advisers to Steve Dandridge. "As some of you are aware, Steve is our senior diplomat attached to Mission Control." Smiling, the President added, "He's the man who has to know what our comrades will do before they know they're going to do it."

After a ripple of laughter, he continued, "We now know the worst, gentlemen. It has been confirmed that the planetoid is on an orbit that would bring it into collision with the earth next Wednesday evening. The impact would occur somewhere in the northeast of North America." He paused to sip a glass of water. "Now for the good news—we can lick this problem. The question is how."

In an effort to put the group at ease, he smiled and added, "I'm looking forward to watching the late movie that night, so I'd be grateful if we could arrange things so that my plans are not disturbed."

As the laughter subsided, he added, "Over to you, Jack. What options do we have?"

The question was directed to General Jack Stonehouse,

Joint Chief of Staff of the U.S. Armed Forces and an expert in nuclear technology.

"Well, we have the tools to do the job. Our latest interplanetary ballistic missile could be launched from the new Nova rocket. The weapon is unerringly accurate and would reduce this planetoid to a dust cloud. It would be a great opportunity to test its capabilities under actual, rather than simulated, emergency conditions—and great fun to press the button."

"How would our Russian friends react to our pulling that baby out of the cupboard?" the President asked Dandridge.

"Publicly, with rage, sir," he replied. "Privately, they'd be delighted to have an opportunity to debase American prestige. They know we have something, of course, but I seriously doubt that they suspect we have such a sophisticated IPBM. They would protest loudly at what they would interpret as a breach of the non-proliferation treaties."

"The alternative," the general interrupted, "would be to let ourselves get blown to smithereens."

"I don't believe so, sir," Dandridge said to the President. "The Russians certainly have some equipment of their own. In the knowledge that the entire earth would be threatened, I'm sure that sooner or later they would be compelled to take action. They are not so foolhardy as to let the world itself be destroyed to gain a political advantage. It might be possible to persuade them that we have followed the treaties to the letter and have dismantled our nuclear equipment."

"Interesting," the President commented. "And how would you propose to do that?"

"I suggest a straightforward lie, sir. How about a direct communication from you to the Russian premier? Dishonest, perhaps, but . . ."

"Perfectly proper in the circumstances. It's brilliant, Steve."

Turning to the general, the President asked, "What is the last possible moment at which we could knock out the planetoid, assuming our comrades hold their nerve or, perhaps more likely, screw it up?"

"About twelve hours before impact is due," the general replied. "That would give us time for another shot if something did go wrong."

"In that case, Jack, prepare for the shot. But before we adjourn, I have one more suggestion."

The President looked around the office, studying the expectant faces before him. "Matt Young, our NASA administrator, has offered an idea. I'd like to throw it on the table. In a nutshell it is this: we cancel the Mars shot, load Apollo-Soyuz with conventional nuclear bombs, destroy the planetoid and avoid letting the world in on our little secret of the new IPBMs. Quite ingenious, I think you'll agree."

The plan clearly took the President's advisers by surprise.

"Steve, what do you make of it?" he asked.

"It's a risk, sir. I believe they would try to prevent the spacecraft being used for such a purpose, particularly if they think we have other methods of destroying the planetoid. But in the final analysis they just might have to agree, if the rest of the world is genuinely convinced that the alternative would be a disaster. I think it's worth a try, sir."

"Anyone disagree?"

No one did.

"Very well. My strategy will be to convince the Russian premier that we have no means of destroying the planetoid other than by using Apollo-Soyuz. In case something goes wrong, the IPBMs will be prepared for firing at 1057 hours on Wednesday—precisely twelve hours before the planetoid would collide with the earth. Now if you would excuse me . . ."

As his advisers left the room the President picked up the hot line to Moscow.

It was 2 p.m. The Mars shot countdown clicked to eight hours, three minutes, zero seconds to liftoff. Young studied the flickering lights on one particular console, which indicated that the computerized check of all Apollo-Soyuz systems was continuing satisfactorily. The technicians, Russian and American, were buoyant with the enthusiasm and excitement that always built up in the last hours before a space launch.

Young lowered his gaze to a red button to one side of the console and to the sign underneath it, also in red—Abort Mission. He found himself wondering when the moment to press the button would come, and what the reaction of the Russians would be at the same moment.

What if they resisted the plan to use the spacecraft to destroy the planetoid? Those KGB officials posing as technicians in the launch control center . . . if he or Kennedy were to be shouldered away from the abort button at the crucial moment . . .

"Let's get some air, Bud," Young suggested suddenly. "I want to check out security."

Kennedy went along unquestioningly. Young hunted out the colonel in charge of the Cape's military personnel.

"We've been alerted to the possibility of interference with the launch," Young said, studying the colonel's face carefully. It gave no indication that the colonel suspected him of lying. The NASA chief continued, "I'd like you to get as many people as you sensibly can near the ship—but discreetly. Nobody, but nobody, Russian or American, is to be allowed access to the spacecraft without my prior approval. And that goes for the astronauts and the cosmonauts."

"Right away, sir."

"If the Russians ask any questions just tell them it's normal routine."

Loudspeakers throughout the Cape crackled into life. "Phone call for Matt Young . . . Phone call for Matt Young," a toneless voice called.

Young stiffened. "This could be it, Bud."

Kennedy ran behind Young back to the launch control center. The call was not the one Young had expected . . . and secretly dreaded.

"This is Akhmerov," the voice said bluntly. Young immediately detected the Russian's annoyance. "I thought we were to share responsibilities and work side by side through this program."

"Of course, Dmitri. Of course. But I always like to be right on the scene for a launch. I thought you would prefer to be at Mission Control. After all, that's where most of the decisions are made."

"I see," the Russian replied. "Nevertheless, I think I'll join you. I would prefer to be, as you say it, where the action is. My plane will arrive shortly."

"Nosy bastard," Young grumbled as Akhmerov rang off. "I hope your children become capitalists."

Young gazed toward Launch Pad 39-A. He noted with satisfaction that a score of soldiers were strolling casually toward the perimeter of the site.

The Politburo assembled for the second time within three hours.

"I have some interesting developments to report," the Russian premier said. "First, we have lost the services of comrade Krotkov. His recent performance was not up to standard and his loyalty was in question. He has been removed before he could do any harm.

"Second, and more serious, the American President has made a devious proposition. The Americans want our agreement to abort the Mars mission and use Apollo-Soyuz as a bomb-carrying vehicle with which to destroy the planetoid. I should add, they emphatically deny that they have other resources capable of destroying the planetoid.

"I should also add that I don't believe them. We've had ample cause in the past to mistrust our capitalist friends." The premier drummed his fingers on the table. "Fortunately, comrade Akhmerov has reported unusual activity at their supposedly secret weapons establishment at Tyndall. Also, the NASA administrator has flown to the Apollo-Soyuz launch site. We have reason to suspect, I believe, that our American friends are up to something."

A dark-bearded figure on the premier's right stood to address the meeting. "Our position seems clear to me. We withhold our approval. Any attempt to interfere with the agreed purpose of Apollo-Soyuz we would regard as an extremely provocative act. The Mars mission must go ahead. And the Americans must take other action to deal with this planetoid."

The proposal was one of the few ever made by Nikita Giorski, chairman of the KGB and one of the most feared men in Russia. He had survived in the office throughout the terms of three Russian premiers. His infrequent proposals were invariably accepted.

"That is the way it shall be," the premier said. "I shall contact Akhmerov now. I shall force the Americans to take action by keeping the President in ignorance of our position until the final moments before liftoff.

"Thank you, comrades."

Three hours, zero minutes, zero seconds to liftoff—the scheduled time for the astronauts and cosmonauts to board the spacecraft.

Young called the colonel in charge of security. Akhmerov, who had now arrived at the Cape, moved a little closer to be sure he could overhear.

"The astronauts and cosmonauts will board the space-craft."

"Yes sir."

As Young hung up he added, "All's well, Dmitri. They're on their way."

"Of course. There's no reason why they shouldn't be, is there?"

Both men, followed by Kennedy, went to join the space-men, who were preparing to enter the ship. Akhmerov drew the two Russians aside.

Out of earshot he told them, "We believe the Americans may wish to abort this mission. The Soviet Union wishes this mission to proceed. In the event of any attempt to sabotage the flight, you will remain in the command module until given further instructions. Good luck."

Soon the formal handshakes were over. The men boarded the elevator inside the spacecraft's umbilical tower and stepped out at the level which allowed access to the command module.

Just like the loading of Noah's Ark, Young thought. Two by two. But this voyage was already sunk if he had his way.

The cosmonauts entered first, followed by the astronauts. The door of Apollo-Soyuz clanged shut.

Two hours, forty-eight minutes, twenty-three seconds . . .

In Firing Room 1—the vital nerve center of the launch control block—Kennedy gave authorization for the fueling of the launch rocket to begin.

One hour, zero minutes, forty-eight seconds . . . forty-seven . . .

Young's intestines were performing a snake dance. A crisis of conscience was beginning to trouble him. It was conceivable that the President would allow the mission to go ahead and use the IPBM. The missile would do the job, all right. But there was no way the Russians could fail to be angered by its performance. Heaven help the future of détente. What would happen, Young wondered, if he alone took the responsibility to abort the mission? It would be the end of his career. But it might prevent a flare-up of the arms race.

He hoped desperately that he would not be forced to make the decision.

"Bud, let's go over to the VIP lounge," he suggested. "This tension is driving me nuts."

Though Jenny had arrived shortly after lunch, Young had so far found time only for a brief hello. In the VIP lounge he and Kennedy found her interviewing a leading actor, who had been invited to the launch along with a group of show business celebrities and politicians. When she saw Young her face remained impassive, except for the lowering of an eyelid—her secret wink, which he interpreted as a friendly "keep away" sign.

"It seems our journalist friend is onto another story and doesn't want to be interrupted, Bud. Let's have a drink."

The senator from Young's home state of Tennessee approached Young and Kennedy jovially. "Hello, Matt. It's going to be a great show, my boy. A great show."

"It sure is," Young agreed. He smiled at Kennedy and added, "One hell of a show."

Zero hours, twenty-nine minutes, forty-one seconds . . . forty . . .

Young and Kennedy sat silently in Firing Room 1. Young had just started on his second pack of cigarettes of the day.

The phone rang.

"Yes," Young almost shouted into the mouthpiece.

"The President wishes to speak with you," an anonymous voice said.

"Matt, are you alone?"

"Just a second, please."

He put his hand over the mouthpiece and looked anxiously at Kennedy and Akhmerov. "Personal call," he said. "I'd like to speak in private."

Akhmerov eyed him suspiciously.

"Sure, Matt," Kennedy answered. "Give us a shout when you're through."

With obvious reluctance, Akhmerov followed Kennedy from the room.

"Yes sir," Young continued.

"I have not heard from the Russian premier, but I take it you have read your sealed orders."

"Yes sir."

"At precisely fifteen minutes before the scheduled liftoff you will abort the mission and act according to those orders."

Young's heartbeat accelerated.

"Yes sir."

"One moment, Matt. I have another call."

A tense two minutes followed.

Zero hours, twenty-four minutes, twenty-two seconds . . . twenty-one . . .

"Hello again, Matt. That was the Russian premier on the hot line. Any attempt on our part to interfere with the Apollo-Soyuz Mars mission will be regarded by our comrades as an act of international piracy."

Young was speechless.

The President continued, "How would you like to be an international pirate, Matt?"

"Certainly, sir."

"You will follow my previous instructions. Abort the mission at fifteen minutes before liftoff. Some, uh, shall we say, fuel problem will be responsible. Then I shall appear on television and announce to the world that our Russian friends have had the bright idea of using Apollo-Soyuz to bomb the planetoid. That should give the Kremlin something to think about."

Young couldn't suppress a laugh.

"Sir, that's genius. Sheer genius."

"I think so, too," the President said. "Go and play Captain Kidd."

Zero hours, twenty-one minutes, seven seconds . . . six . . .

Young called to Kennedy and Akhmerov.

"Let's get to the control desk, gentlemen. This is going to be worth seeing."

Zero hours, fifteen minutes, three seconds . . . two . . . one . .

"Bud, abort mission," Young snapped.

Kennedy instantly pressed the red button. Sirens shrieked. Technicians leapt to their feet in alarm.

"You can't do that," Akhmerov yelled, shaking Young by the shoulder.

Young grinned "I think we've done it. Look at the Soyuz."

The astronauts were now stepping out of the command module onto the umbilical tower. But his grin quickly faded. Seconds later, the cosmonauts had failed to follow.

Young peered intently at the screen showing the interior of the Apollo-Soyuz cockpit. The cosmonaut nearest the hatch had unbuckled his safety harness. Fully suited, he moved clumsily into the escape tunnel that led to the hatch. Only his legs, dangling at one end of the tunnel, now showed on the television monitor. Young looked at the screen showing the exterior of the capsule and breathed a sigh of relief. The Russian's head and shoulders appeared. The astronaut who had just left the command module held out a hand to help the cosmonaut. But instead of climbing out, the Russian grasped the hatch and slammed it shut. The American, startled, stood with his hand outstretched toward the sealed vehicle.

Young wheeled toward Akhmerov. "What the hell are they doing? We have an abort." He grabbed a microphone, jabbed a button on a communications console and thrust the microphone at the Russian. "Get those bastards out of there. Now."

Akhmerov smiled and spoke into the microphone to the cosmonauts. "The Soviet Union is proud of you, comrades," Akhmerov said. "Spasiba. Thank you."

The cosmonauts grinned behind their face masks and gave the thumbs-up sign.

Young realized that he had been outmaneuvered. The game of Russian roulette was to be played until the hammer fell on the loaded chamber. Every second the danger grew that some irreparable international incident might develop. It was vital that the Russians be compelled to play along with the myth of a launch malfunction.

The sirens continued to shriek.

Young snapped at Kennedy. "Make a name for yourself, Bud. Hit the safety release button."

Again, Kennedy acted instantly.

Four simultaneous explosions jolted the command module, unlocking it from the rest of the spacecraft. The small release rocket on top of the capsule roared into life, engulfing the Soyuz in brilliant orange flames. Slowly, the giant spacecraft was beheaded. Soyuz seemed to hover uncertainly, then accelerated.

"Go, baby, go," Young shouted exuberantly.

At 20,000 feet over the Atlantic and nine miles off the Cape, the rocket died. Three parachutes popped open. On board Soyuz the cosmonauts looked at each other in bewilderment. The module gently plopped into the Atlantic.

"My country will . . ." Akhmerov began.

Young patted his chubby cheek and, with a broad grin, his

face a few inches from the Russian's, said, "Fuck off, Akhmerov."

To Kennedy he called, "Fish those cowboys out of the water."

"Right away," Kennedy hollered.

Seconds later, Bigelow phoned.

"Matt, what's happened?"

"No problem, Bob. We had a fuel malfunction. The astronauts were able to get out in time and the cosmonauts landed safely in the drink."

"But . . ."

"No buts, Bob. That's exactly the way it happened. That's exactly the way you tell it to the press."

"Sure thing. I think I've got the message."

To Kennedy Young said, "You handle the TV and newspapers at this end. Malfunction and all that—not another word. I'm going to call the President."

Young found Jenny as she was leaving the press room, surrounded by other journalists. He took her arm and drew her aside.

"How did it go?"

"Not so hot. A brief statement from Bud, but I've got lots of color."

Other journalists, recognizing Young, hovered nearby in the hope of catching further information.

"I suppose there was no factor other than the fuel malfunction," Jenny said.

He placed his hands on her shoulder and looked directly into her eyes. "Honey, don't even think that. Not for a second." He looked anxiously at her colleagues. "It was a fuel malfunction and that was that."

One reporter jostled the others aside. "Can we quote you on that, sir?"

"No. You quote the statement Bud Kennedy gave. But watch the TV at eleven. The President will be on the air."

He turned to Jenny and despairingly held out his open hands.

"Excuse me, honey, but I have to get back to Bud. I guess we've both got work to do. Sleep well. I'll call you when I can."

As he pushed through the doorway Jenny turned and headed for a phone.

At 11 p.m. the President appeared on nationwide TV. Satellite transmissions set up to carry the historic launch worldwide enabled the speech to be broadcast to the Western world's largest ever TV audience. Throughout the communist world the broadcast was recorded on videotape. A decision on which portions should be shown would be made later.

"Less than an hour ago, a malfunction caused the Apollo-Soyuz space mission to be aborted," the President said. "The American astronauts were able to escape from the ship. The Russian cosmonauts, more familiar with the emergency release operation of the Soyuz, chose to splash down safely in the Atlantic.

"The problem with the spacecraft, I am happy to confirm, was a false alarm. One computer system indicated a fuel malfunction. At that moment, with fifteen minutes to liftoff, the mission was aborted automatically. Happily, no one was injured and neither the rocket nor the capsule was damaged."

The President smiled broadly.

"I am delighted to inform you of an even more significant development. Our Russian friends have made a unique gesture that promises to bring our two great countries closer than they have ever been.

"With the mission aborted, the Soviet Union has suggested that, rather than replan the Mars program, Apollo-Soyuz should be reassembed and equipped with nuclear weapons to destroy the planetoid that threatens the earth. The best of the Soviet Union's scientists and technicians are preparing to assist in stripping the Soyuz command module, now on its way back by recovery ship to Cape Canaveral.

"America is proud to accept this gesture of goodwill. We mourn, with the Soviet Union, this backward step from Mars. But we rejoice in this forward leap toward international cooperation.

"We have every reason to believe that our attempt to destroy the planetoid will be successful. There is no cause for alarm.

"Goodnight. God bless you all."

The third meeting of the Politburo was the briefest. A decision was made to broadcast a translation of the President's speech in its entirety.

Obeying the President's sealed orders, Young directed Kennedy to put all hands on the task of reassembling the spacecraft and stripping the command module to create space for the nuclear bombs. Young also instructed him to have a new flight path computed, along which the bomb-laden rocket would be launched at the earliest possible moment.

This time its destination was to be the planetoid.

Chapter Five

After four hundred million years, the planetoid was now within four days of the end of its voyage . . . a mere 13,600,728 miles from the earth.

Powerful floodlights bathed the launch complex as the capsule recovery vessel inched along the canal beside the crawlerway that linked Launch Pad 39-A and the vehicle assembly building. Young and Kennedy, followed by a subdued Akhmerov, left Firing Room 1 to supervise the unloading of Soyuz.

The cosmonauts, still wearing their space suits but with their helmets removed, leapt onto the dockside without waiting for the recovery vessel to be securely docked at the turning basin and ran across to Akhmerov. They began talking excitedly to him in Russian, gesticulating wildly. He silenced them with a few short words and ushered them to a waiting jeep.

Young and Kennedy exchanged smiles as the jeep pulled away. To the tune of the "Red Flag" Kennedy sang softly, "The working class can kiss my ass . . ." Young slapped him jovially on the back.

A massive crane lifted Soyuz from the deck of the recovery vessel and headed for the vehicle assembly building. Kennedy immediately ordered the stripping of the capsule to begin. Only automatic directional equipment was to be left on board. To the foreman in charge of operations in the VAB Kennedy said, "I want this baby as empty as a politician's handshake."

Back in Firing Room 1 a senior technician confronted Kennedy with a sheaf of diagrams and computations.

"We have the new launch schedule, sir."

Kennedy studied the figures for several minutes. "I hope these are right on," he said. "If we're just a whisker wide of the mark, we're in for a headache."

"They're right, sir," the technician assured him. "We've double-checked with Mission Control. And we'll have an opportunity for a mid-course correction."

"Fine." Kennedy dismissed the technician.

"This is it," Kennedy said to Young. "Our most vital launch program ever."

"You better believe it," Young agreed.

The launch was scheduled for 1757 hours on Monday. The rocket would crash-land on the planetoid at 2043 hours on Tuesday. The nuclear bombs would be electronically exploded a split second before impact. At that moment, the planetoid would be a mere 3,777,600 miles from the earth ... a distance it could travel in barely more than a day.

"Let's start the clock," Young ordered.

Kennedy signaled to the officer in charge of all countdowns at the Cape, known officially as the test conductor. The officer got up from his desk beneath the official electronic countdown clock, which had been stopped at fifteen minutes, zero seconds—the precise moment when Kennedy had halted the Mars shot by hitting the abort button. Kennedy handed over the report detailing the new launch program.

"Let's get the clock running, Jim."

The test conductor returned to his desk and began to manipulate buttons on a console. The figures on the countdown clock blurred for several seconds, finally coming to rest at forty-one hours, fifty-seven minutes, zero seconds. At one-minute before one o'clock, the test conductor announced over a loudspeaker, "Countdown will begin on my count at one a.m."

Almost immediately, he added, "At my count it will be T minus forty-one hours and fifty-seven minutes precisely, and counting."

In the jargon used at the Cape and Mission Control, "T" indicated "takeoff." The start of the test conductor's count would be signaled by the single word, "Mark."

Young and Kennedy checked their watches and prepared to synchronize them with the official countdown clock.

"Mark," the test conductor announced abruptly. The countdown clock whirred into life and flicked to forty-one hours, fifty-six minutes, fifty-nine seconds . . . fifty-eight . . .

"Get this shot right and I'll fix you up with an extra pay raise," Young joked to Kennedy.

"If I don't get it right you can forget the raise I'm already due," he answered with a laugh. The flight director would remain in the firing room for several more hours, specifying the new duties of key members of his staff. For Young, the day was over.

"So long, Bud. I'm going to hit the sack."

"Goodnight, Matt. And don't forget that raise. I intend to earn it."

Young set off for his quarters at the Cape, regretting that he had not arranged to join Jenny at her hotel. He hadn't seen her since the press briefing. Now he would have to settle for a goodnight phone call.

In her hotel room Jenny decided to make a final check call to the *Daily News* before going to sleep. She had been exhilarated by her story on the mission abort. Admittedly, other journalists and the wire services had been on the scene and the *News* would have been inundated with copy. But she knew that she had obtained a lot of exclusive detail and extra quotes. Alone among her colleagues she had suspected the true circumstances which led to the abort. Perhaps one day, she thought, there would be time to tell the real story. But for now, she was more than pleased with what she had.

"Hi, Jen," Reynolds answered. "I must admit I was hoping you wouldn't call."

Jenny was stunned. Reynolds had been wildly enthusiastic about her copy earlier in the evening.

"What now, Ken? Did I botch something?"

"You didn't botch a thing, honey. It was terrific. It's just that we're not using your story."

She caught her breath.

"You still there, Jen?" Reynolds asked after a pause.

"Yes, I am," she said weakly.

"Look sweetheart. It's just one of those things. To be specific, it's the Old Man. He's taken your resignation seriously."

"I see . . ."

"Honey, it's . . ."

The phone clicked. Jenny had hung up. She threw herself headlong on the bed and drove a fist into the pillow. After several minutes she lifted the phone off the hook. Tonight she wanted to talk to no one. Not even Young.

For half an hour after leaving home Michael had driven the Chevrolet slowly around side streets. As his confidence grew, he turned onto the main highway and headed north toward New York. He planned to stay with Eleanor for a while at least and get some kind of job, perhaps as a helper in a store.

Shortly before 3 a.m. he passed a sign which read "Washington D.C. 100 miles." Just beyond the sign he drove into a self-service station. Fearful that his youth might arouse suspicion, he had avoided gas stations where he would be served by an attendant. After filling up he went to the cash window and handed over a twenty-dollar bill. He kept his head lowered and accepted the change without comment.

Selecting several dimes and quarters he walked to a payphone alongside the pay booth. By now he had memorized the New York number on Eleanor's birthday card. Repeatedly he had tried to call her, but so far he had been unable to get a reply.

The operator instructed him to put extra money in the box and soon he heard the ringing of the phone at the other end. Michael was about to hang up when a man's voice answered.

"Yeah. What the hell time is this to be making a call?"

"I'm sorry. Is Eleanor Bigelow there, please?"

"Look, sonny." The man almost spat out the words. "You get me out of bed in the middle of the night to ask for that broad. Well, I'm fed up getting calls from you creeps. She doesn't live here any more. Got it? If you want to get your rocks off try looking for her in a sewer somewhere."

Michael flinched as the phone was slammed down. Surely he must have gotten the wrong number. But the man had said Eleanor no longer lived there. Confused, Michael decided to continue his journey and check the number with an operator later in the day.

He drove for another hour before parking off the highway. He pulled a map out of the glove compartment to make sure that his route would bypass the center of Washington—and the many policemen he knew would be on patrol there.

Over the car radio he heard a newscaster giving details of the planned launch of the bomb-laden rocket. For a moment he wavered in his resolve to drive to New York and wondered if he might make it to Cape Canaveral in time for the launch. Checking the mileage he dismissed the idea and decided it would have to be New York after all.

After double-checking his route, Michael swung back onto the highway. A rapidly approaching car behind him swerved violently. The driver leaned on the horn, regained control and sped by, missing his front fender by inches.

Michael cringed. For the second time since leaving home he had almost been involved in an accident.

At 8 a.m., Jenny stepped out of the shower, absent-mindedly dabbed herself and dressed in a calf-length cotton dress which buttoned at the front, a favorite of Young's. She nibbled listlessly at the breakfast that had been brought to the room and phoned down for a dry vodka martini. Though not ordinarily a morning drinker, she decided her morale needed a sharp lift.

At a knock on the door she released the night latch and turned away without waiting to see who had knocked, expecting the room waiter.

"Hello, beautiful."

She recognized Young's voice and swung around toward him. "Matt . . ." She ran into his arms and kissed him.

"I've been trying to call you." He crossed to the phone and replaced it on the rest.

"I'm sorry, Matt. I just didn't want any calls."

She slumped on the sofa and he sat beside her.

"What's the problem?"

"I'm no longer a reporter, Matt. At least, I can't get my stuff into print."

He listened sympathetically as she told him of her call to Reynolds.

"I've had that whole scene, Matt. The *Daily News*, anyway." She put her hand on his knee. "I think I'll take some time off from work to be a wife. And a mother."

Young fumbled for a cigarette. She gave him a gentle look of disapproval.

"Jenny, I want you to be my wife. Badly. But I'm cool on the family part of it." He inhaled the smoke deep into his lungs. "I'm forty-six, honey. I'd be an old man while our kid was still at school."

"Kids, Matt." Jenny corrected him. "I want several. And it's very important to me. I know last time was tragic for you, but it doesn"t have to be like that. I've had a problem on that score, too, Matt. I want to know I can have kids. I want to prove it."

"I don't know, Jenny . . . Maybe."

He kissed her. "Let's see what happens, shall we? Meanwhile, there's a small problem I'd like to get back to at the Cape."

"OK, but think it over, Matt. Please."

They moved apart on the sofa as a waiter brought in the dry martini she had ordered. She smiled with embarrassment at Young and gave the waiter a two-dollar tip. Leaving the drink untouched she took Young's arm and walked with him to the elevator.

Akhmerov had been summoned to an urgent meeting at the Russian quarters of the United Nations building in New York. The choice of venue alarmed him. Had he been in favor, the meeting would almost certainly have been held at the Soviet Embassy. The room in the U.N. building was reserved for meetings that the ambassador, who preferred to delegate some of his less pleasant duties, did not wish to attend.

As Akhmerov drove from the Cape to the airport he wondered if he was nearing his farewell to America. Probably, he decided. Fortunately, his past services to the Soviet Union would stand him in good stead, but he could no longer realistically cherish hopes of further promotion. This was certainly farewell to any chance of being appointed to the Politburo.

Akhmerov had avoided leaving any messages at the Cape about his movements. With luck, there would be time for explanations later.

When he reached the U.N. building he slipped unobtrusively through the main entrance, which was crowded with the usual groups of Sunday tourists. He overheard an official guide remark that this was the building in which rested the greatest hopes of world peace. Aware of some of the behind-the-scenes machinatons at the U.N., Akhmerov knew better.

He almost choked with dismay when he saw the figure who awaited him in the Russian suite offices. Nikita Giorski. The KGB chairman. A man who wielded more power than any of the premiers he had served.

"Sit," Giorski said aggressively. He rose quickly from his desk, clasped his thick, stubby hands behind his back and paced the room. An ugly scar creased his right cheek.

Akhmerov had often wondered what had happened to the person who had caused the injury. It was more than likely, he felt, that the man no longer existed.

"I have flown here to make a personal investigation of the extraordinary events which have taken place," Giorski said. "Already I have determined that your performance has been abominable."

"I can explain . . ."

"You need not explain to me. You will have ample opportunity to explain to your colleagues in your new post. You are to assist at one of our collective farms. You will fly to Moscow this evening and take up new duties immediately. Here is your plane ticket." He flung a paper wallet into Akhmerov's lap.

Akhmerov had served on a collective farm as a student. He had volunteered for the work, excited by the propaganda which promised that the new farming techniques would solve Russia's severe food problems. He had expected to find a band of spirited and patriotic workers; he had found instead a pathetic group of skeletal slaves living in poverty. His new career promised to be a demanding one.

"Meanwhile," Giorski added, "get back to Cape Canaveral. Your government expects you to bid a courteous farewell to your American counterparts. If possible, try to dispel the opinion they inevitably have—that you are a bungling idiot. That is also my opinion. And don't get any bright ideas about missing the plane. You will be watched. Now get out."

Akhmerov's cheeks burned. He heaved his bulk from his chair and stood submissively before Giorski. "Thank you, comrade. I shall do my best to serve my country in whatever task is given to me."

Giorski snorted. "Get out," he repeated.

Akhmerov obeyed promptly.

Throughout New York, life pulsed on at its familiar Sunday pace. A fine drizzle fell. Traffic was light in Manhattan. The few private cars were outnumbered and outpaced by yellow cabs that darted through the crisscross of streets and avenues even more frenziedly than on busy, crowded weekdays. During an occasional lull in the traffic the city seemed strangely deserted. But tomorrow morning, the murmuring of the traffic would grow into a growl, then a deafening roar, announcing the start of another hectic work week.

Eleanor's latest client had paid more attention to the TV news than he had to her. He was an old customer and usually a vigorous performer. Tonight, though, he simply watched television as she lay languidly on the hotel bed. She found herself brooding over the President's statement. She understood only that catastrophe threatened the earth and gained little assurance from the fact that apparently an attempt was to be made to bomb the planetoid. She vividly imagined the worst that could possibly happen.

Eventually her companion took his pleasure rapidly and brutally. He dressed and tossed a $100 bill onto the bed, leaving her to spend the night alone in the suite. She felt thoroughly cheapened.

She poured a glass of water from a pitcher on a night table, reached for her purse and took out a small bottle of dull red tablets. She swallowed three of the pills, slowly submitting to a feeling of euphoria, then swallowed the handful that remained. Soon she slept.

A maid entered the room at ten in the morning and noticed the still form, apparently asleep, the covers thrown back far enough to reveal that Eleanor was naked. The TV had been left on. The President's speech of the night before was being repeated.

"We have every reason to believe," the President was saying, "that our attempt to destroy the planetoid will be successful. There is no cause for alarm."

The maid turned off the set and quietly left the room. She would clean the rest of the rooms on the floor and return later.

The Galiardo brothers had reassembled in Sally's bar and grill. Billy recounted in explicit detail yet another episode of his encounter with Eleanor.

The day before his brothers had greeted Billy's story with derision.

"You lying bastard," Rick had ridiculed him.

At that point Billy had played his master card. "In that case how do you account for this?" And with a flourish he had placed a $100 bill on the table. He had amended the financial details of the transaction to enable him to keep the other $100 for himself. Rick had pocketed the money, but Billy's brothers were suddenly hungry for information. To Billy his new notoriety was worth the price.

"Come on, Billy," Willie now urged him. "Give us some more."

"Well, she was a trick-and-a-half, I tell you."

"Yes, well this isn't getting us anywhere," Rick interrupted impatiently. "What I want to know is, where's my next poke coming from? That hundred bucks ain't going to last long—and it ain't going to last five minutes if Sal sees it. We've got to do a job. And soon."

Billy was the first to make a proposal. He had assumed new status with his brothers since his experience with Eleanor.

"I thought you bums had already decided to knock off Mancini's," he said scornfully. "So let's get on with it."

"Yeah," Willie added. "If they can hit that planetoid, we can sure as hell hit that dump," he said, the boast as lacking in logic as in probability.

"OK, OK," said Rick. "Let's go over the plan one more time."

With a felt-tipped pen he began to scribble on a napkin.

"Billy, Sparks and me'll make our way to the rear entrance by the fire escape here," Rick said. His hand swept across the table to indicate the location of the fire escape and knocked over a cup of coffee.

"Shit," he said, putting the cup upright in the saucer. He mopped up the spilled coffee, realizing too late that he was using the napkin on which he had started to write.

"Hey," whined Billy, the one most likely to need specific instruction, "you'll have to write that out again."

"Aw, to hell—you do it," said Rick, tossing Billy the pen and another napkin.

"Like I said, the three of us go up the fire escape here," Rick continued. He repositioned the pepper shaker, which thus became the fire escape.

"Sparks cuts the burglar alarm wires here," he added, marking the site of the burglar alarm control box with the salt shaker.

"We smash our way into the office here." The ketchup became the office.

"Then, Sparks blows the safe," he forecast optimistically, "we grab the stuff and dash back to Willie's car, here." A bread roll became Willie's car.

"Boom," said Sparks, implying that his part of the job was as good as done.

"Balls," said Sally, totting up the check. "That's $23.49 you owe me."

"No sweat, love," Rick promised. "Have faith. The day of reckoning is near."

He stood to leave, clumsily knocking over his chair. The others followed him through the door, smiling at his discomfort.

Sally put the fire escape, the burglar alarm control box, Mancini's office and the getaway car back where they belonged on the table.

In his home opposite Central Park, Doctor Peters had wrestled all morning with disturbing feelings of guilt. He had added up the week's takings. The sum total of all fees, both earned and unearned, was excellent. But the exercise often reminded him sharply of how different his career had become from the one he had dreamed of in his youth. He now made more money from hookers than from legitimate patients; he swindled more people with charm than he cured with medicine.

"Brunch is ready, dear," his wife called from the dining room.

Peters hurried to the dining table. He still felt a deep regard for his wife, though she had long ago joined the ranks of the nondescript middle-aged. He dreaded the thought that she might one day discover the reason why his practice was so profitable.

"Winston and his family are coming for dinner tonight," she reminded him. "I want to have plenty of time to get everything ready."

The prospect did nothing for Peters' low spirits. His brother was as much of a crook as he was. He remembered that Winston had once been determined to become a good cop. He could well have chosen a career offering a higher salary—but it was doubtful if his earnings would have matched what he had made since submitting to a life of corruption. In the library over a drink after dinner, each would boast about how much he had made in the last week by various devious means. The women would huddle over chores in the kitchen, jibbering on about mundane matters, totally unaware of the reasons why each was given such a generous household allowance.

After brunch Peters lounged in front of the TV while his

wife busied herself about the house. He became engrossed in a program which speculated on the possible consequences if efforts to divert the planetoid failed. Heat-blast injuries, flooding, gas escaping from fractured pipes . . . Peters shuddered. Now that would mean some real doctoring would be needed.

Mrs. Winstanley helped herself to one of the pills Doctor Peters had prescribed. Though the dose was three a day, she had already taken four pills that morning.

"These pills are so good for mommakins," she told her poodle.

The poodle cocked its head on one side.

She ran a bath and liberally sprinkled an expensive shampoo into the water. Cecil scampered suspiciously under a table.

"It's time to make you beautiful, Cecil," she cooed, hauling the dog by its collar to the bathroom. She dipped a hand into the water to test its temperature, then lowered a reluctant, whining Cecil into the bathtub.

The TV set droned on in the living room, unwatched as news of the planetoid continued. The interruption of regular programming had annoyed Mrs. Winstanley.

"No morning cartoons, tootsie," she complained, soaping the dog's back. "I don't know what the world's coming to."

Sergeant Peters and his family sat around the TV, intent on the news.

"What could happen, Winston?" his wife asked, obviously concerned. "I mean, if it really, you know, landed here."

"It's not likely," he assured her. "But you know the drill. Just keep the tube on and stay cool. I guess they'd be able to warn us where it would hit and we'd get the folks out. But the chances of us getting it, even supposing they don't blast it out of the universe, are . . . well, about as likely as a home run hit in Shea Stadium landing in our backyard."

"I don't know," she said, unconvinced.

The sergeant patted the head of his twelve-year-old son. "Simon would handle things for me if I wasn't here. You'd look after your mom, wouldn't you, son?"

"Sure, dad," the boy said absently, absorbed by the TV.

"But they say that even if they blow it up there could be some debris flying around," Mrs. Peters added. "I mean, it doesn't sound safe, does it? What with all these craters and things, and they know it's headed straight for us."

Peters knew it was useless trying to put her at ease. "Honestly, you're the kind of woman who puts on a new pair of panties every time she goes out just in case she gets hit by a car. But that isn't the way things happen."

"Don't be crude in front of the boy, Winston," she rebuked him sourly. "That's not the point."

"So, what do you want me to do? Buy you a tin hat?"

"I want to go to my sister's."

What a terrific idea, he thought immediately. With the old lady and the boy out of the way he could spread around some of the cash he had lying spare.

"Honey, if you want to go to your sister's, go to your sister's. You'd like that, Simon, wouldn't you?"

Simon grimaced.

"Course you would," his mother said.

Mrs. Peters' sister lived in a large house in the suburbs of Toronto with her husband and three children. The man was a bore, Peters had decided long ago, and his kids were a bunch of unruly brats.

"I don't want you worrying if I can help it," the sergeant said. "Let's check with the airport now and see if you and Simon can go first thing in the morning. Just so long as you don't want me to go with you. And at dinner tonight you can brag about how well I trust you."

"Oh, Winston. Thanks . . ."

"OK, that's it. Son, go get me the phone book and I'll call the airport."

Eric Sinclair was desperate to see Eleanor Bigelow again, but flat broke. There was no Vernon to borrow from and the broad wasn't the type to do a favor on credit.

Vernon's departure had hit Eric's pocket badly. His rent had doubled overnight. In fact, his roommate had often paid even more than his share of the rent. When they went drinking, it was Vernon, more often than not, who picked up the tab. And he had been a profitable meal ticket. He had bought most of the food while Eric squandered most of what little money he earned on a succession of women and on wheeling and dealing as he flitted from one salesman's job to another. Looking around the apartment, Eric noted that most of the furniture and fittings belonged to Vernon. If he came back to claim what he owned the place would be bare.

Suddenly a madcap scheme flashed through Eric's mind as he watched the news on Vernon's TV set. He sketched a launching pad, the Apollo-Soyuz, a stock of bombs and a planetoid. Grabbing the Yellow Pages he flipped through in search of toy manufacturers. If he could persuade someone to mass-produce a toy kit . . . Every child in the United States would want one, he persuaded himself. That could mean a fat commission. He wrote down a few company names to call the following day.

He roughly estimated production and distribution costs and an approximate selling price. Guessing at the potential number of orders, he allowed himself a two-percent commission. The figure suggested that Eric Sinclair might yet become an idle millionaire.

The doorbell interrupted his scheming. Vernon and a tall, blonde, Swedish-looking companion pushed past him into the room. Eric decided not to get aggressive.

"This won't take long," Vernon said.

Eric stood aside in silence as the other two hauled out the TV set, the stereo, a batch of records, several table lamps and the last bottle of wine from the fridge.

"You'll be hearing from my attorney," said Vernon. "I'll be back later for the rest of my things."

"I love you," Eric said sarcastically, slamming the door and turning to survey the stripped apartment.

Michael wearily pulled the car into a hamburger restaurant. He drew Eleanor's birthday card from his pocket and checked the number. He dialed carefully on a pay-phone in a corner of the restaurant. Recognizing the gruff voice that answered, Michael hung up without speaking.

There had been no mistake, Michael realized. And the call had cost him half his small change and he now had only two dollars. The meal would take most of that. Without knowing where to find Eleanor . . .

He ran back impulsively to the phone, called Manhattan Information and asked for the number of Miss Eleanor Bigelow.

"I don't know the address, but I know it's Manhattan," he told the operator.

"Yes, I have it here . . ."

With the last of his change he dialed the new number. A woman's voice answered almost immediately.

"This is Eleanor, but . . ."

"Eleanor!" Michael shouted. "El . . ." He stopped short, suddenly aware that he was shouting and that people in the restaurant were looking at him.

The husky voice at the other end continued.

". . . a recorded message. I would love to see you, though. I like tall men, short men, well . . ." Then there was a laugh. ". . . I like all men really, in all sorts of ways. If you would like me to call you, please leave your telephone number and I will be in touch. Remember, this is a recorded message. Please don't begin speaking until you hear the bell."

Michael held the phone at arm's length. The significance of what he had heard dawned painfully. In a moment he heard a bell. He was still staring at the mouthpiece when the message began again.

"This is Eleanor, but this is a recorded message . . ."

The phone fell from his hand, clattered on the wall below the pay-phone and swung on its cord as he ran from the restaurant to the car, unconcerned now about what others might think of his behavior.

He slumped in the driving seat and slammed his palms on the rim of the steering wheel. He switched on the ignition to check the fuel level. Nearly empty. There was nothing else to do, he decided. He would head for the next town and try to get a job. To hell with Eleanor. To hell with his father.

With a fingertip he dabbed the corners of his eyes, then started the engine.

The maid returned to Eleanor's room after lunch and noticed uneasily that the figure in the bed had not moved. "Miss?" she inquired, moving forward and touching Eleanor's arm. She recoiled at once from the cold, stiffened flesh. Her eyes were drawn to the large patch of grayish-blue skin to which the blood in the corpse had drained.

Ken Reynolds sprawled at home in his favorite armchair, surrounded by empty beer cans and the Sunday papers. The *News* was well up to standard, he concluded. He was still angry at being ordered not to use Jenny's copy. In fact, he had used some of it. A lot of the detail was irresistible, and he had recycled it into the copy flow by having it rewritten. He hoped Jenny would gain consolation from recognizing some of her work—even if she wasn't going to be paid for it.

"Can I go and play, daddy?" Susan fidgeted on a chair and swung her legs restlessly.

"Sure, honey. Don't go far."

Reynolds took another can of beer from the six-pack at the side of his chair.

"Let me open it, daddy," Susan pleaded.

He gave her the can and she expertly pulled off the ring top.

"Thanks, beautiful. You'd make someone a terrific wife."

"I'll be in the park, daddy."

Susan skipped out of the door.

In the park the derelict Susan had met two days before pulled up his overcoat to ward off the light rain now trickling down his neck. From a trash can alongside the bench he took out a copy of that morning's *New York Times.* He glanced briefly at the main headline—"Mars shot aborted: Bomb-laden rocket to be fired at earthbound planetoid"—and fashioned a triangular-shaped hat out of the front and back pages of the paper. He placed it on his head for further protection from the weather.

Susan wandered near, stopping uncertainly when she saw the old man. He smiled and picked up a sheet of the newspaper. She watched, curiously, as he fashioned a small hat similar to the one he was wearing. He held it out to her. She came forward shyly, took the hat and smiled at him for the first time. She let him take the hat back and place it on her head. Still smiling, she ran to join her friends.

"Hey," she shouted, "look what I've got."

The old man watched wistfully, oblivious now of the rain that slowly turned his paper hat a soggy gray.

Fearsome Freddie had drawn a small but enthusiastic gathering in the park. Raindrops glistened on his forehead and cheeks as he pounded out his message of doom. The fervent responses of his followers had inspired him even more than usual.

"In the dream of Saint John the Divine as told in the Book of Revelation," he boomed, "we are told, 'And the sun became as black as sackcloth, and the moon became as of blood . . . and there followed hail and fire mingled with blood, and they were cast upon the earth, and the third part of trees was burnt up, and all the green grass was burnt up . . . a great mountain burning with fire was cast into the sea.' "

"Hallelujah!" interjected one of Fearsome's believers. "Hallelujah! Praise the Lord!"

Fearsome nodded solemnly, well pleased with the Lord's preview of the end of the world.

A frustrated John Hutton couldn't suppress a low whistle when Alice bent over the table to serve Sunday brunch, revealing her soft, full cleavage under a loose-fitting blouse.

She looked at him sternly and buttoned her blouse to the top when she turned back to the stove.

Her father, gray-haired, paunchy and affable, grinned at John knowingly. The older man had more than an inkling of his son-in-law's problem.

"Why don't you two visit the crater after brunch. You can take my car. Biggest damn hole you've ever seen. Dug out by a meteorite way back years ago when there were dinosaurs. It'll give you a good idea of what would happen if that planetoid hit the earth. It'd be God help us, I tell you."

"Well, I dunno," John said. "I'd been wondering if we might go there, but Alice wants to stay with her mom."

As Alice sat down at the table, he added, "What do you say, sweetheart? Shall we go?"

Before Alice could speak her mother answered.

"No need to look out for me. You two need some time alone. Me and dad will be just fine."

"That's settled, then," Alice's father said. "That crater's well worth seeing. It's so deep that if you put this town in the bottom and looked down from the ridge you'd think you were looking at us from an airplane."

"Amazing," John said, his attempt at politeness somewhat spoiled as he gulped down the last of his food.

When the others had finished eating, Alice hurriedly stacked the dishes in the dishwasher and announced, "OK, let's go."

She kissed her parents, then held John's hand as he led her to the car.

"Thanks, pop," he said, getting into the driving seat.

"It's a pleasure, son. Oh, these might come in handy." He handed John the car keys.

"Oh, yes. I never thought. Thanks."

John soon decided they were sufficiently far from prying eyes. He stopped the car and turned to kiss Alice passionately. She laughed and leaned back seductively as he pressed the button that lowered the front bench seat to its horizontal position.

"Do leave on the air conditioning, darling," she said. "I'm so hot."

"So am I," John growled, reaching toward her.

Their lovemaking was fast and furious.

"Well, that's more like it," John said as he repositioned the front seat.

"I love you, John. Perhaps later . . ."

Hoping for some sign to confirm the implied promise, he turned sharply to look at her. Alice blew a kiss.

"Wowee!" John shouted, as he accelerated along U.S. 66.

Signs to the crater led him along a six-mile access road. Periodically they passed billboards calculated to entice tourists. One read, "Bigger than the atom bomb!" He eventually reached a parking lot in front of a row of souvenir shops and led Alice through the pay booth. A girl in the booth looked up from a book only momentarily to take his money. A wall behind the booth was all glass. John gasped at the view of the crater.

He and Alice found that they were the only sightseers there. Visitors often arrived by the coachload. Sometimes the crater would be ignored for days on end. This was one of those days.

They made their way through a side door and stood up on the rim. In front of them the ground fell away to the deepest part, 570 feet below. The sides were littered with the debris of some fantastic explosion thousands of years earlier.

"Unbelievable," John said. "Just unbelievable."

At the bottom of the crater lay a tangled heap of discarded machinery, a lone reminder of an attempt years before to drill down below the crater.

"They were hoping to find the remains of the meteorite that caused it," Alice explained. "They never did. Now they think it just blasted to smithereens on impact."

"Good God . . . That must have been one hell of a blast. Let's go and explore."

Halfway down the wall of the crater they reached a small crevice. John sat and saw that the view from the observation room was obstructed by the rim of the crater. "Hey, they can't see us." He patted the ground beside him and winked at Alice.

"John, you wouldn't . . ." she said in mock horror, but smiling nevertheless.

"I would if you would," he said, reaching for her hand and pulling her toward him. "You know, we'll probably be the first since those dinosaurs your dad was talking about."

"John, you're terrible."

"I know," he said, fondling her breasts.

"But what if somebody sees us?" she complained halfheartedly, putting a hand on top of his and crushing it tightly against her. She kissed him eagerly, her fears forgotten.

Michael had driven along a series of secondary roads and, soon after nightfall, reached a park on the fringe of a major town. He had lost all sense of direction and felt too disheartened to bother to check his whereabouts on the map. He drove down an unlit highway toward a forested area—a likely spot to pull in to rest until the following day.

Suddenly his muscles tensed as he heard the wailing of a police siren. He looked quickly in the rear-view mirror and saw a police car speeding toward him, its lights flashing. He tensed his muscles in fear. He might just be able to elude the police and hide the Chevrolet off the forested roadway.

He accelerated, gaining speed rapidly down a winding hill. In the mirror he saw that the police car continued to narrow the gap. Too late, he realized he was travelling too fast to negotiate the bend at the bottom of the hill. He clutched the wheel, his arms stiffened and he slammed both feet on the brake pedal. The wheels locked. The car skidded onto the shoulder, spraying gravel in all directions. Completely out of control now, it smashed into a tree, tumbled over and tore through a patch of tangled brush before coming to rest on all four wheels once again.

Michael heard the hiss of water spewing from the crushed radiator onto the hot cylinder block. A smell of burning rubber stung his nostrils. One headlight shone crazily into the sky. The other had been knocked out in the crash. The hood had crumpled on impact and now almost hid the view from the windscreen. He began to shake uncontrollably. He felt his face and chest anxiously. Miraculously, he was unhurt.

The police siren whined to a stop as he flung open the door

and scrambled up a grassy slope leading from the roadway. As he reached the top, the policeman knocked him to the ground with a flying tackle and they both tumbled down the other side of the slope.

Michael was stunned by the sound of an explosion as flames soared from behind the slope. He realized with horror that the car had exploded and caught fire. The low hill down which he and the policeman had fallen had cushioned them from the blast.

The officer released his hold on Michael and ran back to the top of the slope. "You all right?" he shouted desperately.

"Yeah, I'm OK." The second officer waved a flashlight from the roadway.

His companion called to Michael. "Come on, son. The joyride's over. You're a lucky, lucky kid."

Michael joined the officer sheepishly, and gazed in astonishment at the blazing wreckage.

"I suppose you are Michael Bigelow?"

"Yes."

"We've been looking for you all day, son. Your dad's going to be mighty pleased when he hears what's happened to the Chevy."

Michael stepped back a pace from the heat of the flames, which still burned fiercely.

"No bumps or bruises, son?"

"I don't think so . . ."

The officer patted Michael on the head. "Come on. Let's get out of here. It's too hot for comfort."

In the mid-Atlantic a giant mass of moist, hot air began to swirl, gently at first, then more rapidly. Clouds towered overhead threateningly. Soon the winds rotated at fifty miles an hour, then seventy-five. The circling winds whipped up the ocean waves and flung them toward Florida's east coast. This was the birth of Hurricane Helena.

The hurricane was spotted by the U.S. Tiros and Nimbus weather reconnaissance satellites. Within minutes the U.S. Hurricane Center in Miami was on full alert.

News of the development of Hurricane Helena was telexed to Cape Canaveral. The telex operator immediately delivered the cable to Bud Kennedy. He and Young had remained on duty throughout the evening to supervise the stripping of

Soyuz. Young was preparing to leave to join Jenny at her hotel.

"Oh, Christ," Kennedy groaned. He handed the telex to Young without comment.

"So," Young said, "Mother Nature doesn't seem to be on our side, does she? Though it does seem that the storm will be well clear of the Cape."

"I sure hope so, Matt. You never can tell with those SOBs."

True enough, Young reflected. Forecasting the path of a hurricane was no simple task. Occasionally one would travel in a straight line. More frequently, a hurricane would behave erratically—steer zig-zag paths, dip toward the Equator but then swing away, perhaps halt suddenly and then retrace its path.

"I think I'll leave you with this particular problem, Bud," Young said. His lightheartedness failed to hide his concern. "I know you're not going to let a little thing like a hurricane stop you from getting a pay raise."

"Just what I'd expect from a guy at Mission Control," Kennedy said with a laugh. "If there's a tough job to do, it's always the guys at the Cape who have to save the day."

The waves which lapped the shores of the Cape now grew in strength. Palm trees near the beach began to rustle in a light, warm breeze.

Chapter Six

MONDAY, 5 A.M.

Some 9,496,800 miles now separated the planetoid and the earth. Both planetoid and planet hurtled relentlessly onward, second by second closing the gap between them.

Bigelow rapped on the frosted glass window above the reception counter in the police station. A young officer, alert despite the hour, slid open the window.

"I'm Bigelow . . . Bob Bigelow. I've come to take my boy home."

The officer quickly took in the squat figure of Bigelow. A bit scruffy, the officer thought, but he seemed innocuous enough—not at all the type you would expect sons and daughters to run away from.

"Oh, yes," the officer said hesitantly. "I'd been told to expect you." He drummed a pencil on his desk top as though uncertain how to proceed. "I have a message for you. It's from the FBI—they'd been trying to get in touch with you and the message was passed on here."

"So?" Bigelow was only mildly interested. His prime concern was Michael, and how the boy would react when he heard what his father had to say.

"I'm afraid it's bad news," the officer cautioned.

Bad news? The words stung Bigelow. How could there be bad news? Michael was safe . . . or was he? The officer who phoned had said that the car was a write-off, but he hadn't said anything about Michael being hurt. And how the hell had the FBI gotten into the act?

"What bad news?"

"Your daughter, sir."

Bigelow felt his anxiety begin to ebb away. If the news

concerned Eleanor, it probably couldn't be worse than what he already knew. Perhaps she had been arrested.

"I'm afraid she's dead."

"Dead?" Bigelow dazed, heard himself repeating the word. "What do you mean . . . dead?"

"Suicide, sir. She took a lot of pills. She wouldn't have felt a thing . . . I'm sorry."

Bigelow slid into a seat alongside the reception desk. He tried to feel grief, but was unable to do so. Shock, yes. And guilt. But he was not really hurt by Eleanor's death. It had been so long since he had last seen her.

The duty officer left the reception desk and returned a moment later with two plastic cups brimming with steaming coffee. He handed one to Bigelow.

"Thanks. You know, it's my fault. I was a bastard to that girl and she ran away from home. I probably killed her, in a way. You're looking at a prize bastard, officer. A prize bastard."

Bigelow recalled a long-forgotten and painful episode from Eleanor's childhood. It had been Christmas morning. Eleanor, then aged five, skipped into his bedroom with a large talking doll. He was awakened by the doll's squawking voice, "I want my mommy." Hung over, Bigelow angrily swept his arm out of the bed. A leg fell off the doll as it crashed to the floor. Bigelow yelled at Eleanor in temper. The child bent to lift up the doll and its broken leg, burst into tears and fled from the bedroom. The doll continued its squawking . . . "I want my mommy." He called Eleanor back but she was too afraid to return. It was not a happy day. And it was only one of the many similarly spoiled family occasions. When the child reached her teens Bigelow found it impossible to talk to her. She was so frivolous, and he was always so busy. Or drunk.

"I've been a bastard," he mumbled.

"You can't blame yourself, sir," the officer said. "These things do happen."

"Where is she?"

"I've got all that written down, and information about the funeral. A . . . well, a girl friend has everything set up. I've got her phone number."

Bigelow listlessly accepted the paper from the policeman. He would phone Eleanor's friend and send flowers—but he would not go to the funeral, he decided. There was nothing he could do now for Eleanor; there was much he could do for Michael.

"There's still the boy, sir," the policeman said, echoing Bigelow's thoughts. "A doctor's examined him and he's just fine. Are you ready to see him?"

"I sure am."

"I'll go and wake him."

"No . . . I mean, I'd like to do that. I want to surprise him."

"Sure."

The officer led Bigelow through a maze of corridors to a row of cells. The door to the first was ajar. The officer pushed it open, and Bigelow saw Michael asleep on the bed alongside the wall. Bigelow went alone into the cell and, with a smile of gratitude to the officer, closed the heavy metal door. For a while he sat on the edge of the bed. Michael didn't stir. The boy's face was drawn, and filthy. He obviously hadn't taken time to worry about his appearance during his adventure. He hadn't even bothered to undress before falling asleep in the cell. A heavy gray blanket lay rumpled on the floor. Bigelow put his hand on Michael's shoulder and shook him gently.

"Hi, son."

Michael grunted. Slowly, his eyes opened.

"Hi, son. How's it going?"

"Hi, dad. Oh, I'm all right."

"A fine place you chose to stay." Bigelow grinned. "I'm the guy who should be in here and they should throw away the key."

He ruffled Michael's hair. "I know you don't like it son, but we can't just shake hands, can we? It's great to see you."

"The car, dad . . ."

"To hell with the car. I can always get another. I've only got one son."

Suddenly Bigelow was gripping Michael in his arms. The hardness of Michael's chest against his own reminded him that it had been a long time since he had felt the warm softness of a woman.

Michael was unable to hold back the tears. Bigelow was unable to force back the lump that rose in his own throat and he too gave way to tears.

"I'm going to make things up to you, son. I really am.

What say we go home? You can watch the launch with me from Mission Control."

"Great. Yes, that would be neat, dad."

Bigelow pulled a handkerchief from his pocket, quickly wiped his eyes and smilingly handed it to Michael.

Father and son walked arm in arm from the cell. The officer, waiting outside the cell door, smiled and held out an arm directing them back to the reception area. Bigelow happily slapped the officer on the back.

"There are some papers to sign," the officer said when he returned to his desk. "And the boy's things."

He placed a plastic bag on the desk containing the belongings which had been taken from Michael as a matter of routine. The officer tipped the contents on the desk and began checking off each item against a list. Bigelow's eyes fixed on a pack of cigarettes. Michael blushed. But Bigelow simply ruffled the boy's hair and laughed.

"That's a good brand, Mike. I smoke them myself."

"I've been meaning to give it up," Michael said tamely.

"Sure, son. Sure."

The officer checked off the last of the items and Michael swept them into his pockets, except for the cigarettes.

"You have them, dad. I don't really need them."

Bigelow laughed again at his son's embarrassment. "Sure thing, son. But let me know if you're going to smoke, eh? From now on it's no secrets between you and me. Things are going to be different, Mike."

The officer referred to a heavy ledger on the desk top. "There may be charges," he said to Bigelow. "Taking the car, driving without a license—they're serious offenses. The captain will have to decide whether we go ahead."

"I understand."

To Michael, Bigelow added, "If we have to face the music, we face it together. This has been more my fault than yours."

The officer handed Michael a form to sign acknowledging receipt of his property, then pushed a form across to Bigelow. It advised him that charges might be laid. Bigelow signed with a flourish.

"Thanks, officer. Is that it?"

"Yes, sir."

Bigelow grinned at Michael once more and led the way into the twilight.

Young awoke at six after a troubled sleep in his quarters at the Cape. He pulled back the drapes and squinted in the fiery-gold morning sunlight. The stunted spacecraft, still without the Soyuz command module, loomed like a headless giant and cast a long, grotesque shadow.

In less than twelve hours the ship would have to be reassembled, loaded with bombs and launched, Young reminded himself anxiously. He switched on the radio to catch the weather forecast.

"Hurricane Helena appears to be losing strength north of the West Indies," the announcer reported. "A hurricane alert has been issued for the entire east coast of Florida, but it now seems likely that the storm may veer across the Atlantic and blow itself out."

"Thank God," Young muttered.

"Nevertheless, Florida can expect heavy rain and possibly severe thunderstorms later today, caused by the same weather system."

"Terr-if-ic," Young grumbled.

He looked again at the cloudless sky, which seemed to make nonsense of the forecast. But Young knew only too well how dramatically the weather in the area could deteriorate. Black storm clouds could race in within minutes, as though from nowhere.

In the cafeteria Young found Kennedy already experimenting with what the chef had decided was suitable for breakfast.

"Hi, Matt. It's Russian day, I'm afraid."

Out of deference to the Cape's guests, Russian dishes were offered on alternate days.

"It's sort of like porridge," Kennedy explained, "only worse."

Young ordered toast and coffee.

"I'm afraid I'll never be able to take things their way, especially the food," Young said. "No wonder the cosmonauts were so reluctant to get out of the ship. Perhaps they were hoping the Martian grub would be better."

Young liberally spread his toast with peanut butter.

"Our comrades seem to have recovered from their shock at the 'malfunction,' " he said.

"They sure have. They've been swanning around preening themselves as though the whole deal was their idea."

With a frown Young motioned to Kennedy to break off the

conversation as Akhmerov approached. The Russian's bald
head had become burned and blistered in the unaccustomed
Florida sunlight and was now redder than his florid face. He
tugged gloomily at his drooping mustache as he sat down.

"Morning, Dmitri," Young said sociably. He couldn't resist
the temptation to add provocatively, "I'm glad you're still
talking to us. I was afraid I might have done something to
annoy you."

Akhmerov ignored the taunt. Kennedy softly whistled the
first few bars of the "Red Flag."

"My work here is almost done," the Russian said. "I am
returning to Moscow tonight after the launch."

Young and Kennedy, taken aback, immediately regretted
teasing him. Both appreciated that the future for Akhmerov
was uncertain following what the Politburo would regard as
his failure on the mission.

"I'd honestly hoped that it wouldn't be so soon," Young
said. "I wanted at least to buy you a drink."

"Perhaps some other time," Akhmerov said with affected
politeness. "Of course, the technicians will remain to assist in
every way possible."

"That's fine," Young said. Offering his hand to Akhmerov
he added, "You know, all's fair in love and war. No hard
feelings, Dmitri?"

Akhmerov accepted the handshake.

"Yes, I'm sorry you're going so soon," Kennedy added.

The three completed breakfast with only sporadic attempts
at conversation. Thankful to avoid further discussion of
Akhmerov's departure, Kennedy peered at the spacecraft out
of the cafeteria window.

"Soyuz should almost be ready for reassembly," he said.
"Half an hour ago the stripping was all but completed."

"Good," said Young. "The sooner this show is on the road
the sooner I can get back to Houston to tie up a few loose
ends." Rising from the table he winked at Kennedy and
added jokingly, "It'll be good to be back where the real action is."

Akhmerov stoically joined in the laughter.

The three men reached Firing Room 1 at 6.40. Kennedy
phoned the vehicle assembly building, where Soyuz had been
hauled.

"How goes it?"

"We've just finished, sir. She's all stripped as bare as a newborn babe and ready to go."

"Ok. Get her over to 39-A."

The whole operation would take more than three hours, leaving Young and Kennedy with little more to do than worry.

Soon the massive doors of the VAB slid apart. The vehicle that would haul the Soyuz to the launch pad rolled on its eight oversize tires into the VAB. Low and squat, with a fifteen-foot-high steel brace at each end, it looked like an outer-space dune buggy.

It was moved into position beneath the Soyuz and hydraulic arms lowered the command module onto the vehicle. Soyuz nestled securely in the vehicle's two braces, then the entire assembly emerged slowly into the blazing sunlight.

At its top speed of four miles an hour, the vehicle carried Soyuz across Merritt Island's sand-blown and palmetto-lined roadway—two parallel forty-foot-wide strips of reinforced concrete built to support the mammoth crawler which had earlier transported the entire Apollo-Soyuz spacecraft. Soyuz moved toward the causeway which crossed the Indian River Lagoon. Ahead of the lagoon lay Launch Pad 39-A.

In the launch control center Young took a key from his pocket and looked inquiringly at Kennedy. The launch director nodded, producing a similar key. The two men approached a wall safe. Young placed his key in one of the two locks. Kennedy placed his key in the second lock, then Young turned both keys at the same time. The door swung open. Inside was a red telephone. A red light flashed on the dial as Young lifted the receiver.

"This is the NASA administrator, acting on special instructions from the President," he announced. He listed a set of numbers known only to the President, himself and the colonel at the other end of the line. The colonel, who was in charge of the Tyndall Air Defense Weapons Center, replied by listing another set of numbers.

"So much for the James Bond stuff," Young said. "It's go. Let's get those bombs on the road. Now."

The route from Tyndall had been closed twelve hours earlier. At the base two groups of twelve tanks, each group in three rows of four, lined up at opposite ends of a fifty-yard area marked out on the roadway. Around the area were a thousand motorcyclists and two thousand armed troops. Now the section of roadway between the tank formations began to rise. The reinforced concrete surface hid a three-foot layer of protective lead. A massive nuclear carrier, itself with floor, walls and roof reinforced by lead two feet thick, rose slowly into view. A ramp on which the carrier had been assembled clicked into position, fitting precisely into the gap left by the road surface, which now towered overhead.

The files of troops in front of the forward group of tanks parted, clearing the roadway. The thousand motorcycles thundered into life and were ridden to form a dense cover around the entire convoy. Soon the massive contingent began to move forward. As it advanced, the roadway began to subside.

The bombs were on their way.

The VIP lounge at Cape Canaveral was unusually deserted for a launch day. The timing of the rearranged launch had left no opportunity for the usual batch of politicians and celebrities to be invited to watch the liftoff. Kennedy had taken advantage of the situation to invite his wife and son to join him, Young, Jenny and Akhmerov for lunch.

The boy, about six, was a startling miniature of his father. Both had crew cuts, both were stocky and both had wide, toothy grins. Kennedy's wife, in her early forties, was pudgy and contented and made no effort to disguise her age. Her laughter was infectious and Kennedy was obviously enraptured by her.

"Shall we have a little boy like Bud junior, Matt?" Jenny asked politely. "He might grow up to be an astronaut."

"I'd be delighted—if we could guarantee that we'd have a young man like Bud junior."

It wasn't much of a concession, Jenny thought, but she had begun to believe that she could persuade Young to let her have a child. The strange longing was with her virtually all the time now. Married or not, she wanted desperately to be a mother.

She cupped a hand around Young's ear and whispered, "I think I'd like a baby soon, Matt."

"I'd like a brandy," Young said, laughing and motioning to the waiter.

Before a final round of drinks could be served, a military policeman approached his table.

"The cargo has arrived, sir," he announced.

At that moment the motorcycle troops escorting the bombs roared into view and headed toward Launch Pad 39-A.

Young, Kennedy and Akhmerov rose to leave.

"We want to be sure you get a good show, folks," Young said. "Excuse us while we go and check the fireworks."

The first drops of rain began to fall as Young greeted the colonel in charge of the convoy. Young looked anxiously at the clouds gathering overhead, then led the group back to the launch control center.

"Let's get this baby loaded as soon as we can, colonel. And let's get your troops and vehicles out of the way on the double so we can roll out the lightning shelter. If our spacecraft gets hit the planetoid isn't going to simply go away."

A TV set recorded the scene at the launch pad as the nuclear carrier backed to the elevator entrance at the foot of the service tower alongside the spacecraft. Three times the elevator rose with a heavily guarded load of bombs. Four soldiers with oxyacetyline equipment then rode up to the Soyuz. Within half an hour they returned and entered the nuclear carrier. Now empty, it began to pull away from the launch pad on its return journey.

"That should do it," the colonel said. "She's all set."

Dark clouds now tumbled above the Cape, hiding the sun. Rain suddenly washed down, swept by twenty-mile-an-hour winds.

"What's the latest on that hurricane, Bud?" Young asked anxiously.

Kennedy had been making frequent checks with the weather bureau on Hurricane Helena's progress.

"The nearest part of the hurricane is fifty miles due east and the storm is heading northwest—which means we're in for quite a lashing from the tail end."

Lightning suddenly fractured the sky and rolling thunder reverberated through the launch control center.

"Roll out that damn lightning shelter," Young ordered. "If that baby gets hit we're in big trouble."

"She's already on the way. I'm keeping my fingers crossed until she gets there."

"Do that—but don't hold your breath."

Thunderbolts now flashed from cloud to cloud and, more menacingly, from cloud to ground. Apollo-Soyuz blazed into brilliance with each lightning flash. If a thunderbolt should hit . . .

Young had once been asked at a Press conference what precautions had been taken at the Cape to withstand the worst of the hurricanes and tornadoes that frequently battered America's sunshine state. He admitted that, largely because of the haste with which the Apollo program was conducted in the race to land man on the moon, most structures would probably not withstand winds exceeding a hundred miles an hour.

"But hurricanes can produce winds stronger than that," the reporter said.

"I know. And tornadoes bring winds even stronger."

"So what would be the effect," the reporter persisted, "if a hurricane swept directly over the Cape?"

Young ended the interview with an abrupt, "We'll just have to wait to find out."

Now he began to wonder if he might not have to wait as long as he would have hoped.

"Ok, let's check out Soyuz," Young said, reaching for a raincoat on a coat rack. "Grab your coats, boys."

The howling wind, now gusting at forty miles an hour, blasted hail into the control center as Young opened the exit door. He ran to a waiting jeep and heaved himself into the seat next to the driver. Kennedy, Akhmerov and the colonel tumbled into the rear seats. The driver pulled forward, seemingly into a solid mass of hail, the windshield wipers flailing frantically back and forth. He was guided more by the sporadic lightning flashes than the useless headlights.

Grateful for the jeep's four-wheel drive, Young braced himself against the dashboard as the jeep was buffeted by a specially severe wind blast and skidded. The engine raced as the wheels spun crazily, then gripped again as the jeep rose up the ramp to the entrance of the Apollo-Soyuz service tower.

As the four men scurried toward the service elevator the lightning shelter had inched from its location near the junction at which the crawlerway split into two—one section leading to Launch Pad 39-A and the other to 39-B. The shelter had been built specifically for possible use during the Mars mission. Constructed of steel scaffolding, it supported an aluminum-alloy mast that stood ten feet higher than the launch tower. The assembly was drawn along a railway track by huge steel cables attached to diesel-powered windlasses— one at each launch pad. Winched along at the pace of a slow walk, the shelter could be hauled into place in about fifteen minutes.

The service tower elevator slowed to a stop at the level of the Soyuz command module and the four men disembarked. Although the elevator car was walled in, the walkways and the outer portion of the tower consisted of open scaffolding. All four men grabbed for a nearby handrail as the tower swayed and rocked in the storm. Lightning flashed more frequently now, illuminating the tiny buildings below and the looming shape of the lightning tower as it moved steadily closer.

Young led the three men along an open gangway which projected along the south side of the tower and joined up with the command module. Only railings enclosed the sides of the gangway.

He turned to wave encouragement to his colleagues.

"Come on, Dmitri. Get the lead out."

The Russian looked in puzzlement, not understanding the expression. "Sorry?"

"Aw, skip it," Young yelled, turning once more toward the command module.

"Skip . . . ?" Akhmerov queried, even more puzzled. The rest of his words died in the roaring wind.

Suddenly the sky blazed a brilliant blue as a jagged streak of light struck the approaching lightning shelter—now some three hundred yards from the launch tower. The sharp smell of ozone stung the nostrils of the four men.

Young hauled open the hatch to Soyuz. The wind tore it from his grasp and it clanged against the side of the command module. He grabbed again for a handrail as a gust of wind all but swept him off his feet. The other three men hunched forward against the onslaught and followed him into the relative safety of Soyuz.

"Shut that damn hatch," Young said to Akhmerov.

The hatch banged shut and Akhmerov twisted the metal locking handle. His ruddy face, whipped by the winds, glowed like a neon light. His mustache, usually combed, hung soggy and limp, obscuring his small, thin-lipped mouth.

Soyuz, which had been cluttered with equipment, now resembled the interior of a cargo container more than a space vehicle. The seating, manual guidance controls, communications and life-support systems had been taken out. On the floor around the perimeter of the nose cone were nine square metal boxes, each one containing a one-hundred-megaton bomb.

The colonel checked the metal mountings which had been welded to secure the containers, then traced the intricate wiring mechanism which would explode the bombs on an electronic impulse activated at Mission Control.

"She's looking good, Matt. This payload's going to make one hell of a bang. Your planetoid is in for quite a jolt."

"If the planetoid knew about the weather here it'd probably go somewhere else," Kennedy said, mopping his forehead with a handkerchief.

"Maybe," said Young, "but let's not take that chance." Looking around Soyuz he added, "Everyone happy?"

The other three looked inquiringly at each other. No one spoke.

"Ok. Let's go back and battle that storm."

A sheet of rain flooded into the command module as Akhmerov pushed open the door. He bent forward and shuffled along the gangway. Kennedy and the colonel followed. Young began to pull himself through the Soyuz hatch.

"Move your butt, Dmitri," he shouted.

Akhmerov turned and shrugged, indicating that once again he hadn't understood. Kennedy and the colonel halted behind the Russian on the gangway.

The sky suddenly shattered into a million brilliant fragments. A thunderbolt lit up the lightning shelter—now less than a hundred yards away—and the service tower. An explosive cracking sound blotted out the roar of the storm as the thunderbolt hit the gangway, halfway between the service tower and the spacecraft. The bolt flashed into brilliant whiteness, engulfing the gangway in a white-hot shower of molten sparks. One section of the gangway railing collapsed.

The colonel, his hand on the railing, died at that moment in a quivering frazzle, his hair leaping horribly on end, then singeing. His body was flung into Akhmerov, then hit the railing across from the one that had been destroyed. For an instant the corpse hung suspended there. Then, slowly, his feet lifted off the gangway floor and he toppled to the wet concrete more than four hundred feet below.

Young had been knocked spinning back inside the command module. The interior was plunged into darkness, then lights flicked on again as automatic circuit breakers reset themselves. Before he hit the floor he caught a glimpse of

Kennedy seeming to reach toward him. Kennedy's face was ashen and his mouth gaped as if he were trying to catch his breath.

"Bud!" Young yelled. "Bud, are you OK?"

Young scrambled out of Soyuz, slammed shut the door and reached out to grab a railing on the gangway. He noticed that one hand was covered in blood. With the other hand he wiped it away, exposing a jagged cut on the back of his hand. Ignoring the wound he pulled himself with the help of the railing toward where Kennedy had fallen, then retched at the sudden stench of scorched flesh.

"Bud! Oh Christ, Bud . . ."

Kennedy lay crumpled about six feet away. A horrible burn had erupted along his left arm and the side of his face. He moaned—and Young shouted frantically.

"Hang in, there, Bud. You're going to be OK."

Kennedy gave no sign of having heard.

Akhmerov stood as though paralyzed at the end of the gangway, clutching his right thigh and shaking with shock.

"Can you make it back to the elevator?" Young shouted.

Akhmerov nodded weakly and clung to the railing.

"OK," Young shouted again. "I'll bring Bud."

Young reached Kennedy's side, knelt down and put an ear close to Kennedy's mouth. He could barely discern the unconscious man's breathing.

"For God's sake, hang in," he whispered. He lifted Kennedy onto his shoulders and carried him to the interior of the service tower. Akhmerov met them at the doorway and tried to help, but the pain in his leg stopped him short. He mumbled an apology as Young laid Kennedy awkwardly but gently onto the floor. Young paused to tie his necktie around his injured hand to stem the bleeding.

"Sorry, Matt, my leg . . ." Akhmerov said. "I can barely walk."

Young jabbed the elevator call button.

"Let's just get Bud down fast. He needs a doctor. The poor colonel didn't have a chance."

"The elevator's not working. I've already tried it. The lightning must have burned out the motor."

"Christ."

The only alternative route to the ground level was down an emergency stairway, which was wide open to the storm.

"It's going to be tough, Dmitri. Can you make it?"

"I think so . . ."

Akhmerov helped lift Kennedy onto Young's shoulders. Young grimaced with pain as Kennedy's legs swung limply and hit his injured hand.

"Are you OK?" Akhmerov asked.

"It's my hand . . . just a cut. We'll make it."

Akhmerov limped behind as Young headed for the stairway and descended two flights of stairs with cautious haste. He noted with alarm that Kennedy's rapid shallow breaths seemed more labored than before. He shifted Kennedy on his shoulders and reached for the railing.

"OK, Dmitri?" he hollered.

He heard Akhmerov's voice only faintly over the roar of the storm. "Fine. You go ahead."

He gripped the railing more tightly as he was lashed by the wind. The driving force of the rain stung his face, and the slippery-wet steel stairs forced him to concentrate on each step he took. His legs and back began to ache. Mercifully, his injured hand had become numb.

Eventually he heard someone shouting and the military policeman who had driven the four men to the launch pad climbed to meet him. Below, sirens wailed and red lights flashed as half a dozen ambulances arrived at the foot of the service tower.

"Let me help you, sir," the policeman shouted.

"This man's badly hurt," Young yelled. "I can't risk handing him over here. Akhmerov's up there—he's hurt too."

The military policeman ran past him and took the stairs three at a time.

As Young arrived at the second-floor landing he was met by four ambulancemen carrying a stretcher. With smooth, practiced efficiency they placed Kennedy on the stretcher, covered him with blankets and strapped him in. One attendant quickly checked Kennedy's pulse and respiration and frowned. He unclipped a small oxygen respirator from the side of the stretcher and fastened its mask over Kennedy's face.

On the ground three ambulances were grouped around the spot where the colonel had fallen. An ambulanceman with a shovel walked toward a tiny mound, which had been covered with a plastic sheet.

As Kennedy was loaded aboard an ambulance two attendants climbed into the rear. A third closed and locked the doors and ran to the driver's seat. Young yanked open the other door and climbed into the seat beside the driver.

"I'm coming with you."

"Yes, sir. Hold on."

The siren screamed to its top pitch as the ambulance swept forward, Young turned to face the attendants in the rear. One was checking Kennedy's respiration and heartbeat with a stethoscope. The other was preparing to attach the electrodes of a portable electrocardiograph to Kennedy's chest.

"How is he?" Young asked.

The question was ignored. The attendant with the stethoscope picked up a small penlight, opened Kennedy's eyelids with a thumb and played the light across one eye, then the other. The second attendant attached electrodes to Kennedy's chest.

The attendant with the stethoscope opened a drawer and took out a hypodermic syringe. As he plunged the needle into a small bottle and drew back the plunger of the syringe, he said to Young without looking at him, "I'm afraid he's in trouble, sir. His heartbeat is weak and unstable. He must have received an awful kick from that lightning."

The electrocardiograph was switched on and began to trace a series of jagged lines along a moving strip of graph paper. The machine gave out a steady bleeping sound. The attendant finished preparing the syringe, then studied the record of Kennedy's heartbeat while the other attendant clicked a dial on the machine to several different positions.

Young kept his eyes fixed on Kennedy as the ambulance wailed along the crawlerway, past the launch control center and along the rain-soaked roadway toward the military hospital at Patrick Air Force Base.

One of the attendants punctured Kennedy's arm with the hypodermic needle, discarded the syringe and held the stethoscope once more to Kennedy's chest. He turned his head to watch the heart monitor at the same time. The machine still traced an erratic pattern. Then, as the drug began to take effect, Kennedy's breathing became slower and somewhat deeper. The tracing pens of the electrocardiograph bounced more strongly across the paper. The bleeping continued steadily.

The attendant with the stethoscope leaned back and smiled.

"He's doing better. We'll have him at the hospital in a few more minutes."

The ambulance sped past a large green-and-yellow road sign: "Patrick Air Force Base. Authorized Personnel Only."

Suddenly Kennedy exhaled sharply and groaned as if he had just been punched in the stomach. He gasped for breath. The electrocardiograph went wild, then just as abruptly traced a quiet pattern of thin straight lines. The bleeping of the machine became a continuous, monotonous tone.

Both attendants leapt toward Kennedy. One increased the flow of oxygen to the face mask, then reached for a hypodermic. The other immediately straddled the stretcher and placed his hands, one on top of the other, on Kennedy's breastbone. With arms stiff the attendant rocked forward and pressed sharply on his chest. The needles on the electrocardiograph jumped. The attendant rocked back. The needles traced thin straight lines again. The second attendant plunged the hypodermic into Kennedy's arm.

Young's knuckles whitened as he gripped the back of the seat and watched Kennedy's chest.

"Come on, Bud," he murmured. "You can make it."

The ambulance wheeled up to the emergency entrance of the hospital. The driver and Young jumped out and ran to the back of the vehicle. While one attendant remained astride the stretcher and continued to massage Kennedy's heart, the three other men slid the stretcher out of the ambulance. Its wheels dropped to the ground and Young helped to push it up a ramp and along several corridors to the intensive care unit. As they raced past the reception area of the emergency entrance, one attendant barked, "Cardiac arrest. Alert intensive care." Seconds later, three loud blasts of a horn echoed through the hospital. The alarm was still blaring when the men burst through the swinging doors of the intensive care unit.

A waiting intern took hold of the stretcher and, without slowing it, guided it across the room to an equipment-filled alcove. Two doctors followed the stretcher. One motioned to the attendant astride Kennedy. The attendant stopped pumping Kennedy's chest and climbed off the stretcher. At the same time, the doctor put a stethoscope to Kennedy's chest.

Seconds later he reached toward the other doctor, who handed him two cup-shaped metal objects, each attached by coiled wires to the nearby equipment.

"Now!" he said. The second doctor pushed a button. A

needle on the machine jumped. An electric shock ripped through Kennedy's heart muscles. The portable electrocardiograph attached to the side of the stretcher, still monitoring the heartbeat, zig-zagged crazily, then traced smooth even lines. Kennedy's back arched clear of the bed. His legs and arms stiffened. Then he flopped back like a puppet with its strings cut.

"Again," the doctor ordered.

Three times in succession, the doctors tried to jolt Kennedy's heart back to life. Each time his body bucked as if he had been struck with a sledgehammer. Not once was there any variation of the continuous tone of the electrocardiograph.

Finally, the doctors pulled a white sheet up over Kennedy's body and face. The older of the two doctors walked over to Young.

"I'm sorry. It's hopeless. We did everything we could."

Young said in a quiet voice, "Thank you. He was a good man."

"Good God, man. You're hurt too."

The doctor had noticed Young nursing his injured hand.

"It's just a cut."

The doctor had begun to clean the hand when Jenny burst into the room.

"Oh, Matt. We saw it on TV in the VIP lounge. It was horrible." He put his arm around her shoulder.

"I know, honey . . . I know."

"Matt, you're hurt."

"It's OK, but Bud . . . the colonel . . ."

She stood back, noticing for the first time the covered form on the stretcher. She had seen the colonel plunge to his death but had assumed that Kennedy was not badly hurt.

"Bud? Is that . . . ?"

She continued to stare at the form on the stretcher.

"Yes, he's dead," Young said. "He never knew what hit him."

"Oh, Matt, his wife and boy are outside. They came with me."

A nurse entered. "Mrs. Kennedy is here," she said. "She's asking about her husband."

The two doctors looked inquiringly at Young.

"Yes," he said softly, "I'll tell her."

He slipped down from the bed where he had been sitting,

his hand securely bandaged, and walked with Jenny to a waiting room. Mrs. Kennedy sat with her son on her knee.

"Matt, thank God you're all right," Mrs. Kennedy said. "How's Bud?"

Young swallowed. Jenny went to her and put her arms around her neck.

"Oh, I'm so sorry . . ."

Bud junior leapt from his mother's knee. "My dad," he said, running to the door. "My dad . . ."

Young caught the boy. "Let's get your mom home, son. She's going to need your help. I'm afraid your dad . . ."

Bud junior walked to his mother who was weeping silently.

"Come on, mom. It'll be OK." The boy's voice faltered. He was unable to stop his own tears.

"Yes, let's go home."

It was Mrs. Kennedy who had spoken. Arm in arm with Jenny, she made her way out of the waiting room.

The countdown was approaching the final half hour when Young returned to Firing Room 1. He reached for the microphone that would enable him to address the four hundred technicians in the room over a loudspeaker system.

"This is the NASA administrator. I have sad news. I regret to tell you that your launch director, Bud Kennedy, died a few minutes ago. He was a great man . . ."

Tears moistened Young's eyes. He swallowed deeply, then added, "He was a good friend. I don't need to tell you that there's still a job to be done. Let's get to it. When Apollo-Soyuz lifts off it will commemorate the efforts of men like Bud. I'll be taking over his job for the rest of the countdown."

Several minutes of silence followed, to be relieved at last by the voice of the test conductor.

"On my mark it will be T minus three-oh minutes, and counting."

He was reminded that Kennedy had frequently suggested a revision of the jargon used during a launch. Much was precise and meaningful; a lot was stilted and reminiscent of a World War II recruitment center. Young vowed silently that Kennedy's revisions would be made.

A senior technician reported matter-of-factly, "All systems go, sir. All coordinates confirm impact at twenty-six hours forty-six minutes into the mission."

Young seized the microphone and announced, "This is a hot count. Absolute discipline will be maintained over the intercom and within the area."

The statement was traditional—a warning that the time for wisecracking was now past. Young had acted mechanically, and immediately regretted it. Today that warning was totally unnecessary, he realized sadly.

The test conductor continued examining the winking lights of a console that indicated that the continuing checks of all systems were satisfactory. The countdown clock, placed high in view of all personnel, flickered down from 31.09 . . . 08 . . .

At precisely thirty minutes before take off the test conductor announced "Mark." The countdown clock confirmed that there were exactly thirty minutes to go.

At just before twelve minutes to liftoff Akhmerov entered the firing room on crutches. Overcome by Kennedy's death, Young had forgotten about the Russian, who had traveled to the hospital in another ambulance.

Young motioned to a nearby seat.

"Matt, I'm sorry . . ." Akhmerov said. "I'm sorry for the loss of your friend."

Young looked carefully at Akhmerov. There was no doubt that the Russian was sincere. Young wondered how many deaths Akhmerov was personally responsible for. That he should feel sadness at the death of Kennedy, Young felt, was a tribute to both men.

"Thanks, Dmitri. Thanks."

Young helped him place his crutches against the desk.

"How are you feeling?"

"I'm fine. Just torn muscles. I'll be off those crutches in a day or two. But your hand . . ."

"Oh, it's OK. It's nothing."

The test conductor announced, "Man stations for the terminal count. On my mark it will be T minus one-oh minutes, and counting."

A pause, then, "Mark."

At T minus three minutes, automatic launch systems would take over. The myriad flashing of lights, the whirring of computers and the digits of electronic gauges confirmed that all was well.

Central Control reported that the Atlantic Missile Range

was all set—the intricate system of tracking stations that would record the spacecraft's flight path.

On the launch pad an activated control loosed a Niagara of water. The cold liquid washed over the enormous flame deflector tube below the Saturn first-stage rocket to help protect the steel against the fury of the rocket's fire as it grabbed its first moments of life. All missile control circuits were switched to internal power sources.

"T minus ninety seconds and counting."

The test conductor checked again with panel operators.

"Command on internal," he snapped.

"Roger."

"T minus sixty seconds and counting."

"Range safety lights on."

"Roger."

"Range ready."

"Roger."

"Ignition systems ready."

"Roger."

Young walked to the section marked "Weather Observation."

"How's Helena?"

"Well clear, sir. It's quite a storm we've got, but no problem."

Anxious eyes swept dials and charts in the fleeting moments before the launch.

A rumble grew in the launch area. Spray flew as the water flow over the flame bucket increased to its full power of 35,000 gallons a minute. Automatic cameras around the launch pad whirred into action.

"T minus ten seconds and counting . . . eight . . . seven . . ."

Flames spewed into life. The spacecraft was alive. The rumblings created by the initial thrust of ten million pounds echoed across the Cape.

"Two . . . one . . . we have ignition."

Great clouds of gray-black smoke billowed from beneath the rocket while fifty thousand gallons of water a minute poured in a sheet down the sides of the Saturn and vaporized in a hissing white blanket of steam. Orange and red flames seared through the holocaust. The towering rocket stood motionless, amid the fury of its unleashed jets, for a full nine seconds while the Saturn's mighty engines built up thrust.

Then the four twenty-ton restraining arms released their grip on Apollo-Soyuz.

The rocket stirred. Agonizingly, it lifted off the pad. It seemed to hover as it moved upward, balanced on its fiery tail. Then it surged skyward, gulping fifteen tons of fuel a second and trailing a brilliant shaft of flame nine hundred feet long.

"We have liftoff."

Apollo-Soyuz climbed swiftly now, disappearing into the still-raging storm and arcing over the Atlantic.

"All systems are go."

It was a perfect launch.

Firing Room 1, normally a bedlam of excited shrieking at the moment of a launch, remained subdued. No one had forgotten even for an instant the death of Kennedy.

The second stage ignited on schedule, one hundred and fifty-four seconds after liftoff, kicking the spacecraft onto the course computed to bring it into collision with the onrushing planetoid.

A technician checked the paths of the spacecraft and the planetoid.

"It's looking good," he said to Young. "We're right on target, sir."

Akhmerov joined Young and Jenny at the bar of her hotel for a farewell drink.

"This is goodbye, Matt," Akhmerov said. "I'd like you and Jenny to have something."

Akhmerov placed one crutch against the bar, leaned on the other and fumbled in a pocket. He produced two small velvet boxes and handed both to Jenny. In the first was a jeweled Russian wristwatch.

"But Dmitri . . . It must have cost a fortune."

"It's value is much less than that of our friendship, I hope," the Russian said gallantly. "I'd noticed you didn't wear one . . ."

Jenny kissed him on the cheek.

She began to open the second box and Akhmerov said, "That's for Matt."

Young lifted the lid and took out a set of diamond-studded cufflinks.

"Dmitri, this is marvellous," Young said. "I'm afraid I have nothing to offer in return. Your decision to go was so sudden."

"I'll accept the crutches, Matt," Akhmerov said, smiling. "And I will take home many, many memories. Good luck."

He shook hands with Young and Jenny, picked up his second crutch and hobbled toward the door.

Jenny slipped the jeweled watch onto her wrist.

"It looks gorgeous, Jenny," Young said.

Akhmerov turned at the door of the bar and waved. Suddenly he was gone.

Chapter Seven

TUESDAY, 9 A.M.

In outer space, the planetoid zoomed on unerringly, offering a target no larger than a pinhead on the infinite backcloth of the universe.

It was now 5,464,800 miles from the earth.

Warning lights flashed on a console at Mission Control and a horn blared irritatingly. A technician flipped a switch, silencing the alarm. A pre-programmed message from a computer appeared on the screen in front of him. He scanned it quickly, then spoke immediately into the slim microphone he wore, attached to a lightweight headset.

"We have a Level Three fuel leak from the port jet valve. Flow rate three hundred and fifty gallons per minute. That is three-five-oh gallons. Pressure is holding."

At other consoles, technicians concerned with particular aspects of the rocket's performance and equipment fed the new information to computers. In seconds, it was confirmed that fuel from the leaking valve was being safely exhausted into space, but that the rocket's sensitive balance would be affected if the leak remained unplugged for three minutes.

In spite of the immensely powerful gyros that stabilized the rocket, it depended on the proper distribution of its fuel load to keep its flight true.

While conversations crackled between technicians and scientists, computers calculated the cumulative effects of the escaping fuel on the rocket's trajectory.

Sweat formed in beads on the brow of flight director John Sykes as he evaluated the data that flowed through his central console. Then, his voice calm and firm, he spoke into his headset.

"Activate starboard bypass valve seven degrees."

A technician fed the instructions to a computer.

On board Apollo-Soyuz, a valve hissed open and fuel from the starboard tank flowed across the ship into the port tank. The additional fuel pressure increased the flow of leaking fuel, but now the loss would be from both tanks and the spacecraft would remain in equilibrium.

Sykes removed his headset, mopped his brow and approached Young, who had returned with Jenny to Houston on an early flight.

"Well, it looks like we got our fuel malfunction after all, Matt."

Young smiled. "Can we live with the leak, John?"

"No problem. But luckily it's only a short hop to that planetoid. With fuel belching out like this it would have been touch and go on making the trip to Mars and back."

"Jesus . . ."

Young pondered the furor that would have erupted had a manned Mars mission been cut short. Recriminations would have been thrown back and forth. The new era of American and Russian cooperation would have again been in jeopardy.

Sykes moved to return to his post. "Back to give my ulcer another workout," he said to Young with a grin as he walked away.

"John," Young called, "let's hit this bastard smack on the nose, eh?"

Sykes raised his hand in a friendly salute, then hurried to his console.

The countdown clock showed eleven hours, twenty-eight minutes and seven seconds still to go before the bombs were to be detonated.

> *"Happy birthday to you*
> *Happy birthday to you.*
> *Happy birthday, dear Bob,*
> *Happy birthday to you."*

Bigelow sat next to Michael in the Mission Control cafeteria as a group of friends and colleagues sang and laughed. Bigelow blushed and grinned awkwardly.

The surprise party was Dandridge's idea. On his return to Houston he had destroyed the films of Eleanor that the CIA had recovered from Krotkov's hotel room. He had also persuaded the police chief handling the case of Michael's joyride not to press charges. Sympathetic to the torment he knew Bigelow must have suffered in the last few days, Dandridge had hurriedly arranged a noontime birthday party with the willing help of some of his associates.

Young stepped forward with a large chocolate cake. On top of it was perched a scale model of Apollo-Soyuz on a miniature launch pad.

"Happy birthday, Bob," Young said as he set down the cake and reached across the table to shake Bigelow's hand.

"Speech, speech," someone called. The rest of the group applauded and repeated the chant.

Bigelow stood up. As the din died down he coughed.

"Naturally, I don't know what to say . . ."

"Congratulations," someone retorted, "that's the first time in fifty-five years."

Bigelow laughed with the others and began to relax.

"This is great," he continued. "I can't thank you enough. I'm particularly proud and pleased that Michael is here to share this with me."

He put his hand on his son's head and ruffled his hair. Michael looked up at his father and smiled.

"I'm glad, too, dad. You know I love chocolate cake."

The crowd laughed and applauded again.

"I know most of you came here for the same reason as Michael so I'll make this short, then we'll cut the cake. They say as you get older you get wiser. Well, there's nothing I can do about getting older. But with the help of a fine son like Michael here and with the kindness of friends like all of you, getting wiser is beginning to look a little easier. Thank you all. Thank you very much."

Michael stood with the others and clapped and cheered the loudest of all.

"Three cheers for Bob Bigelow," one of the group shouted. "Hip, hip, hooray . . ."

Again Michael's voice could be heard above the others.

Bigelow picked up a knife and prepared to cut the cake. Dandridge stepped forward. "Not yet, Bob. We've got another surprise."

Dandridge motioned to a technician. A bearded young

man, carrying a box of wooden matches, approached the table.

"We knew that if we gave you a rocket ship, it would have to be more than a toy, and Ron here has made sure of that," Dandridge said.

Taking his cue from Dandridge, the bearded technician waved everyone back a few feet, then withdrew a match from the box.

"Well, Bob, Apollo-Soyuz eventually lifted off without a hitch," the technician said. "Let's see if its little brother can do the same."

"Well, I'll be damned," Bigelow exclaimed.

Michael's eyes were wide with anticipation.

"On my mark, it will be T minus ten seconds and counting," the technician said. He struck the match. "Mark. Ten . . . nine . . . eight . . . seven . . ."

Michael joined in the count and soon everyone in the cafeteria was marking time.

"Five . . . four . . . three . . ." they roared. "Two . . . one . . ."

"Ignition," the technician called as he set the flaming match on the miniature launch pad beneath the rocket.

The rocket, designed to spew flames and brightly colored smoke like a tiny inverted Roman Candle, belched fire. It toppled over and, with a loud bang, skimmed off the cake and along the table. Icing was splattered over the technician and the rocket smoldered to a halt about three feet away.

"Abort mission," Bigelow said with a loud hearty laugh. "Fuel malfunction."

The technician gingerly picked up the hissing rocket, dunked it into a glass of water, and handed the model to Michael. The boy accepted it happily.

"Come on, everyone," Bigelow said. "Let's eat what's left of this cake before Ron turns it into a UFO and sends it flying out the window."

As Apollo-Soyuz and the planetoid streaked toward each other, the entire world waited anxiously for each news report of the progress of the mission. Hundreds of tracking stations plotted the advance of the meteorite-scarred mass from outer space and the course of the bomb-laden command module.

At Mission Control a sky map was projected on a large overhead screen. A green diagram of Apollo-Soyuz and a red circle of light the size of a baseball, representing the planetoid, moved at relative speeds. Inch by inch, the two tiny voyagers plummeted closer to each other.

The voice of John Sykes boomed over the loudspeaker system.

"Stand by for mid-course burn. Full burn for seven seconds."

A course correction was required to counter the effect of the fuel leakage.

"We'd never have made the Mars landing unless that leak could have been plugged manually," Sykes said to Young. "We've already lost far too much fuel."

Over the loudspeaker system Sykes added, "On my mark it will be ten seconds to mid-course burn. Full thrust for seven seconds."

"Mark," Sykes announced. ". . . Three . . . two . . . one . . . ignition."

"Ignition on."

In outer space, Apollo-Soyuz sped on silently, trailing a thin luminous line of vaporized fuel like an enormous umbilical cord from its leaking valve. Its engines ignored the command from Mission Control and the spacecraft continued on an increasingly wayward course.

"Ignition inoperative. We have no burn."

"Roger, stand by," Sykes replied, running his moist palms down the front of his sweat-soaked shirt. He punched a message into his computer console.

Onto the console screen appeared the words, "Ignition input negative. Instructions inoperative. Error."

The technician across from Sykes groaned. "Hell, my fault," he said.

Sykes requested new instructions from the computer for a second attempt at a mid-course burn.

"Let's take a deep breath and relax," he said into his headset. "Proper codes and sequences are now displayed. On my mark we will have a hot count for five seconds. We will burn for nine seconds. Repeat, burn for nine seconds at full thrust."

To the technician who had made the previous error Sykes said, "Confirm code and sequence."

The technician repeated the instructions and tagged, "Sorry, John," onto the end of them.

"OK, stand by."

Sykes intently watched the countdown clock.

"Mark," he called. ". . . Two . . . one . . ."

After precisely nine seconds, the brilliant flame from the engines of Apollo-Soyuz flicked out. In the coldness of space, the jets cooled rapidly from red to orange to black.

Apollo-Soyuz was again on target.

At 7.30 p.m., a little more than an hour before Apollo-Soyuz was scheduled to detonate its nuclear cargo mere feet above the surface of the planetoid, the White House announced that the President had prepared a speech announcing the success of the mission. The President's message would be broadcast worldwide on television and radio as soon as he received confirmation of the planetoid's destruction from Mission Control. The broadcast had already been taped—and the President had prepared only one speech, the White House statement added. He was unshakeably confident Apollo-Soyuz would succeed.

At 7.35, journalists at Mission Control were clamoring for the official reaction of NASA chiefs to the White House announcement.

At 7.40, Dandridge informed Young of the announcement, and of the persistent requests by journalists for a press conference.

"I guess I've got the time to make a brief statement," Young decided.

As he entered the press room he was besieged by reporters, photographers and TV cameramen.

He noted sadly that Jenny was not among them. She had insisted that she would prefer to watch the progress of Apollo-Soyuz on the TV set in her hotel room, rather than from Mission Control. Following her latest clash with Reynolds she had decided that to file more copy on the planetoid story would be futile.

Young shielded his eyes for a moment from the glare of the lighting and walked to a podium at the rear of the room. Behind the podium was a large TV screen showing the constantly narrowing gap between Apollo-Soyuz and the planetoid. The babble of voices died down as Young switched on a microphone on the podium.

"As you all know, Apollo-Soyuz will be exploded a short distance above the surface of the planetoid about an hour from now," he began. "And I fully share the President's confidence in the ability of Apollo-Soyuz to do its job. The damage to the planetoid will be considerable. As soon as the effects of the explosion are estimated I will call the President."

The reporters began waving their hands in the air and shouting questions. He asked for quiet and looked at the countdown clock behind him.

"I will answer questions for fifteen minutes." He acknowledged the waving hand of one of the reporters. "You first, and let's keep the questions brief."

The reporter rocked forward on tiptoe and said in a loud, cynical tone, "Mister Young, so far there have been two fuel malfunctions and a burn that failed to fire. In view of those complications, on what do NASA and the White House base their unqualified optimism?"

Young frowned in irritation. "The flight to the planetoid requires only a fraction of the spacecraft's capability. The fuel problems have been minor, not serious. Every valve that has ever been made leaks—it's just a question of how much. With the pressures and temperatures to which valves are subjected in a spacecraft, it sometimes amazes me that they hold at all. But this is a situation we are constantly prepared for. Apollo-Soyuz is the product of the world's most sophisticated technology. Our confidence and the President's is based on an exhaustive examination of the performance of the spacecraft, and the bombs it contains. The screen behind me shows that confidence to be well-founded."

All eyes focused on the screen. The drawings of Apollo-Soyuz and the planetoid were less than a foot apart. Both were traveling unerringly toward each other.

Most of the reporters continued to compete for Young's attention and he fielded their questions confidently.

"What exactly will happen to the planetoid when the spacecraft hits?"

"Apollo-Soyuz will not 'hit' the planetoid. It will make a controlled descent. Less than twenty-five feet above the surface the nuclear devices in the spacecraft's nose cone will be activated by an electronic signal from Mission Control. They will explode six feet from the surface at 8.43 precisely. The planetoid will be all but obliterated. Since it is primarily composed of iron and nickel it will be almost entirely vaporized in the explosion."

"You said 'almost,' Mister Young. And earlier you spoke of 'estimating' the effects of the explosion. Are 'almost' and 'estimates' good enough?"

"I'd be less than honest if I pretended there wasn't a degree of guesswork involved," Young admitted. "But we have estimated that the mass of the planetoid will be reduced to one-tenth of what it now is. The remainder will be shattered and the fragments will hurl into space on orbits that will not cross that of the earth. A giant dust cloud will be created from the vaporized material and that will likely cause a spectacular meteor shower. But it will be just that—a spectacular meteor shower—and as safe to view as a Fourth of July fireworks display."

"Won't the dust cloud be highly radioactive?"

"Yes, but the earth is bombarded daily by far more powerful radiation every time a solar flare erupts from the sun. The earth's atmosphere will filter out most of that radiation."

"Will any particles in this dust cloud be large enough to strike the earth?"

"That is extremely unlikely. Such particles would have to be quite large to survive friction with the atmosphere. Every year, the earth is bombarded with hundreds of thousands of meteoroids. Only a very few are large enough to blaze into fireballs and strike the earth. Rarely are the surviving masses larger than a baseball and still more rarely does one strike near a populated area. Those are about the same odds we face with the remnants of the planetoid. And they're extremely safe odds. You've been living with them every day of your lives."

Young looked at the countdown clock again, then said, "One last question." He pointed to a television reporter.

"How soon will you be able to assess the results of the explosion, and why is Apollo-Soyuz carrying only nine nuclear bombs when there was room in the command module for many more?"

"That's one question?" Young said good-humoredly. Everyone laughed. "I'll do my best to answer it.

"Detonation of the bombs will be recorded within seconds. INSITE and other orbiting astronomical units will analyze the effects of the explosion by X-ray and spectral analysis and radio telemetry. That data will be interpreted within minutes.

"As for the number of bombs, well, nine was the number calculated to be necessary to destroy the planetoid. They will certainly deflect it from its orbit. I think you'll find we did our homework properly."

As he left the room several reporters continued to hound him with questions. He firmly brushed them off with, "No further comment, gentlemen."

Young arrived back in the control room as the countdown to impact clicked to forty-three minutes and eight seconds. He conferred briefly with Bigelow and Sykes. Since the burn error, the flight of Apollo-Soyuz had proceeded without incident.

At 8.07, Apollo-Soyuz began to gather speed as the gravitational pull of the planetoid began to tug at it.

"We have pull of 1/20g," a technician announced.

"Almost home free," Sykes said with a grin. Into his headset he announced, "Stand by to fire retro rockets."

At 8.15 the firing of small jets on the front and sides of the command module would turn it around so that its large bulbous end faced the planetoid. The main descent rocket would then reduce the speed of the spacecraft by more than half. Unless slowed down it would risk overshooting the planetoid—the rocket's speed overcoming the planetoid's slight gravitational pull.

"On my mark it will be ten seconds and counting to retro firing," Sykes said. "Mark . . . nine . . . eight . . ."

In outer space, the spacecraft was but a tiny speck looming over the large dark mass of the planetoid. On command, the retro rockets fired in sequence, first correcting the capsule's yaw and pitch, then orienting its bulbous end toward the toppling mass.

"We're in the clear," he announced. "We'll be down in seven minutes four-oh seconds. Stand by for detonation at altitude of two-one-two feet. Gently does it."

With Soyuz some 3,778,000 miles from the earth it would take the detonation signal from Mission Control more than twenty seconds to reach the spacecraft. During that twenty seconds the spacecraft would descend at about ten feet a second under power of its main engine.

At three minutes and twenty-six seconds before detonation, the capsule's main rocket engine fired and Soyuz braked rapidly into the controlled descent stage of its flight. It was six seconds before 8.39 p.m. Soyuz was positioned almost exactly over the short axis of the planetoid.

"We have ignition," a voice called.

The bomb-laden command module slowed progressively as it plunged toward the planetoid.

"Coming down at fifty thousand feet," Sykes announced. "Looking good. We are under control."

Forty thousand . . . thirty thousand . . .

"Looking good . . . we're coming down nicely."

"We have a slight yaw."

"Confirmed, we have retro firing," a technician replied.

"Coming down at eighteen thousand," Sykes continued. "We are holding steady now . . . drifting slightly to the left . . . slowing now, still slightly wide left but we're OK. Coming down nicely at six thousand . . . five . . . two thousand now . . . Still on axis and holding. Come on baby. Ease on down. We're slowing. Thrust to eighty percent . . . We have full burn, coming down to terminal descent speed . . . down fifty feet per second . . . almost there . . . twenty feet per second . . . fifteen . . . stand by for detonation . . . five hundred feet . . . ten feet per second and holding . . . stand by for detonation . . . Steady, steady . . . drifting left again . . . terminal speed holding. On my mark it will be detonation minus ten seconds . . . three-thirty feet, three-twenty . . . Mark. Nine, eight . . . three, two. Now!"

"Confirmed," a technician shouted.

"It's out of our hands," Sykes said. "Still drifting left. Down at one-sixty, one-fifty . . . one-ten . . . we'll know in a few seconds. . . . Down at forty, thirty, twenty, ten . . . that's it. Stand by and monitor. We'll have confirmation of detonation in eighteen seconds . . . all systems reading . . . sixteen seconds and standing by . . . This is it . . . four, three, two, one . . ."

A fraction of a second later, the last signal from the command module reached Mission Control. The banks of computer screens monitoring the spacecraft's performance all went blank simultaneously.

Sykes collapsed into his seat. A wild roar of jubilation ripped through Mission Control, Cape Kennedy and tracking stations around the world. Scientists, technicians and administrators whooped and shouted.

Young, standing with Sykes and Bigelow, hugged both men unashamedly. Then he shouted, "Well done. Congratulations everyone. Terrific job."

He ran a hand through his hair. "I'd better give the chief the good news." He picked up an open line to the President's office.

"This is the President."

"We did it, sir. We did it. Thank God we did it." Young realized he was laughing. "I'm sorry, sir. I had a more rational statement prepared, but it's bedlam here. We've done it, sir. You can tell the world we've done it."

"Thank you, Matt. Well done. We all thank you. I'll stand by for satellite confirmation."

"Thank you, sir," Young said, regaining his composure as he talked. "We've got a bunch of crazy, wildly happy people here, but we'll calm them down enough to have that confirmation to you in minutes."

"I'll be holding."

"Yes sir."

Far above the Atlantic Ocean, the INSITE astronomical observatory was trained on Apollo-Soyuz and the planetoid.

Gamma ray radiation was the first record of events in outer space to arrive at the satellite. Then light from the explosion and slower-moving radiation particles bombarded the orbiting station. Its radio telescope emitted an intermittent signal that bounced off the planetoid and back to INSITE. The returning signals had been of regular intensity and frequency until shortly after detonation of the bombs. Then their intensity suddenly diminished. INSITE's radio telemetry equipment swept an arc back and forth across the sector where the planetoid had been. With each sweep the size of the arc increased and the intensity of the returning signals varied irregularly from weak to moderately strong.

On the ground, scientists plotted data from the complex jumble of signals received from INSITE, other satellite observatories and ground-based radio and optical telescopes. Gradually, the scientists were able to piece together a reasonably accurate picture of the planetoid's destruction.

Preliminary findings indicated that when the bombs exploded the planetoid fractured and a large part of it was deflected out of its original orbit. That mass, some three hundred miles across, would careen endlessly through space unless captured by the pull of a larger planet. Tracking devices proved conclusively that the fragment would miss the earth by tens of millions of miles.

The remainder of the planetoid grew rapidly into an expanding cloud of dust and debris. Much of it turned to molten metal and was vaporized. Although X-ray and radio telemetry could not decipher the actual content of the dust cloud, or determine the maximum size of solid fragments within it, scientists felt reasonably certain that no sizeable fragments could have survived the explosion.

As soon as the scientists agreed on an interpretation of the data—which they would continue to revise as new information became available—a summary was delivered to Young, who again spoke with the President.

"Mister President, we have confirmation. All observations coincide. The planetoid has been destroyed."

"Thank you, Matt."

The President turned to his press secretary, who had remained in the Oval Office throughout the call.

"Tell the networks to release my statement."

For the third time within a week the President's face filled the nation's TV screens. Behind his desk was draped the Stars and Stripes.

"My fellow Americans and people everywhere," he said. "This is the happiest duty I have ever performed as President of the United States. In the last few minutes the National Aeronautics and Space Administration has confirmed that nine one-hundred megaton hydrogen bombs have been successfully exploded directly above the surface of the planetoid which had threatened to collide with the earth. The planetoid has been destroyed. After these anxious days, we can now look forward to life returning to its normal course."

The President sipped a glass of water.

"I need hardly add that this threat to the earth has been eliminated due to a joint American and Russian exercise. It is painful to me—and, I am sure, to our Russian friends—that our two great nations have not always confronted danger side by side. Sometimes, indeed, we have been in conflict. But this unique exercise has brought us close together. At last, we can truly claim to be allies. To our Russian friends go my heartfelt thanks—and those of all Americans. I firmly believe that the closeness we now share is only the beginning of an even more meaningful relationship."

The camera panned in closely as the President continued. "I must also congratulate my countrymen everywhere. Your confidence in our ability to deal with this danger has been inspiring. It has not been a time of serious panic. You faced this danger with composure, and courage. Tonight I am prouder than ever to be an American. To Americans everywhere, I say another thank you.

"To our magnificent team at NASA, ably assisted by some of the greatest scientists of the Soviet Union, we owe a debt of gratitude that can never be repaid. They are the men who truly saved the world."

The broadcast was followed by a news report speculating on the possibility of a spectacular meteor shower the following evening at around eleven p.m.—approximately the time when the planetoid would have collided with the earth.

"The explosion has created a massive cloud of dust and debris in outer space and some of it is likely to continue along the original orbit of the planetoid," the newscaster reported. "In a report issued only moments ago, NASA confirms that this debris holds no threat to the earth. It is expected to be decades before the cloud dissipates. Consequently, it will continue to orbit the earth and a meteor display of unprecedented brilliance will recur regularly.

"Again, the NASA communiqué states that the planetoid has been destroyed. A meteor shower will occur tomorrow evening, but will pose no danger. Any particles large enough to flame into meteors are expected to burn up in the atmosphere. A few may survive friction with the atmosphere and fall as meteorites, but they are expected to be of a small size."

Because the earth was covered mostly by water, the newscaster added, the chances of a meteorite falling on land were remote.

After the broadcast the President phoned Joint Chief of Staff

Jack Stonehouse. "Cancel preparations for the superbomb launch," he ordered. "She won't be needed."

In Moscow, the Russian premier summoned The Dancer. "We won't need to launch the interplanetary missile, Alexis," the premier said. "Call off the alert."

Chapter Eight

WEDNESDAY, NOON.

In outer space, when the bombs detonated, the planetoid blazed silvery white, like a newborn star. The initial shock of the blast tore through the solid mass, jarring an old wound in its once molten interior. The planetoid fractured almost cleanly in two. The largest section, some three hundred miles across, streamed molten metal behind as it was kicked into depths of space.

The remainder of the planetoid was blown apart and vaporized or scattered, except for a mile-wide fragment which continued on a course nearly identical to the original orbit of its parent body.

The mile-wide fragment hurtled toward the earth, undetected in the huge cloud of the shattered planetoid. In less than eleven hours, the fragment would become a blazing fireball.

The speedometer hovered at ninety as Young's T-bird sped along the highway toward Houston International Airport. Jenny leaned back in the passenger seat, humming in tune with a cassette tape Young had bought that morning, a re-recording of "The Shadow of Your Smile," by Johnny Mathis.

Though for years the song had reminded Young of his first wife, lately the image of her had become more difficult to recall. Instead, whenever he heard the song, it was Jenny's smile that he saw.

"You're sure you'll be able to join me in New York tomorrow, Matt, aren't you?"

"You bet. We're both due for a long, relaxing break with nothing to do but make love."

Young moved the gear shift from overdrive into third to

negotiate a sharp curve. Jenny placed her hand on his as it rested on the gear shift.

Jenny was anxious to return to New York to wind up her affairs with the *Daily News* and to prepare her apartment in Fort Lee for Young's arrival the following day. He had decided to remain at Mission Control until all possibility of debris from the planetoid entering the earth's atmosphere had passed. The two then planned a long weekend. Young had resolved to discuss with Jenny a date for their wedding.

At the airport he pulled up beside a "No Parking" sign near the departure lounge and decided to risk getting a ticket. From the trunk of the car he took a cellophane package and handed it to Jenny. It was a dozen yellow roses.

"Matt Young, I love you very much," she said, kissing him on the cheek.

"I love you, too, honey. Happy anniversary."

"Anniversary . . . ? But . . . ?"

"I thought it was women who always remembered special dates," he teased.

Jenny checked the date on her watch and the significance finally struck her . . . it was twelve months ago to the day that they had their first date . . . the Italian restaurant . . . the song . . . the yellow roses the next morning . . . "Oh, Matt, I feel terrible. There's been so much happening. I completely forgot."

Young kissed her cheek. "I forgive you. Just have a safe journey."

A porter arrived at the car to help with the suitcases. The couple followed him to the airline desk, then strolled to a cocktail bar to await Jenny's plane.

"Do you really expect much of a meteor show, Matt?" she asked, gazing thoughtfully at her glass.

Young had been disturbed that morning by reports of the latest radar soundings from the vicinity of the explosion. Though no large solid mass was recorded, the soundings indicated a considerable quantity of swirling debris—much more than previously expected, and much of it apparently en route to the earth.

"I wouldn't be surprised, honey. We've bounced the bulk of the planetoid to heaven-knows-where, but there's still a hell of a lot of junk flying around. It's more than likely that much of it will enter the earth's atmosphere. I don't want to scare you, but watch the meteor shower from indoors, will you? With luck all that junk will burn up in the atmosphere, but some of it just might reach the ground. You're the one very special person I don't want any harm to come to."

"Don't worry, darling. I'll look after myself . . . just for you."

An airport announcer called on passengers for New York to board the plane. Young led the way to the boarding gate. He kissed Jenny before she handed over her ticket. As she passed through the gate she blew a kiss.

"Hello, ugly. Remember me?"

Jenny had stood for several seconds in front of Reynolds' desk at the *Daily News*. He had remained engrossed in a piece of copy.

"Jenny! Home is the prodigal daughter. It's great to see you."

"Thanks for the welcome, but I don't need it. There's a small matter of some holiday money I'm owed. Cashiers are acting dumb and they've referred me to you. So, I want my check. Fast, Mister Reynolds."

"Sure, sure, Jen. But first how about a chat? Ace girl reporters like Jenny Corbett don't grow on trees around here. Let me make a quick call."

Reynolds picked up an internal phone and dialed 111—the number reserved for urgent calls direct to the publisher's office.

"She's here, sir."

Jenny was puzzled by his behavior. She had assumed that her career with the *Daily News* was at an end, so why the call to the Old Man?

"Right away," Reynolds said.

He took Jenny's hand. "The Old Man wants to see you. Shall we go?"

"Tell him to . . ."

"Why don't you tell him, Jen? Come on, there can't be any harm in seeing what he wants. I have an idea he's not too happy at losing the services of Jenny Corbett."

"Well, he can go and . . ."

Reynolds led the way to the elevator without waiting to hear what Jenny had to say. In the elevator he simply grinned at her obvious surprise.

"What's this all about, Ken?"

"We don't want to lose you. It's as simple as that."

"You should have thought of that earlier. You and the Old Man can go to hell. The *Daily News* isn't the only paper in the universe."

Reynolds ignored the protest and took her arm as the elevator doors opened.

The publisher was waiting at the door of his office. He greeted Jenny warmly.

"My dear, come in, come in. I am glad to see you."

She warily declined an offer of a drink. At a sign from the publisher, Reynolds helped himself to a tumbler full of rye with a dash of ginger and poured a weaker version for the boss.

"I want to say how much I regret our little problem," the publisher said. "I can only tell you that my actions seemed right at the time and, on reflection, I think I would do the same again. But our future interests me more. Especially yours. How much were you earning with us?"

The publisher would be well aware of the amount, Jenny realized.

"Thirty thousand dollars," she said, "but . . ."

"Mmmm . . . not bad, eh? But not exactly top rate. Your salary will be increased to forty thousand." He sipped his drink, then added, "As of last week. We'll regard the time in between as an extra, well, paid vacation. I'm sorry it couldn't have been more pleasant for you."

She straightened her skirt in an attempt to compose herself. Perhaps the baby could wait another couple of years. "I never imagined for a moment that . . ."

"No, of course not. As for now, I'd consider it a personal favor if you would prepare a wrap-up of the week's events. The whole scene at Mission Control and the Cape, the 'I was there' touch and whatever you want to throw in—except for our small tiff, of course. I know of no one better qualified for the job. What do you say?"

"I think I'd like that drink," Jenny said, smiling her broadest smile. "And thanks for the raise."

"Good, good. Then it's decided."

Reynolds poured Jenny a gin and tonic and surreptitiously replenished his own glass.

"Here's to us," the publisher said. "And especially to our top reporter."

"I'll drink to that," Reynolds said.

The three finished their drinks, then Reynolds escorted Jenny back to her desk in the newsroom.

"OK, honey, get that typewriter clacking."

"Whatever you say, ugly. Right away."

She fed a sheet of copy paper into the typewriter, tapped out the date and wrestled to find the first words of her story.

A young reporter who had the desk next to hers said, "Hi, beautiful. Welcome back."

"Thanks," she said with a smile.

It was just as though she had never been away, she thought.

In anticipation of the meteor shower, the Minor Planet Center at Cincinnati, in cooperation with astronomical societies, had organized official meteor watches throughout North America.

Scientists were hoping for a unique opportunity to document a wealth of detail on any falls. Even now, little was known with certainty about meteors, their orbits and origins. Because of the suddenness with which they appeared, few were recorded by camera and eyewitness accounts of sightings varied considerably. Though often eloquent, the reports would be sketchy on directions, angular elevations and durations. Untrained witnesses usually had only the haziest concepts of direction, even in familiar surroundings. Many would report that a meteorite had fallen "in the next block," "behind that row of houses" or "in the next field," when it might actually have fallen several hundred miles away.

Eight observers, eight clerks and eight photographers formed each official watch. The observers and photographers lay on cots at a distance of one mile from a central point, toward which each observer and photographer faced. The clerks with each watch would record what, if anything, the observers reported, and the time and duration of any sightings. Each report would contain the estimated stellar brightness of any meteor, the point at which it was first seen, the duration of its flight, its direction, the area of the sky it crossed, its color and estimated speed. When possible, sightings would be recorded on movie film.

The clerks in each group were to keep in touch with a central control station by a two-way radio. For all involved in the watch it was to be a busy—and for some, perilous—evening.

The first of the meteors flashed into the sky over the mid-Atlantic at 10.54 p.m. Only a few passersby in New York saw the first flashes. A couple of people pointed excitedly to the sky, but within a fraction of a second the meteor had burned up in the air.

Three meteors followed in rapid succession about thirty seconds later. They also blazed into view over the Atlantic. This time there was excited shouting in the streets of a dozen east coast towns and cities. Those meteors also burned out miles above the earth.

At 10.55 a host of shooting stars swept into the sky, increasing in intensity until more than fifty exploded simultaneously into view—only to be followed almost immediately by another dense throng. Each was minute in size and none reached the earth. The display was spectacularly beautiful— and disquieting. No scientist had anticipated a phenomenon of such alarming density.

The sky flamed crimson and orange with fiery sparks as the meteor shower turned into a storm. East of New York City, several large particles shattered with an explosive crack less than ten miles above the earth. A dozen golf-ball sized meteorites rained down on a barren stretch of highway in Maine, pitting the asphalt and turning it molten before the globules of smoldering iron cooled. A mass the size of a baseball thudded into a cultivated field, punching a crater as large as a child's wading pool in the soft brown earth

In downtown Manhattan shouts of excitement turned into cries of fear. Someone at the junction of East 42nd Street and Third Avenue shouted, "Get indoors . . . Get off the streets." The cry was taken up by others and people began to flee to nearby doorways. Soon, panic took hold. A swarm of terrified people fled in a thousand directions. The elderly and the frail were knocked aside. Traffic was halted.

Almost as suddenly as it had begun, the intensity of the meteor shower decreased. The panic subsided as the number of meteors dwindled to fewer than half a dozen a second. For a moment an uneasy calm returned.

The mile-wide fragment of the planetoid burst into the sky as a fireball of blinding brilliance at precisely 10.57 p.m. Like the meteors that had preceded it, the fireball tore through the atmosphere at forty miles a second as the earth, traveling at its own unrelenting speed of eighteen and a half miles a second, swung directly into the fireball's path.

In an instant, almost incalculable friction heated the surface of the meteorite from 2° Centigrade to almost 6000°. Night exploded into day with a dazzling incandescence—ten times brighter than a clear full moon—from the eastern seaboard to as far west as Dakota. Thousands of tons of air were compacted and intensely heated in front of the fireball, melting its surface and flinging globules of molten iron and nickel into the atmosphere. These were swept into the wake of the fireball and formed a vivid trail. The fiery tail streamed for 125 miles behind the fireball.

An ear-splitting sonic boom reverberated across the sky to be followed quickly by an even more startling explosion. The intense heat at the surface of the fireball and the intense cold at its core produced stresses that tore it asunder as it arched toward the earth. Its speed had slowed only marginally as the bulk of the mass plummeted toward the heart of Manhattan, thrusting a scorching heat blast ahead of it.

Twenty-one seconds after it first appeared, the fireball hit Central Park. In those twenty-one seconds, millions were paralyzed with terror. On impact, as the fireball's forward motion was halted in a split second, the outer parts of it and the ground below were compressed, heated and partly vaporized. The vapor and steam from the suddenly heated water present in the ground expanded in an explosion as devastating as that of a hydrogen bomb, blasting much of the fireball back out of the ground and tearing an ugly, gaping crater nearly three miles wide and 483 feet deep at its center. Fragments of the shattered fireball were scattered widely over the surrounding area. Then an intensely hot air blast burned and destroyed nearby life and vegetation. Simultaneously, shock waves spread from the crater, warping and shattering surrounding rock strata. Millions of gallons of water were blasted from the Hudson River into the Atlantic, eventually to be hurtled back in a massive tidal wave that was to swamp east coast regions. The shock waves rippled across the continent, carrying a threat of new destruction that would soon tremble the earthquake-prone regions of the Californian coast.

As the billowing cloud caused by the impact mushroomed miles into the air, a scene of the greatest devastation any city had ever known was unshrouded.

The crater had virtually severed the section of Manhattan south of Central Park. The rim extended from West 115th Street down along the miraculously still-intact Franklin D.

Roosevelt Drive, and across from near East 56th Street to West 58th Street.

The shattered northernmost section of Columbia University teetered on the rim of the crater. At the south of the crater, the Rockefeller Center had been partly flattened. Central Park had been obliterated. A three-mile section of the Henry Hudson Parkway had vanished.

Countless life-giving arteries of New York had been ruptured. Power and gas lines were cut. Half-way down one side of the crater the remains of a subway train peeped through the crushed tunnel along which it had sped only moments before. Here and there the crater was curiously honeycombed, bearing the holes of what had been other subway routes.

Around the perimeter the fragmented remains of buildings, their superstructures undermined, leaned crazily forward on the verge of collapse.

A wall of water some ten feet high now rushed up Upper Bay, swamped Liberty Island and the Fort Jay U.S. Coast Guard Station, swept up the Hudson and East rivers and hurtled into the gaping crater. The water rushed up the sides of the crater until it reached sea level, then the force of the torrent subsided.

The crater had become a water-filled grave.

Young had been watching TV coverage of the meteor shower at Mission Control. He had been startled by the frequency of the meteors and had frozen in horror as the fireball blazed into view.

The TV commentator screamed frantically, "My God . . . Look at it! Christ, what the hell . . . ?" The screen went blank.

Young desperately grabbed the channel selector knob. Reception had vanished on all channels. Finally the voice of another news reporter came through.

"It's hit New York . . . Christ, it's hit Manhattan." He was clearly trying to shout, but his voice was a nervous high-pitched squeak.

Moments later a picture of Manhattan came into focus. Awestruck, Young watched the mushroom cloud—a swirling, choking mass of concrete, metal, life and limb.

"Jenny . . ." Young whispered hoarsely. "Jenny . . ."

The announcer had regained his normal voice. "It's hit Manhattan somewhere near Central Park. My God, thousands must have been killed. Probably millions. Oh, God, my wife is somewhere . . ."

The screen continued to show the Manhattan scene as the newscaster struggled to describe the devastation.

Young's eyes remained fixed on the screen as he dialed the *Daily News*. Desperately he prayed that someone there might know where Jenny was. The line was dead. He called Jenny's apartment in Fort Lee. There was no reply. In desperation he hit the buzzer on his intercom and yelled at his secretary.

"Get me New York. Any police precinct in New York."

As though hypnotized he stared at the screen.

"I have the New York 17th Precinct, sir," Young's secretary reported.

"What is it?" a voice snapped. "Make it fast."

"The *Daily News* building . . ." Young began.

"I don't know that there is any *Daily News* building," the officer said. "I don't have the faintest idea of what's left of Manhattan. I'm sorry."

Young ran to his secretary's desk.

"I'm going to take the VTO. Tell them I'm on the way. Get the crew jumping."

Young's secretary used a scramble call normally used only in war alert exercises. The engines of the VTO were screaming up to full pitch as Young sped across the runway and ran up the stairway to the passenger door.

"New York," he yelled to the pilot as he pulled the doorlock handle behind him. "Land anywhere you can, but get me to Manhattan."

Reynolds had persuaded Susan's nanny to babysit while he took Jenny for a celebration dinner at a third-floor restaurant in the Rockefeller Center.

"Welcome back to the fold," he toasted.

Jenny had completed a two-thousand word wrap-up of the week's events which was to occupy, with pictures, more than six pages of the *Sunday News*.

"That piece you did today is fantastic, Jenny."

Other reporters had been speculating that Jenny might win a Pulitzer prize for her vivid reporting of the planetoid story. Jenny was surprised when she first heard the speculation, then she began to long secretly for the award. It would be a tribute she could look back on with pride.

"A Pulitzer has got to be in the bag, Jen," Reynolds said.

"It's the greatest story of the decade, and your handling of it was superb."

"I hope so. I've got to admit it would give me a great kick."

"Story of the decade . . ." she thought, reframing the words in her mind. It had a compelling ring to it.

But even the most pessimistic experts had failed to foreshadow just how devastating the planetoid story was to become. Soon it would be labeled as the disaster of the century.

Jenny and Reynolds hurriedly joined other guests at the windows of the restaurant when the meteor shower began.

"It's like stars raining on the earth," Jenny gasped.

"That's a great line, Jenny," Reynolds enthused. "A great line—you've got to get that into copy."

As the shower increased he added, "Hey, it would even make a great headline . . . 'Stars rain on earth.' It'd fit like a dream, too. Right across the front page."

As the meteor downpour lessened, Reynolds and Jenny returned to their table. Both had just sat down when the room was lit by a searing flash as the fireball entered the earth's atmosphere.

The windows rattled from the sonic boom. Chairs were knocked over as customers dived for cover. Holding both hands to her ears as the fireball exploded, Jenny wondered if she had been deafened.

A pillar near the table protected her as the windows shattered. A hundred glass fragments pierced Reynolds' eyes, nose, mouth and throat. The lights went out as Jenny reached forward toward him, numbly hoping to help. Somehow he remained on his seat. She touched his face, then felt the warm blood pulsing from his jugular vein. His throat made a gurgling sound as though he were trying to speak, then he tumbled to the floor.

The room rumbled with the falling of masonry as the ceiling collapsed. A waiter was relighting candles on the tables, providing a faint light on the gruesome scene. His skull was crushed by a falling chunk of concrete and twisted metal.

A whimpering voice came from a mound of rubble alongside Jenny.

"Help me. Help me."

Jenny realized that, like others, she was half buried. She kicked and clawed in a futile effort to free herself.

"Help me . . ."

Jenny, though still trapped, was able to reach out to the rubble from which the voice came. First she found a hand. Soon the face was uncovered.

"It hurts," the woman murmured.

Pulling away more debris, Jenny shrunk from the sight of what remained of the woman's chest.

"You'll be fine," Jenny said encouragingly.

"I don't think so," the woman said. As her voice trailed away her eyes glazed over and her head rolled to one side.

Another survivor called to Jenny.

"Hey, give me a hand. This guy's in trouble."

Jenny again tried vainly to free herself.

"I can't . . ."

Suddenly, she stiffened and sniffed anxiously. A menacing, deadly smell began to fill the room. It was the smell of smoke. Jenny heard the crackle of flames.

Susan cringed in bed, clutching the paper hat the old man had made. She wondered why her nanny hadn't come to her. Susan crept from her room and fearfully peered through the settling dust in the littered hallway. The door to the living room was jammed. She could no longer hear the TV set.

"Nanny," she called. "Nanny . . ."

Perhaps her nanny had walked to the corner delicatessen for an evening snack, as she sometimes did when Reynolds was expected home late. Susan ran back to her bedroom and stumbled over the litter to the window, which overlooked the junction of East 52nd Street and First Avenue. Below, where the road to the park should have been, water swirled down a massive hole. She wondered about her father . . . and the old man who had made the hat. She decided to run to the delicatessen.

The water had begun to subside by the time she reached the street. Totally confused, she waded along the road, keeping well clear of burning buildings. She reached the edge of the crater, now full to the brim.

Among the debris and bloated corpses floating in the murky water was a painting. It was a large portrait of an old man and reminded her of the new friend she had made in the park. She picked up the painting and tucked it under her arm.

Other survivors ignored her, too numbed by their own

shock and injuries to be of help. Bewildered, Susan turned back for home.

The old derelict had spent the evening in the company of a bottle of methylated spirits. His thoughts lingered drunkenly on one of the few pleasures life had given him—the sweet, innocent smile of a little girl. The bottle finished, he sprawled on a park bench.

The flash barely aroused him. His unkempt hair and beard were singed, then burst into flames as his flesh began to scorch. The life was crushed from him by the pressure blast.

Fearsome Freddie was visiting one of his followers, an elderly man whose ramshackle apartment faced away from Central Park. The man listened intently as Fearsome replayed his latest sermon.

From Psalm 18 Fearsome quoted, " 'Then the earth shook and trembled; the foundations also of the hills moved and were shaken, because He was wroth . . . He bowed the heavens also and came down; and darkness was under his feet . . . At the brightness that was before him his thick clouds passed hailstones and coals of fire. The Lord also thundered in the heavens . . . He shot out lightnings . . . Then the channels of waters were seen, and foundations of the world were discovered.' "

"Hallelujah," the old man mumbled.

When the flash brightened the room Fearsome dropped his Bible to the floor. The old man sat up in his bed when the sonic boom rocked the building. The mid-air explosion of the planetoid and the shattering impact blast followed.

" 'And the Lord came down in a chariot . . .' " Fearsome whispered reverently.

He opened the door and looked out. Where there should have been a hallway, there was now a sheer drop to the street. Half of the building had vanished. A small remaining section of the floor directly in front of him groaned, split away and tumbled into the emptiness. Clouds of dust billowed into the room as Fearsome ran back to the old man's bedside.

"Let's get out of here," he urged, uncharacteristically concerned about his precarious existence on the earth.

"You go," said the old man. "I'm staying. I'm OK where I am."

"Am I to turn my back on a Christian brother?" the preacher asked. He pocketed his Bible and hauled his friend onto his back.

The old man, overcome by fear and shock, protested violently. He pummeled Fearsome's back and kicked wildly as the preacher tried to carry him.

Fearsome stopped at the bottom of the fire escape and let the old man stand. Both stared silently at the dead and dying that littered the street.

"How terrible is the wrath of the Lord," the preacher said.

As they tripped and scrambled over the ruins in the street, Fearsome noticed an ominous new sound. At first it seemed like the gentle rustling of leaves in the wind. Then it changed to a loud hiss. He stopped and looked around when the noise grew into a roar, drowning out the crackle of flames. Startled, he let go of the old man's hand. A wall of water, sweeping debris ahead of it, rushed toward them. Fearsome ran to a nearby lamp post and shimmied up, out of reach of the water. The flood hit the old man at waist height. He struggled to keep his balance but a wooden packing crate, carried by the current, struck him on the chest. He fell, arms thrashing, and disappeared down the flooded street.

"Home to Jesus," Fearsome whispered.

The water, still ranging and swirling down the street, flooded into basements and subway entrances. Fearsome clung in panic to the lamp post, his teeth chattering an incomprehensible stream of Bible verses and exhortations.

The flood waters rose rapidly underground. Slowly, the roadway began to crumble into the subway tunnel.

"Glory be to the father, the son, and . . ."

He never finished the quotation. His sanctuary leaned sharply, then toppled into the widening crevice. Fearsome's stream was cut short.

Mrs. Winstanley, her drapes drawn across the windows, was awakened by the explosions. The foundations of her apartment block were undermined and she plunged down two flights as the building partially collapsed. Her first thought was to marvel that somehow she was still in her bed. A section of the ceiling, a light fitting still attached, lay across her legs. She couldn't feel her feet. The pain, cruelly intense, started a moment later.

She called for her dog. There was no answering yelp.

"Cecil," she repeated. "Cecil, I'm hurt."

This time another voice answered.

"Where are you? I think my back's broken. Please help me."

Somewhere in the gloom, one of Mrs. Winstanley's neighbors also lay buried.

"I can't help," Mrs. Winstanley said. "I think my feet . . . Who is it?"

"I'm Mrs. Moore—number 306."

"I'm Mrs. Winstanley—305. I'm sorry, but I'm afraid I can't move."

Neighbors for seven years, it was the first time the two women had exchanged more than the rare, "Good morning."

The pain was burning mercilessly now, shooting up Mrs. Winstanley's legs like fiery needles.

"Oh, my feet . . . my legs . . ." she cried, and passed out.

Some time later she heard footsteps overhead. Debris was being hauled away. Then the head of a mud-grimed young boy appeared in the gaping hole above her. Flashlights held by other rescuers bobbed about behind him. One light swept the boy's face and she noticed that his forehead was terribly bloodied. A knotted rope snaked through the hole and the boy slid down. He hauled Mrs. Moore free. She found that her back was not broken after all. He knotted the rope around her waist and other rescuers pulled her to safety.

The boy approached Mrs. Winstanley. Sweat dripped on her as he heaved at the concrete and iron that pinned her legs.

"Come out," he encouraged. "You'll have to struggle."

"I can't . . . I think my feet . . ."

She plucked up the courage to continue.

"I think my feet have been cut off," she said numbly.

Others were now helping the boy. She heard one say, "It's no good. We'll never shift it."

The helpers moved back and whispered together.

The boy returned.

"We'll go and get a doctor for you. Just hold on."

Mrs. Winstanley, her face pale and drawn, began to cry.

No one ever returned. Hours later flames raced through the building. The smoke choked her as she lay unconscious. The fire consumed her broken body.

Doctor Peters was flung to the far wall of his living room, his head and arms punctured by flying glass. He regained consciousness minutes later to find his wife leaning over him.

"Dear, you're all right, you're all right," she simpered.

"I'm fine," Peters assured her. He got up, removed some of the glass fragments from his face and arms and staggered to his adjoining office. Hurriedly, he stuffed his black leather bag with syringes, morphine, bandages, and splints.

In the street outside he gazed in dismay at the enormous crater and understood the impossibility of the task that confronted him.

Wounded people wandered aimlessly, sidestepping those already dead. Peters was puzzled for a moment when he noticed that many of the survivors had little clothing and walked with arms curiously outstretched, forearms and hands dangling. Their clothing had been burned in the heat of the flash. He realized that they held out their arms to prevent the painful rubbing of raw, burned flesh. On the naked back of one young woman he noticed that the pattern of her dress had been scorched into her skin.

"Are you a doctor?" a harassed policeman, nursing an obviously broken arm, asked Peters angrily, nodding at the black bag he carried.

"Yes, I am."

"Well, don't just stand there. Get to work, you fool. People are dying."

Peters placed his bag on the ground, opened it and reached to examine the policeman's arm.

"I'm all right, for Christ's sake. Help some of those other poor bastards."

Peters stared about him, horrified by so much broken flesh. Soon he was working like an automaton . . . wiping, daubing, bandaging . . . wiping, daubing, bandaging.

After a while he began to ignore the critically injured. He knew they were doomed. His duty was to help those who might live.

Suddenly he heard screams.

"The crater's filling with water," one man shouted. "It's flooding."

Peters watched the water lapping the sides of the crater. The doctor was among the survivors at the north of Central Park, all of whom escaped the roaring torrent that swept in from the Hudson estuary.

Shaking his head in bewilderment, Peters returned to his task.

Sergeant Peters had switched to late duty. He was once again in his favorite bar, performing the ceremony of placing the flower from his buttonhole into the empty glass. The sonic boom shook the windows. Another blast as the fireball exploded in mid air . . . and the front of the building was blown inward. The band's amplifying system wailed and died, its power cut.

The building groaned and teetered slowly into the crater as the weakened ceiling of the New York subway began to give way. The wooden surface of the bar split, almost in slow motion. For a second, the sergeant and other customers stared at the growing crack. Several customers clung to the bar as the floor tilted, just as a drowning man would clutch a straw. Their desperation was just as ineffective. The bar and the twenty-four floors above it collapsed and tipped into the crater, vanishing in a cloud of dust.

In Toronto, Peters' wife and son had watched the disaster on television.

"Don't worry, mom," the boy comforted her. "Dad will be OK. He'll be calling soon."

Eric lay asleep in the apartment. He was awakened by the flash and the sonic bang. Lurching to his feet he instinctively shielded his eyes from the glare. His right ear-drum burst with excruciating pain as the fireball exploded in midair. He grasped his ear and a warm liquid trickled through his fingers. He cursed, "Jesus . . . Jesus Q. fucking Christ."

An instant later the fireball hit.

Vernon and the tall Swede waited for the flood waters to subside. The Swede had agreed to accompany Vernon while he checked his old apartment, a mile north along First Avenue. Vernon insisted he was merely curious about the few belongings he had left there, refusing to admit that his real anxiety was for Eric. The old affection born of a long friendship was dying hard.

Some distance from his destination he saw that the block where he once lived no longer existed.

"I guess he's had it," he said.

Envious of the regard his new friend still felt for Eric, the Swede answered, "I thought it was your belongings you were worried about. I guess they've had it, too."

Vernon felt the heat of the fires on his face. A hundred feet away, one of Manhattan's few single-storey buildings, a bar-restaurant, burst into flame as if it were a match that had been struck. This time the heat was severe. Updrafts caused by the heat produced fierce local windstorms, which howled at times at hurricane force. As the freak scorching winds whipped through shattered buildings the flames burned even more ferociously. The two friends turned to cross Franklin D. Roosevelt Drive and joined other survivors who were struggling toward the comparative safety of the East River. Heavy globules of warm rain now began to fall as the burning air suddenly condensed on meeting the cold air above the city.

More people streamed toward the river until the crowd was a dense throng, jostling nearer to the river's edge. Fighting desperately now, Vernon lunged to grab the Swede. Both men toppled only feet from the water. The crowd continued to surged forward.

Vernon had never learned to swim. For more than an hour, his companion searched for him in the murky water. Finally, the Swede swam to the twisted supports of the Queensboro Bridge. He stretched out on a beam and gasped for breath after his exertion in the water. A broken portion of the bridge's superstructure collapsed on top of him.

The raid at Mancini's went with only the occasional hitch. As they drove past the front office, the four Galiardo brothers noted with satisfaction that the guard had gone for a drink.

Rick, Sparks and Billy left Willie in the car at the back of the building and tiptoed up the fire escape. Billy slipped on the top step. His jimmy fell, clanging loudly on each step all the way to the ground. All three froze, breathlessly expecting to be nabbed in the act once again. When it became apparent that Billy's clanger had not been heard, Rick kicked him vindictively on the knee cap. Billy suppressed a scream.

Sparks located the burglar alarm control box and drew out the four wires leading to it. He scraped away the insulation, attached two sets of clamps and snipped the exposed wires. The box was out of action.

Rick opened the office door by forcing back the catch of

the lock with a stolen credit card. The threesome crept to the safe without further difficulty.

Sparks drilled two holes above and two below the combination lock and set the charges. He lit all four fuses and fled to join his two brothers, who were crouched at the far end of the room.

The door blasted open with a satisfying boom. The brothers grinned at each other and ran toward the safe. They were stopped in their tracks by another boom—the sonic blast of the fireball. In seconds all three were crushed to the thickness of a dollar bill.

Outside, Willy had leapt from the car to gaze in consternation at the fireball. He joined his brothers in eternity at the same instant.

Mancini's had stood directly inside the impact area.

The familiar urge overwhelmed John Hutton as he and his bride sat eating in the restaurant at the top of the Pan Am building.

"Let's leave quickly," he suggested.

With a smile, his bride agreed.

"We can always watch the meteor show on TV—if it happens," John added, signaling to a waiter to bring the check. "I'll be able to appreciate it a lot more after we've . . . you know."

They took a cab to the Carlyle and went straight to the room they had booked earlier. Undressing quickly, John pulled Alice toward the bed. Both laughed as she writhed beneath him, teasingly.

"You'll always love me, won't you John?"

"For ever and ever—honest."

He arched upward in astonishment as the flash lit up her face. Her skin shone gleaming white. Her mouth opened in terror.

John and Alice Hutton died in each other's arms.

Through a side window of the VTO Young studied the dazzling phosphorescent trail left by the fireball. A mile across, the trail began at a point over the mid-Atlantic and vanished in the cloud of debris over Manhattan. In the moonlight the trail reflected a dazzling array of colors. At its highest point the trail had been buffeted by winds and now writhed in a zig-zag pattern.

Young joined the pilot in the cockpit and saw Manhattan directly ahead, the familiar skyline flickering in the light of a million fires.

"I don't believe it," the pilot muttered. "It can't have happened. I just don't believe it."

"Jenny . . ." Young whispered. "Please be all right."

For the first time he questioned whether sufficient measures had been taken to destroy the planetoid. Obviously not, he reflected bitterly. The superbombs packed immensely more destructive power than the nine bombs which had been detonated. But politics had dictated the decision not to use the superbombs. . . .

"Where to?" the pilot asked.

"Fly overhead," said Young. "Anywhere will do, but get me near the point of impact."

The VTO began its descent and Young caught his breath as the plane flew northward, directly toward where Central Park had once been. A whole section of the skyline had vanished. From the south of Harlem to near Times Square was, unbelievably, just empty space. Carnegie Hall . . . Lincoln Center . . . they had simply disappeared. So too had Cleopatra's Needle, the Metropolitan Museum of Art and a host of other historic buildings. The Queensboro Bridge writhed like a massive snake in its death throes.

As the plane spiraled lower over the disaster area Young impatiently pointed east of the ruined Columbia University.

"The park . . . can we put down there?"

The pilot studied Mount Morris Park, to which Young had pointed.

"I guess so. Here goes."

Young silently cursed the fact that though the park offered a good landing area, it was at the opposite end of Manhattan from the *Daily News* building.

The engines screamed as they were thrown into reverse. The VTO needed an area only slightly larger than its own dimensions to land. As the jet descended Young and the crew noticed that some of the trees on the edge of the park had been flattened and now lay like the spokes of a wheel, all pointing away from the center of impact.

"Don't wait for me," Young yelled above the roar of the engines. "I'll call Houston when I know the score."

He slid down the VTO's emergency escape chute.

Helicopters hovered over the impact zone. The crew had

given up all hope of finding any survivors in the area, but now measured the extent of the devastation. A million wailing sirens shrieked through the night as ambulances and police cars ferried dead and dying to emergency mortuaries set up in buildings on the perimeter of the impact zone.

As Young fled from the park he dodged between the debris of shattered buildings. Cars and trucks had been flung hundreds of yards along Madison Avenue. The trunk of a station wagon lay wedged in the third-storey window frame of an insurance block. The front wheels, teetering over the street, spun slowly in the breeze.

The buildings now gave way to a vast, open space. On East 116th Street, on the northernmost rim of the crater, all that remained of a jewelry store was its second-floor bathroom, perching on top of a slender pillar.

Young heard himself repeating Jenny's name softly. He forced himself to acknowledge the probability of her death. He remembered her excitement when she had called to tell him she had been given her job back at the *Daily News*. He knew she and Reynolds had planned to go to dinner. But where . . . ?

Spilled on the doorway of a shattered bar was a heap that Young recognized as human remains. A group outside the immediate impact area had first been crushed by the advancing pressure wave, then had sizzled in the murderous blast of heat created by the force of the thousands of tons of air which had been compressed on impact. Nearby a motorcycle lay on its side, its driver hunched over it. Young approached the man. A wide wound was smothered in congealed blood where the man's head had been almost severed by the bike's windshield. Young pulled the body clear and lifted the bike upright. Its clutch handle and a foot rest had been bent, but otherwise the machine seemed to be undamaged. He thrust his foot down on the kick start and the engine fired.

He headed over rubble and debris toward the East River Drive and the southern section of Manhattan . . . the area in which Jenny was most likely to be. Or what remained of Jenny, he thought wretchedly.

Despite the breeze caused by the bike's speed he began to choke on the dust-laden air of Manhattan as he weaved around the clutter on the roadway. At one point he leapt from the bike to haul it above a mountain of shattered concrete. On his left a section of the Queensboro Bridge rose vertically, the bridgeway now starting at a point some fifty feet in the air. He turned the bike toward the East River and accelerated to eighty miles an hour before reaching the Pan Am building. Mud deposited by the floodwaters made the roadway treacherous, but this section of Manhattan, protected from the blast by the size of the Pan Am building, was relatively intact.

On reaching the *News* building he let the motorcycle drop to the pavement. A scene of horror met him inside the foyer. The building had been turned into an emergency mortuary and rows of corpses, covered with crude plastic sheeting, crowded the floor. He was unable to suppress the thought that one of them might be Jenny. A police captain had commandeered the desk normally occupied by a receptionist and was rummaging through some of the victims' belongings.

Young flashed his identity card to the captain.

"Are the phones working yet? I want to call upstairs."

"Feel free," the captain said.

From a directory on the desk Young read the news desk number and dialed.

"Jenny Corbett. Is she there?"

"Miss Corbett isn't here. I'm afraid we haven't heard . . ."

"Ken Reynolds. Is he there?"

"No, he went for dinner with Miss Corbett."

"Where the hell did they go?"

"The Rockefeller Center. I believe it's damaged . . ."

Young was on his way. He leapt through the main doors and kicked the bike into life once more. He roared alongside East 42nd Street and up Fifth Avenue, ignoring the one-way signs. A heavy sense of gloom oppressed him when he saw the massive extent of blast damage at the Center. Slowly, in terror of what he might discover, he ran toward the section of the Center that was still intact.

Fire hoses played on the now-smoldering third floor.

"The restaurant . . .?" Young rapped inquiringly to a fireman. "I know someone in the restaurant."

"I dunno what the chances are. We kept the fire under control there, but there's been a lot of smoke. We're still looking for people in there."

Young ran across the rubble-strewn forecourt of the Rockefeller Center to an exposed flight of stairs.

Guessing his intention, the fireman shouted urgently, "Come back, you idiot."

Ignoring the shout Young scrambled up the stairway to a third-floor emergency exit. The door was locked. He hit the door with his shoulder. It didn't budge. He stepped back and kicked at the door. It all but gave way. With his next kick the door was flung inward and he choked on the hot blast of smoke that wafted out of the room. Grabbing a handkerchief to his mouth he lowered his head and charged through the doorway.

"Jenny . . . Jenny . . ."

His shouts were unanswered. The far end of the restaurant was relatively free of smoke, which billowed out of the shattered windows. He made his way toward the clearer air, stumbling on a body. He bent to feel the man's pulse but, at the first touch of his flesh, realized that he was dead.

"Jenny . . . Jenny . . . Oh, Christ, Jenny . . ."

The answer was barely audible.

"Matt . . ."

"Jenny . . . It can't be . . ."

"Matt?" The voice was stronger now. "Matt, I'm here."

Jenny lay behind the pillar which had protected her from the shattering window panes. Her face was smeared with dirt, smudged by her tears.

"Oh, Matt."

Young bent to her and kissed her roughly all over her face. "Thank God."

"Matt . . . Matt . . ."

Finding almost superhuman strength, he heaved a slab of cement from her as though it were a pebble. Gently, he swept the remaining debris from her legs, looking anxiously for some sign of injury.

"Can you move your toes?"

"I think so . . ."

She flexed both feet back and forth.

"I don't think anything's broken," she murmured.

He carefully examined her legs and saw that her right leg was cut and bruised. Jenny winced as he touched it.

"I'm sorry. Let's get you on your feet."

He placed his arms around her and helped her to stand. He kept hold of her while she tested the strength of her legs uncertainly.

"My right leg hurts, but I think it's OK."

She coughed, suddenly swallowing a fresh blast of smoke.

Young swept her in his arms and, sidestepping other bodies

in the restaurant, headed for the exit. Two firemen met him at the doorway.

"Let me have her," one said.

"No way," said Young, laughing almost hysterically. "I found her and I'm keeping her. There may be others back there."

The two men slipped on facemasks and rushed into the room.

At the foot of the stairway Young helped Jenny to stand once more. She placed her feet on the ground gingerly, then stamped her right foot.

"It's just bruised, I think. It's . . ."

He was suddenly kissing her forcefully. She responded eagerly.

The firemen who had tried to stop Young going into the building watched and grinned. An elderly man being hauled on a stretcher to a waiting ambulance gave a wolf whistle. Young turned and laughed, then kissed the old man playfully on the head.

"I love you, too, you wonderful son-of-a-bitch," Young said.

He returned to Jenny and grabbed her hand.

"Oh, Matt . . . I thought the bombs had worked. It was . . . just horrible. So many dead. Ken was sitting opposite me when . . ." She buried her face in his chest.

"Ken? Ken Reynolds?"

"Yes. He's dead. He . . ." Suddenly she pushed against Young and gasped, her eyes wide with alarm. "Oh Matt . . . the girl. His daughter. Susan."

"Where was she?"

"At home with the nanny. She . . ."

"Come on. Show me where." Young took her hand and pulled her toward the motorcycle. He straddled the seat and thrust a foot down on the kick-start.

"Get on," he shouted. "Let's go."

"But the bike? Where . . . ?"

"Forget it. It's a long story. For Christ's sake, are you coming?"

Jenny climbed onto the pillion.

"This is the block." Jenny shouted in Young's ear and pointed. He switched off the engine and coasted to a halt.

Mentally he rehearsed the words of comfort he felt convinced he was going to have to give Jenny. The building was badly damaged. Chances of finding the girl alive looked remote.

"Second floor," Jenny said anxiously.

He led her up the rubble-strewn stairway. He ran ahead on hearing a child's whimpering voice. The apartment door was slightly ajar. She pushed it open and over her shoulders Young saw a small girl, clutching a large painting and sitting in the center of the floor.

"Susan . . . remember me?" Jenny spoke softly. "It's me . . . Jenny. Jenny Corbett."

She hoped Susan would recognize her. The two had met during Jenny's early days at the *Daily News*.

The little girl scrambled to her feet and rubbed her nose with the back of her hand.

"Susan, are you hurt?" Jenny asked.

"No."

Jenny laughed with relief and hugged the child to her breast. The painting dropped to the floor.

"My picture," Susan complained.

Young recognized the painting. It was one of the many that he and his first wife had admired on their many visits to the Metropolitan Museum of Art. Astonishingly, it was Rembrandt's self-portrait. A priceless masterpiece.

"Where did you get this?" he asked.

"I found it in the water. It's mine."

Young's eyebrows raised. "Jenny, do you realize . . ."

"Later, Matt. Not now." To Susan she added, "How would you like to come to my place? It's safe there."

"My nanny," Susan pointed to a door leading off the room.

Young was able to heave the door apart only an inch or two. Behind it was a heap of fallen masonry. The ceiling had collapsed, bringing with it the floor and part of the walls of the apartment above. It was hopeless. He looked at Jenny and shook his head.

"I don't think your nanny's here," Jenny said to Susan. "Let's go to my house."

Young lifted Susan into his arms.

"My painting," she said, holding out her hand toward it. Jenny looked at him questioningly.

"Suppose so," he said, uncertainly. "We can explain how we got it later."

Jenny picked up the Rembrandt and followed Young and

Susan to the motorcycle. He started the engine as Jenny and the girl climbed on board.

"Here we go," he shouted above the noise of the bike. "You know . . . stolen painting . . . stolen bike . . . we could get arrested for this."

Chapter Nine

THURSDAY, 6.30 A.M.

A heavy blood-red sky shrouded the broken New York sky-line. The cloud of smoke and dust that still lingered fractured the rays of the rising sun into a blazing tapestry of vivid red, gold, violet and purple.

For days to come, similar sunrises and sunsets would appear, as dazzling as the fireball had been destructive.

Jenny stood naked at the bedroom window, her body glowing in the sunlight. She turned toward the bed where Young lay sleeping.

He awoke as she kissed his forehead.

"Matt, come and see."

They crossed to the window and gazed at the kaleidoscope of colors.

"It's beautiful, but so terrible. So many people have died."

She shuddered involuntarily.

Young held her close and stroked her hair.

In the other bedroom Susan tossed fitfully in her sleep and called, "Daddy . . . daddy . . ."

About the Authors

Vic Mayhew has previously been an editor for Britain's *Daily Mirror* and *The Sun*. He has also worked for both *The National Enquirer* and *Reader's Digest*.

Doug Long has been a journalist with the Canadian Press news service, public relations manager with a large insurance company, and is now an Associate Editor in the Special Books Department at *Reader's Digest*.

Big Bestsellers from SIGNET

- [ ] **NIGHT SHIFT** by Stephen King. (#E8510—$2.50)*
- [ ] **CARRIE** by Stephen King. (#J7280—$1.95)
- [ ] **THE SHINING** by Stephen King. (#E7872—$2.50)
- [ ] **'SALEM'S LOT** by Stephen King. (#E8000—$2.25)
- [ ] **COMA** by Robin Cook. (#E8202—$2.50)
- [ ] **DEADLY PAYOFF** by Michel Clerc. (#J8553—$1.95)*
- [ ] **DANIEL MARTIN** by John Fowles. (#E8249—$2.25)
- [ ] **THE EBONY TOWER** by John Fowles. (#E8254—$2.50)
- [ ] **THE FRENCH LIEUTENANT'S WOMAN** by John Fowles.
  (#E8535—$2.50)
- [ ] **A ROOM WITH DARK MIRRORS** by Velda Johnston.
  (#W7143—$1.50)
- [ ] **BLOCKBUSTER** by Stephen Barlay. (#E8111—$2.25)*
- [ ] **SHADOW OF A BROKEN MAN** by George Chesbro.
  (#J8114—$1.95)*
- [ ] **LOVING STRANGERS** by Jack Mayfield. (#J8216—$1.95)*
- [ ] **THE INFERNAL DEVICE** by Michael Kurland.
  (#J8492—$1.95)*
- [ ] **DYING LIGHT** by Evan Chandler. (#J8465—$1.95)*

* Price slightly higher in Canada.

THE NEW AMERICAN LIBRARY, INC.,
P.O. Box 999, Bergenfield, New Jersey 07621

Please send me the SIGNET BOOKS I have checked above. I am enclosing
$_____ (please add 50¢ to this order to cover postage and handling).
Send check or money order—no cash or C.O.D.'s. Prices and numbers are
subject to change without notice.

Name _____

Address _____

City_____ State_____ Zip Code_____
Allow at least 4 weeks for delivery
This offer is subject to withdrawal without notice.